W9-AHV-135

Eurotrash Deceptions

Eurotrash Deceptions

Eric Bercovici

A division of Shapolsky Publishers, Inc.

Eurotrash Deceptions

S.P.I. BOOKS
A division of Shapolsky Publishers, Inc.

Copyright © 1993, 1990 by Epipsychidion, Inc.

All rights reserved under International and Pan American Copyright
Conventions. Published in the U.S.A. by Shapolsky Publishers, Inc. No parts
of this book may be used or reproduced in any matter whatsoever without
written permission of Shapolsky Publishers, Inc., except in the case of brief
quotations embodied in critical articles or reviews.

Previously published as *Tread Lightly, My Dear,*
in hardcover by Birch Lane Press.

ISBN 1-56171-202-7

For any additional information, contact:

S.P.I. BOOKS/Shapolsky Publishers, Inc.
136 West 22nd Street
New York, NY 10011
212/633-2022 / FAX 212/633-2123

Manufactured in the United States of America

10 9 8 7 6 5 4 3 2 1

This is truly a work of fiction. None
of the characters or the events portrayed
herein are based on real people, living
or dead, or actual happenings, past or
present. Except for any accidental
straying into accuracy regarding only
historical persons or dates, any resemblance to reality is purely coincidental.

"Things are never as good or as bad as they seem."

—JOHN MCENROE
(Television interview)

LONDON

1

The Victorian red brick building on Henrietta Street appeared ready for either demolition or preservation under the National Trust, but it seemed a proper home for Farrow & Farrow, Ltd., old, traditional and solid. I wasn't sure about the bright green Rolls-Royce Corniche parked in front. Eclectic. Red brick, green Rolls, gray sky, May rain. It could be a London postcard, I thought as I splashed my way across the sidewalk, an ugly postcard. But that was only personal grievance on my part. Once my heart was shattered here. More than once.

Inside, Farrow & Farrow, Ltd. had clearly decided the furnishings should maintain the stylistic and historic nature of the exterior, and there have been few exceptions less comfortable than of that strangled reign the English hold so dear. Has Fiona made me an anglophobe? From behind her desk, the receptionist (also a period piece) could not keep her eyes from filling with that familiar confusion my name usually produces, as her lips tried and failed to form a puckered response. I decided to give her time so I peeled off my wet raincoat to reveal my Turnbull and Asser shirt, regimental tie and Jermyn Street suit, an outfit that Fiona picked out for me when I last saw her on my way to Italy a year ago. "When in Rome, dress like an Englishman," she said in her constantly irresistible way. I found a vacant hook on the coatrack and left my wet Burberry among the dripping Aquascutums, typical costumes for a London spring. Or summer. The receptionist hadn't made any noticeable progress, so I tried again.

"Amicus Maltese."

"You do what, sir?"

"For Mr. Rupert Farrow." I took out my card and placed it in front of her. "He's expecting me."

When the British get confused, it can become hopeless. My card just made it worse.

A. MALTESE
Provenance

"Oh," she said, then leaned over to whisper into a vintage intercom. "There's a Mr. Malteezee to see Mr. Rupert. Says he's expected."

The last phrase was spoken with obvious doubt, the woman having a practiced eye for author types and I clearly did not belong. Old London publishing firms were not my usual venue, though no one has ever accused me of looking particularly at home in a museum, either. For the past year I had been back and forth between New York and Rome almost on a monthly basis in an attempt to determine the origin of a questionable 16th century sketchbook that had been "found in a cellar in old Rome" (like so many "discoveries") by a priest who also was a professor at the University of Naples. Not only a Man of God, but a Paragon of Virtue. And a connoisseur, the world's (self-proclaimed at least) authority on Michelangelo, whose divine hand he detected in these cartoons.

For only $6.5 million US, this invaluable work of art could belong to the Met. So, the Met sent me. Instead of flying directly, I routed myself through London for that last disastrous attempt at reconciliation with Fiona, so by the time I arrived in the Eternal City, the National, the Cleveland, the Frick and, of course, the Getty were already nicely settled in. The *professore* gave us a feathery touch of his hands, a glimpse of the sketchbook, but refused any scientific testing. *Caveat emptor.* One by one, the other museums decided not to gamble, but the Met was determined.

So, spurred on by my rejection by Fiona, I pursued the *professore*. After two months, he agreed to allow a single page to be X-rayed. Very healthy. Several months later, another page was put under ultra-violet inspection. Healthy again. At last, the Met wanted carbon-dating. The paper came up a definite quattrocento. The *professore* even showed me the cellar where he had uncached this treasure (in a building, it turned out after some investigation, owned by his cousin).

In between these adventures, the *professore* returned to enlighten his students in Naples, while I continued my obsessions with Fiona, eloquent imaginary phone calls, unwritten letters of great persuasion, and trying to explain to the Met what was taking so long in acquiring this coveted work of art. My "Well, I'm just not convinced" didn't sit too well, but without my authentication of provenance, they would look like fools if they bought the sketchbook and it later was revealed to be a fake. It had happened too many times to the Met. And just about every other museum as well. They needed the guarantee of provenance. That's what I was supposed to supply, and something kept holding me back.

Finally, on this last trip to Rome, the *professore* took me to the Vatican and there used his sacramental authority to gain us sole audience, actually inside the protective cage, with Michelangelo's great Pieta.

"I will confide in you, my son," the holy *professore* spoke gently as my fingers touched the Madonna's smooth marble toes—we'd gotten rather chummy over the past twelve months, it being the nature of my profession to ingratiate myself with people. "You see, it was she who told me where to look. For after God, His son Jesus is the most divine, and after Jesus, it is Michelangelo who is closest to God himself. Right now, we are in the presence of the Divine and it is through that Divine intervention that the Blessed Santa Maria, created by our great Michelangelo, revealed to me in my deepest prayers the location of this treasure."

"Did she quote the price, too?" I asked.

The Met was understandably disappointed and sufficiently grateful to keep me on expenses for the rest of the day. There had been, it came as an afterthought, an inquiry regarding my services from Farrow & Farrow, Ltd. in London, which might be worth investigating, as the Met had no foreseeable plans to inflict me on their payroll again. London! Fate was sending me back to Fiona!

"Ah, Mr. Maltese," it was a plummy voice. "This is indeed a

pleasure."

He was tall, thin, the suggestion of a chin, lanked forelock dripping elegantly. His perfect pinstripe made me feel like a fraudulent tourist, a gauche interloper, the haberdasher's disgrace. Why hadn't Fiona taken me to Savile Row?

"Mr. Farrow?" I offered a clumsy paw.

"So glad you could make it on this short notice," he craned down toward my face, "as this is rather urgent."

"Have you bought a painting?" I went right to the point. "I mean, have you paid for it?"

"A painting?" Farrow blinked. "Heavens no. Why should I buy a painting? You are Mr. Amicus Maltese from the Metropolitan Museum of New York?"

"Sometimes," I said.

"Provenance?" he asked.

"Provenance," I assured him. "Are we talking about a marble?"

"No, no, no," Farrow waved his hands. "It's something of a totally different nature. Why don't we go into the conference room. It's much more comfy."

Comfy? Well, the receptionist had said Mr. Rupert, so this had to be the young, very young Mr. Farrow. Where was the real Mr. Farrow, I wondered, following him up the narrow staircase.

"You see, I'm afraid my father's had a bit of a stroke," Rupert read my mind. "So you'll have to suffer me with this problem. Of course, we have our own experts, but in the end, it will have to be your word that counts."

Not a painting, not a marble, my mind was climbing faster than my feet. What else could it be? A primitive Sienese bookbinding? An icon? Ancient Roman coins?

"Just tell me that it's nothing Etruscan," I said.

"I'm afraid that you're missing the point, Mr. Maltese," Farrow dropped the words over his shoulder. "It's nothing as simple as that."

Egyptian? I remembered reading something about the prying open of a pyramid. Catherine the Great's lost jewels? The Magna Carta? Persian miniatures? The golden plates from the Angel Moroni? But young Farrow's sangfroid was greater than my curiosity. Perhaps they do learn something besides buggery in

English schools. (Actually, Fiona once said that, so I'm quoting).

"Here we are," Farrow opened the double doors at the head of the stairs.

If the conference room was his idea of comfy, then he must have had a bed of nails in his office. Six hardback chairs around a small table. A jowly man and a woman whose hair was pulled back into a severe gray bun were sitting opposite each other, eyeing the cardboard box in the center as if waiting to see if it would move. The *objet* in question.

"Mrs. Bettina Sachs, who has been kind enough to travel down from Oxfordshire, and Stephen J. Thurston, our solicitor," Farrow made the introductions. "Mr. Amicus Maltese of the Metropolitan Museum."

"Part time," I added.

"As you are no doubt aware, sir," Thurston launched right into it, "the publishing firm of Farrow and Farrow has been privileged to have a long association with Oliver Godolphin. You do know Oliver Godolphin?"

"The writer," I nodded.

"The author," Thurston amended. "And the recipient of the Nobel Prize for Literature."

In my mind, I could see the books in airport shops everywhere. Godolphin was a tough name to avoid, though I'd never read him. Oliver Godolphin. The name was in such large type, I used to think it was the book's title. Then I remembered.

"He's dead."

"Seven years ago this month."

"Plane crash," I recalled dimly.

"Helicopter, actually. Mr. Godolphin and his wife both perished. The bodies were never found."

"Tragic," Farrow said, just as I began to wonder why the lawyer was doing all the talking.

Mrs. Bettina Sachs from Oxfordshire was still staring at the cardboard box. Godolphin's skull? Farrow and Thurston looked at each other, as if deciding whether or not to continue.

"What follows, Mr. Maltese, must remain absolutely confidential," Thurston spoke with great solemnity. "Do I have your assurance of that?"

"Yes, you have my assurance, but if you have to ask me for it, then perhaps I shouldn't be here," I let the irritation show: people can question my virtue, but not my honor.

"Of course. You're quite right, and I do apologize," Thurston didn't seem sorry at all. "Rupert?"

"This firm, Farrow and Farrow, was founded by my great-grandfather and it has been under direct family management ever since. There has never been a question of our professional integrity, never even the possibility of a scandal."

Until now, I thought.

"Until now," he said. "And that is something we simply cannot afford. Oliver Godolphin was one of our greatest authors. Perhaps our very greatest. A man whose talent had both the finest literary qualities and mass popular appeal. A rare combination. My father was his first publisher and, of course, that novel was an immediate success here and then an even greater success in the United States. But out of loyalty, Oliver Godolphin always insisted that Farrow and Farrow be the first publisher, even though the Americans paid far more. And to this day, over a million Oliver Godolphins are sold in soft cover each year. It's an extraordinary shelf-life."

Shelf-life, I assumed, was not the same as on the shelf.

"In point of fact," Farrow went on, "Oliver Godolphin remains our best selling author."

"Translated into twenty-two languages," Mrs. Bettina Sachs spoke for the first time.

"Yes," Thurston sat forward, "so if you add in the foreign rights, the Oliver Godolphin royalties are more than substantial."

"The royalties? Who gets them?" I interrupted, suddenly feeling on familiar ground: *Cherchez l'argent.*

"His daughter, Alexis Godolphin," Farrow sounded a little defensive. "We send her all the statements and very promptly."

"No go-between? No dealer? No agent?" the familiar ground fell away.

"Oliver Godolphin detested agents on principle. He always negotiated for himself," Farrow said. "Except for the last book. Alexis met with my father on that. Not that it was much of a negotiation. She named the price and we paid it."

"So you can just imagine, Mr. Maltese," Thurston pressed on, "if there were a new novel by Oliver Godolphin how much it would be worth?"

"No. Actually I can't."

"Easily a four-million dollar advance, between us and the Americans," Farrow said. "With the Americans paying most of it, of course."

"Too bad he didn't live to write it," I said sympathetically.

From the long pause, I knew we had finally arrived at the meat course. Farrow and Thurston looked at each other for final confirmation, then Thurston pushed the cardboard box across the table to me. Mrs. Bettina Sachs's eyes didn't leave it for an instant. With my fingertips, I eased off the cover.

SAKURA
by
Oliver Godolphin

The photo-copied manuscript looked about seven inches thick and I touched it as if it were a medieval vellum, letting the pages ripple like water off my thumb. The typing was erratic, wandering margins, words and sometimes entire lines crossed out and the page below the title page contained only the words "Page Missing," which made no sense since the following page was captioned "Chapter One." I glanced up to find all three of them staring at me.

"When did you get this?" I asked calmly.

"A week ago," Farrow answered. "Eight days, actually. It gave my father a stroke. The shock, you know."

"How did it arrive?"

"By courier."

Obviously no one was going to volunteer the details, just like museums. If you want to know the answer, you had to ask the right question.

"From where?"

No one answered. Finally, Thurston picked up his briefcase and opened it to extract a plain envelope. Inside there was a letter and reluctantly he handed it to me.

Rougemont & Cie
Geneve, Suisse

Reginald Farrow, Esq.
Farrow & Farrow, Ltd.
London

(undated)

Dear Mr. Farrow:

I am sending you this manuscript at the request of Oliver
Godolphin. He says as follows:

"Reg,

The old contract will do, plus ten percent. Please make out
your cheque to Rougemont & Cie."

With best wishes,
(scrawl)
Pierre Rougemont

I smoothed the letter out on the table, then read it again. The
instructions seemed quite clear. Now I knew why Farrow & Farrow needed me.

"And you require provenance on the book," I said.

"I'm afraid so," Farrow nodded.

"You think it's a forgery?"

"Nonsense," Mrs. Bettina Sachs snapped. "It is without question one of Oliver's best works."

"Obviously you've read it," I was just trying to make it all
clear.

"Of course, I've read it. The book has Oliver's unique stamp
on every page," she declared. "No other writer could imitate
that."

And no one could draw like Michelangelo, either. I decided to
move away from Mrs. Sachs, but not quickly enough.

"I know his work better than anyone," she went on.

"You see, Bettina—Mrs. Sachs—was Oliver Godolphin's editor." Farrow stepped in, "From the first book till the last. Well,
the last one published. There was no one else's literary opinion
Oliver Godolphin valued more than Bettina's."

"He really listened to me," she added. "That's why I retired when he died. There was no other author for me, no one like Oliver. No one."

"I'm sure," I started to look away.

"So don't you ever imply that this masterpiece is a forgery," Mrs. Sachs was not giving up.

"Mr. Thurston," I spoke over her. "I take it that Rougemont and Company is a private bank in Geneva."

"Yes," he said.

"And have you spoken with Pierre Rougemont?"

"Of course, I have."

"What did he say?"

"He said that he had been instructed not to say anything," Thurston said with a gesture of dismissal. "You know the Swiss. No point in even attempting a conversation when they're not forthcoming."

"I take it that this manner of manuscript submission and requested method of payment is unusual," I persisted, delaying my inevitable return to Mrs. Bettina Sachs, who clearly had several more opinions to reveal.

"Nothing in publishing is unusual, Mr. Maltese," Farrow sounded resigned. "But insofar as Oliver Godolphin, no, we have never experienced anything like this. As I said before, our dealings have always been direct. Oliver Godolphin, and now his daughter, Alexis."

In attempting to prove provenance in the art world, obvious questions generally provided the easiest answers, though not always the most truthful ones. Particularly when dealing with thieves, buyers and sellers, time and patience were usually on my side. The artists, when they could be found, who actually forged ("created" was their preferred term) the work were quite often proud and even eager to discuss their inventions. I decided to decelerate and turned back to Mrs. Bettina Sachs.

"Tell me, Mrs. Sachs, is there anything different about this new book by Oliver Godolphin?"

"Different? Of course it's different," she pounced on the question. "Do you think that Oliver wrote the same book all the time? His imagination was unbounded, the ground of his creative mind so fertile that a thousand stories could grow. His people, his characters, they were all so alive, so pulsing, so vibrant."

"But this book, Mrs. Sachs, what makes it different?"

"Oliver wrote this book. I know he did. I can feel him there," she was still adamant.

"The title, *Sakura,*" I inched forward, "that's very interesting. Is that an unusual title for an Oliver Godolphin book?"

"Oliver was brilliant with titles," she said. "Just brilliant. He had a special gift."

"But *Sakura* is an unusual title, isn't it?"

"Absolutely not. It means cherry blossom in Japanese."

"Is the book about Japan?"

"Absolutely not. Oliver never wrote about Japan."

"Then why is the title in Japanese?"

"You'll have to read the book to find out." I knew she'd say that.

"Bettina," Farrow was almost imploring, "Mrs. Sachs, didn't you tell me that this was by far the most, ah, most personal, I believe was the phrase you used, book by Oliver Godolphin?"

Mrs. Bettina Sachs glared at Farrow for a full minute, scorning him for his treason, before she turned her furious eyes back to me.

"I may have said something to that effect," she admitted.

"In what way personal, Mrs. Sachs?" I smiled pleasantly. "What's the story about?"

"Well, and I can hardly do justice to the texture of Oliver's writing, it is about an American journalist in Vienna, a man, I might add, who has seen many terrible events in the world, wars, famine, the deaths of children, all the horrors of this modern world, and whose own emotions have been numbed by all these terrible experiences, his own soul wounded . . ."

I had the feeling I'd already seen the movie on a plane, so I drifted off. But then I had never been a connoisseur. Being able to determine what was real art and what was forgery was not the same as knowing good from bad. Personally, some of my favorites were fakes. Giovanni Bastianini's bust of Savonarola, attributed briefly to both Michelangelo and Luca della Robia and fleetingly acclaimed as one of the great works of the Renaissance, is still my favorite terracotta regardless of the fact that it was created only slightly more than a hundred years ago.

". . . until one day when, unexpectedly, he saw her in that cafe on the hill overlooking Salzburg, her face pale as alabaster, her hair red as the setting sun, she was dressed in an exquisite silk kimono. And in that instant, this man who could feel nothing was engulfed by love, an all consuming, all obsessing passion for this beautiful woman . . ."

Oh my God! Oliver Godolphin (or someone) had written the story of me and Fiona. It was on the bridge in St. James's Park instead of Salzburg and she wasn't wearing a kimono, but everything else was the same. One look at Fiona was all it took. I had found the only woman I would ever love. Fiona Hazeltine-Taylor. The name shimmered then with a magic happiness. It still does. I can't see red hair without thinking of Fiona. Or green eyes. Or the Victoria and Albert Museum. She is in my dreams. Once, for eighteen months, she was in my bed.

We were married in May on the riverside in Richmond and then lived in her parents' flat in Belgravia while they were on a three-month summer cruise. Fiona's eyes were always filled with wonderful green laughter and it seemed the sunlight was always in her hair and she always wore that thin, clinging white silk negligee.

"Mr. Maltese?" Farrow's voice came from somewhere.

I was standing at the window. Somehow Fiona had lifted me up and carried me across the room. Farrow and Thurston were staring at me, Mrs. Bettina Sachs having evidently finished her recount. I knew that it was time to stop messing about.

"Have you spoken with Alexis Godolphin regarding the unexpected appearance of this manuscript?" I asked Farrow.

"Yes, of course," he bobbed his head up and down. "Immediately."

This was my big moment.

"And Alexis Godolphin said that her father, Oliver Godolphin, did not write the manuscript entitled, *Sakura.*"

"That's right," Farrow's head stopped bobbing. "How did you know?"

"She'll sue if we publish," Thurston added.

"But Oliver wrote the book!" Mrs. Bettina Sachs had lost none of her resolve.

It was very clear that they needed A. Maltese Provenance. Perhaps I needed one, too.

2

People have said that since Fiona left me, I have been unbalanced. There may be some small truth to that, but, with the exception of my involuntary walk across the Farrow & Farrow conference room, there is no noticeable manifestation. The Art World accepts, and probably expects, some mildly idiosyncratic behavior. Besides, my being in love with my ex-wife harms no one, certainly not Fiona. I suspect she rather enjoys the fact and my lingering feelings in no way inhibited her two subsequent marriages, nor did my continuing emotions influence her divorces. Somewhere, I was convinced that she would return to me. How did Oliver Godolphin find out about us? Did he know Fiona?

"I beg your pardon?" Farrow peered at me over his grilled sole in the Les Ambassadeurs Garden Room.

"Yes?" I peered back over my grilled sole.

"You just said, 'Fiona.' "

"I did?"

"Quite distinctly."

"I can't imagine why."

"It's my wife's name, you know," Farrow said, then forked a piece of fish up to his mouth.

It couldn't be. I would have heard something. Still, it had been over a year. The earlier events of the day, however, made anything seem possible. After Mrs. Bettina Sachs repeated her positive identification of the manuscript's authorship several more times, she had left to travel back to Oxfordshire, and Farrow, Thurston and I went through the formalities. Talking about money is never easy, but since there was so much of it at stake, my advance fee and expenses were agreed upon fairly quickly.

I, of course, agreed to be accurate in my accounting and diligent in my investigation, though I made it clear that digging out a solid provenance could not be done with the clock ticking, particularly in this situation where the work in question had already been pronounced definitely real and no less definitely false. It was, I pointed out, a very delicate matter.

Then, of course, I needed their official letter of authorization, the names and addresses of the connected people, a few sample pages of the manuscript (copied off their copy) and a synopsis of the story, which Mrs. Bettina Sachs had already done. After we agreed to all that, Rupert Farrow decided we should have lunch at Les A to wish me Godspeed and give Thurston time to get back to his office to legal it all up. The green Rolls, of course, was his and he was kind enough to give us a lift to Mayfair.

"Red hair?" I asked casually.

"Hmm?"

"Does she have red hair?"

"Does who have red hair?"

"Your wife."

"Good gracious, no," Farrow somehow seemed offended at the thought. "Why do you ask?"

"It just popped out, actually."

"Sort of an intuition, eh?" he chuckled. "Wrong this time though. But let's try holding to the facts on our project, shall we?"

"I only deal in facts, Mr. Farrow, but sometimes facts can be very disappointing. That's part of the risk. You've hired me to establish the provenance of our project, but what you really want is for me to prove that, in fact, Oliver Godolphin is the author." Farrow winced when I spoke the name, but it just slipped out. "So if it turns out that he is not the author, the facts will disappoint you."

"I'm quite certain Bettina, Mrs. Sachs, is right," Farrow said stiffly.

"But not certain enough to publish in the face of a lawsuit," I pointed out. "Particularly in light of who would be suing you."

"No," he dabbed his mouth with the napkin, then pushed his plate away, half a sole remaining. "How do you intend to resolve this?"

"I don't know. I've never done a book before."

"What do you usually do?"

"Paintings and sculptures mainly. Generally Renaissance through to the European Moderns. Not much worth forging or stealing after Utrillo, though some people would argue."

"No. I mean how do you usually establish provenance?"

"Well," I didn't want to go into a long description, "it's sort of like tracing a family tree. Who did what, where and when. Long absences are usually suspect."

"I see," he nodded. "And how did you first become involved in this type of work. It does seem an unusual occupation, if you don't mind my saying."

This was not easy to explain. Wars, at least European wars, are very good for the art market. Paintings are stolen or sold or hidden during the hostilities, then reappear slowly during peacetime, usually quite far from their place of origin. As a result the dealers have a field day, museums being as avaricious as they all are, which is one reason that most of the world's great paintings are no longer in Italy, Spain and Holland. If the Sistine Chapel were transportable, it would have been long gone.

I had checked the 1923 edition of Elie Faure's *History of Renaissance Art* out of the Yale Library for some light reading on the train from New Haven to New York and made it all the way to page twenty-two before I fell asleep staring at a small black and white photograph of Andrea de Castagno's "The Crucifixion," which the caption said was in the Uffizi in Florence. There was no point in going into detail about why I happened to visit the Met that afternoon, and since he knew nothing about my father, I had no reason to bring it up, but there hanging on the wall of the Metropolitan was what should have been in the Uffizi, de Castagno's "The Crucifixion." A recent acquisition. Like the good Art History major that I had been, I asked a few curious questions and was told to mind my own business. The Met did not discuss its policy nor reveal its sources, and even the suggestion of forgery was sufficient to make me distinctly unwelcome.

Of course, this did not have the effect on me that the Met had intended. After a number of overseas calls, it turned out that the Met was right to be offended at the suggestion of forgery. The de Castagno had been stolen from the Uffizi sometime before 1945. A little over a month later, I (with, to be honest, a little outside help) had tracked down the source. A dealer had arranged the sale for $150,000 and a shaky provenance, having paid $25,000 to its previous owner, a Dutch immigrant to Canada who was down on his luck and had simply driven the painting across the border and down to New York City and who turned out to be a former Sergeant of the Waffen SS.

It was a newsworthy story, and de Castagno went back to the Uffizi and I took his place at the Met. They hired me out of embarrassment as it was the only thing they could do to repair their image, at least from a PR point of view, but my reputation was made.

For the next two years, I prowled and provenanced, only to discover how lucky I had been my first time out. I came up with several dubious purchases, but they were simply moved to the basement and I was encouraged to move on. By now, everyone had forgotten my grand success with the de Castagno caper and the Met decided to put me on a free-lance basis, which turned out to be the watermark on the paper of my life. The next day, I was hired by a dealer to fly with him to London and check the provenance of an Old Master he was about to bid for on behalf of a private party. And that's when I met Fiona.

"You've met my wife?" Farrow interrupted.

"No," I looked at him blankly. "I've never met your wife."

"You just said you met Fiona."

Obviously, I'd slipped. Just as I was about to explain that his Fiona was not my Fiona, Thurston arrived.

3

For me, Room 46 at the Victoria and Albert Museum became the significative exhibition at the moment of discovery. More of a corridor than a gallery, it contains some of the finest forgeries ever created, including my beloved Savonarola by Bastianini, displayed alongside his brilliant busts of Marsilio Ficino and

Lucrezia Donati—all three of them on a rather shabby counter—
and, therefore, since these are proven fakes, it is a tribute to
provenance, both accidental and intentional. Every piece is a
work of genius, misguided perhaps, but nevertheless undeniable.

Art forgery has a long tradition, only slightly shorter than art
itself. After the first cave-drawer exhibited his original creation,
other latent artists were hot on his heels. Even Michelangelo in
his youth couldn't resist the forger's temptation, hammering out a
sleeping Cupid in the Greek style which, after antiquing, he took
to Veii and, with the connivance of Lorenzo di Pierfrancesco de
Medici, pretended to discover. The Cupid was then sent to Bal-
dassare del Milanese, an art dealer in Rome, who sold it to
Raffaele Riario, the Cardinal of San Giorgio, for two hundred
ducats, of which Michelangelo received only thirty, dealers being
then what they are now.

Lunch at Les A had mercifully ended shortly after Thurston's
well-timed arrival and I walked through the rain, protecting under
my trusty Burberry the thick envelope Thurston had given me, to
Barclay's Bank where I deposited Farrow & Farrow's handsome
check before plodding on (not a taxi to be found) all the way to
my hotel, the Rembrandt, naturally, on Cromwell Road. There,
sitting in a hot bath, I looked over the various papers.

The letter of authorization seemed fine, on the Farrow & Farrow letterhead, "The bearer of this letter, Mr. A. Maltese, is
empowered to determine the literary provenance of the
manuscript *Sakura*. On behalf of Farrow & Farrow, Ltd. (signed)
Rupert Farrow, Managing Director (acting), for Reginald Farrow
(Chairman)."

Then, on separate pieces of paper, two sample manuscript
pages (109 and 323), the address and phone number for Pierre
Rougemont, Rougement & Cie, Geneva, and the same for Alexis
Godolphin in Cap d'Antibes. The remaining pages consisted of a
single document, Mrs. Bettina Sachs's synopsis of the work in
question.

It was basically a longer version of the story Mrs. Bettina
Sachs had related in the Farrow & Farrow conference room,
except now the characters had names—Jordan Leander, our
American journalist, and Lulu von Hofmannsthal, our beautiful
red-haired lady of the kimono, and on and on and on, another

thirty characters at least. There was also a lot of information about Austria, the Hapsburg monarchy, the collapse of the Austro-Hungarian Empire right through the Anschluss, when Germany annexed Austria, a joyful time in Vienna, in 1938. At least according to the synopsis, World War II is sort of glossed over, but Jordan Leander is ironically amused by the political compromise that somehow left Austria pictured as a victim of the war, rather than as bad, if not worse, a villain as Germany.

Now stationed in Vienna and not feeling particularly good about anything, the singular Austrian attitude of surface amnesia covering a deeper murderer/criminal personality enrages Leander, as if the entire nation was still pretending that Hitler was a German and Johann Sebastian Bach an Austrian and that they had nothing to do with all those terrible events. Soon, Jordan Leander is "filled with a deep and abiding detestation" (Mrs. Bettina Sachs's words) for all things Austrian. Enter Lulu.

"Es ist interessant," she says when Jordan Leander asks why she is wearing a kimono.

The bathwater had cooled down and I decided to leave the rest of my research for later. Besides, I knew Jordan was falling obsessively in love with Lulu and I needed to prepare myself for that part, so I put on some dry clothes and my wet Burberry and plunged out into Cromwell Road, heading for the emotional safety of the V & A. Fiona and I had been to Room 46 dozens of times, but she never understood my fascination with these forgeries, preferring the two huge adjoining galleries, Rooms 46A and B, packed with official reproductions of European sculpture (how they got the enormous imitation Trajan's Column in there I could never figure out). Finally, she refused to come with me, but the association remained.

The first time I talked her through the exhibit, I know she was interested. It was the repetition that wore her down. But standing in that familiar spot in front of Savonarola (a man who cried out that the worship of beauty led men away from the search for God), it was neither Bastianini nor Oliver Godolphin who beckoned me. I was in London and the temptation was too great to resist.

A taxi had just pulled up in front of the V & A and I grabbed it, directing the driver to 123 Ebury Street. Since the Gallerie

Naif was open to the public, at least I knew Fiona couldn't just slam the door in my face, not that she had any real reason to be angry at me. I had only tried to kiss her lips on our last parting, managing to plant one on her nostril when she turned away. And it couldn't be a total coincidence that she had chosen Ebury Street for the location of the Gallerie Naif—featuring, naturally, the works of "naïve" artists, of which I was not overly fond—as this was where we had once lived together in our own tiny flat after leaving her parents' larger one in Belgravia. Ebury Street, a place as close to Heaven as the hills of Jerusalem.

I handed the driver a fiver and was too excited to wait for change, bolting across the sidewalk to the gallery entrance, barely glancing at the rather awful paintings in the window as I hurtled through the door.

"Well, fuck me with a fiddle, if it isn't Mickey Maltese," Sally Morgan said. "My bleeding heart."

Sally Morgan, better known as Morgan the Organ, was, for reasons that I could never understand, Fiona's closest friend and partner in the Gallerie Naif. She had also been maid of honor at our Richmond wedding, which she capped by bending over and flipping up her dress to give Fiona and me a view of her naked backside on our departure and which Fiona found hysterically funny. Being, understandably, in a totally euphoric mood at the time (hadn't I just married the girl of my dreams, the woman of my life, the full partner of my heart and soul?), I laughed as well, taking the gesture as an intimate nude salute to our union and meant to hurry and inspire us toward our nuptial celebration. How was I to know then that Morgan the Organ, this foul-mouthed woman of slender education and outrageous behavior, was soon to become the viper in our happy nest? Her mean little eyes, framed by her spiky blond hair, glinted with evil satisfaction, but I was not about to be intimidated.

"Oh, hello, Sally," I let the words drop casually, as my eyes darted around the empty gallery. No sign of Fiona.

"She's not here," the Organ spoke. "Shitty timing as usual. Christ, what an asshole."

"How's business?" I gestured indifferently at the hangings, all pastoral scenes that appeared to have been painted by gifted children under the age of six.

"What are you doing in London?" she didn't bother to answer my question. "You're supposed to be safely farting about with the guineas."

"Where's Fiona?"

"Just passing through?"

"Is she in town?"

"Going back to New York?"

"Where is Fiona?"

"None of your fucking business."

"I'll find her."

"Rot in hell, Mickey."

"Heute mir, Morgan dear."

That went right over her head. There was no valid, as I saw it, reason for Sally Morgan's hostility and I had done nothing, from my point of view, to instigate it, other than marrying Fiona. But other men had done that as well. Yet, to my knowledge, the Organ reserved all of her animosity for me.

"Fuck you in the brain," she said, then turned away to answer the telephone.

"May the fire of St. Anthony fly up thy fundament," I was not about to descend to her level. "Though God only knows what's been there before."

"Gallerie Naif, good afternoon," the Organ modulated into the phone, her head snapping around to glare back at me. "Oh, hi."

I knew it was Fiona on the other end of the line, and just the thought of being so close, even with such an unpleasant intermediary, was enough to make me tingle.

"What's worse than death?" the awful Organ asked. "The Maltese curse. Yes, he's right here, oozing all over the fucking floor. Christ, you can't be serious. Fiona."

The name, that name, was spoken as a whining complaint, then dreadful Sally turned away to listen, but not before I saw her expression start its unhappy contortions. I would see Fiona in the flesh, but no clearer than the Fiona in my mind. The precise red of her hair, the exact curve of her lip, her earlobes, the unique timber of her voice, the blood vessels in her eyeballs, toes, fingernails, the whiteness of her bottom, the whole exciting collage was about to tumble back into perfect order. The miserable Morgan's back was quivering with rage and I could just imagine her furious expression, the repugnance in her weasel eyes. It was wonderful.

"You are bloody insane," suddenly Sally was laughing, and she turned back to face me with something close to joy. "All right, I'll tell him. Bye."

The Organ's cheerful countenance clicked off at the same instant she disconnected, but even so there was no sign of anger, the usual loathing astonishingly absent. Humming some cheerful tune, Sally busied herself tidying up the desk for a minute or so, then glanced up as if surprised to see me standing there.

"Ah, Mickey," she smiled venomously. "So glad you haven't gone."

"What are you supposed to tell me?" I phrased the question in a way that she had to answer.

"Tell you? Oh, that's quite right, there was a message for me to pass on. Let's see. Fiona said, now what was it exactly? Fiona said that you should be at her house at seven-thirty, if that's convenient. Of course, if you happened to be hit by a bus in the meantime, I'm sure she'll understand. Or was it eight-thirty?"

The Organ's concept of humor was not exactly *comedia del'arte,* but lightness was never her forte, unless, of course, her ease and eagerness to dive into indiscriminate beds ("Warren Beatty is the best fuck in the world," was once her motto, which she claimed was tattooed on some part of her anatomy as a challenge to all other players) can be classified as a form of farce. Nevertheless, I was vividly aware that some telephonic collusion was responsible for the feeble attempt at jocosity, which created an atmosphere of suspicion in my psyche. Not that Fiona lacked a sense of jest, wicked in fact, but never cruel.

"Seven-thirty," Sally was defeated by my silence. "Now get the fuck out of here."

"Thanks awfully for your help," I smiled.

"Die," the Organ said.

4

Fiona's house, which she had somehow acquired from her last husband, a stocky oilman named John Lipscomb, was on Chester Square, only a few blocks from Ebury Street. So faced with the steady rain and a good two hours (I could arrive a little early) to kill, I headed for the old neighborhood pub where Fiona and I had spent so many happy hours years ago. I pushed open the door and instantly froze in emotional stasis. Nothing had changed, there had been no passage of time, even the publican's face was the same and for a moment I hoped that I had stepped through a glorious time machine. It was, of course, nonsense and I snapped right out of it.

"Help you, sir?" the pub keeper said as I approached.

"A pint of cider, please."

"And a pink gin for the lady?" he asked.

"The lady?" I failed to make the leap. "What lady?"

"Your missus. Haven't seen her for a while."

Oh my God! I jerked around, anticipating that Fiona would be there, which, of course, she wasn't. It took a moment for me to collect myself, past and present having become a bit confusing in the last minute.

"I'm meeting her later," I answered truthfully, not seeing it necessary to add the unfortunate details.

The pub keeper drew my pint of cider, then I retreated to a corner table to avoid further conversation. It was a natural mistake on his part, an understandable error, and publicans are well known for their feats of memory, drink preferences, faces if not names. Besides, Fiona was not only easy to remember, she was unforgettable. Calmer now, I glanced around, nodded pleasantly to anyone who caught my eye, and sipped my cider as warm thoughts of my married life swept over me.

"I don't know why I can't, Mickey," I remember Fiona saying

to me here one night. "God knows, I never had trouble popping off with anyone else."

This was in response to my feeble joke that if she were a Navaho, her name would be "Woman-Who-Never-Comes." There had been a slight problem in the conjugal bed, but we had discussed it openly, though both of us remained baffled by her inability to climax. Still, her reference to past orgasmic performance was, I thought, a bit tacky. In a totally lovable way, of course.

"And please don't keep blaming it on your roger," she had gone on, taking adorable bites out of her pink gin. "I know you're sensitive about that."

Sensitive? As well as Fiona knew me, there was no way she could have truly known what it was like during my adolescent years in boarding school. "Mule dick Maltese," was one of my classmates' favorites, that and "Crowbar," and the endless fun they had with the fact that I always wore a tight jock-strap under my underwear. They even tried to persuade me to exhibit myself to their girlfriends, "Come on, Mickey, she won't believe me. Show her the big baloney," and once the football team held me down while the town tart, Four Finger Sally Sears, manipulated me against my will into a full extension.

It wasn't until my second year in New Haven that I realized what I had considered my deformity was something of an attraction, though still a social embarrassment as I was easily stimulated. Merely the most fleeting glimpse of Fiona's naked shoulder reflected in the bathroom mirror was enough to tumefy me after a year and a half of marriage. 19.0500381 by 8.89001778. Fiona had once laughingly measured me in centimeters, but my failure to satisfy her soon brought that laughter to an end, and we argued, each of us trying to assume the blame, Fiona claiming that it was all an emotional block on her part and I knowing that it was a physical problem on mine.

Whichever, we never resolved it and when she finally left me, she departed as sexually unsatisfied as she had been on our first night together. After Fiona's subsequent remarriage only a few months later, an act which I put down to bodily need rather than heartfelt emotions, I brought up the subject of our past difficulty.

"Difficulty?" she had blinked as we were standing outside of

Fortnum's after an accidental encounter. "Oh, Mickey, are you still chewing on that old bone?"

Of course, I was.

"Believe me, it was just some silly mental thing I had about having sex with you. Honestly, darling, there's no problem now," she stroked my hand consolingly, then glanced at her watch. "I've got to run."

I was devastated. Since that time, I have wisely stayed off that subject with Fiona and she has felt no need to discuss it with me. But still it is hard to keep totally out of mind, particularly since I have chosen to be celibate since the break-up. Sleeping with Fiona or sleeping alone seemed the only two options, and since I only had one of them, the choice was thrust upon me. I suppose all that unexpressed desire is what catapulted me so intensely into my work, so my post-Fiona life has had its satisfactions. In a way.

During these last reflections, I had sipped all my cider away, so I carried my glass back to the bar for a refill. There was still considerable time before I could make my appearance at Chester Square, but already my anxiety about the encounter was rising. Running into Fiona by chance was one thing, but seeing her by appointment was something else entirely. Was there something she wanted to discuss with me? "I know this is unpleasant for you to hear, Mickey, but we simply have to talk about it," I could imagine her saying gently. But what? And why the Organ's sudden shift to laughter on the phone. There was something I didn't know. A plot? I put that quickly down to paranoia.

"Seen Ted lately?" the pub keeper asked as I handed him my empty pint.

Ted? I drew a total blank. Ted who?

"Ted, the writer fellow," the pub keeper continued, refilling my glass.

"Not recently," I fished out some coins and spread them on the bar.

"In here with the missus once or twice."

'Ah, probably."

After all, Fiona did know practically everybody. But Ted, the writer, here in our local? While we were still married? Had Fiona been unfaithful, perhaps seeking some physical relief? Was there a hidden liaison, the secret shared with the awful Morgan, that was behind their laughter? And how many details had Fiona revealed about our relationship? Women do tend to exchange these pieces of intimate information. Could that be the reason terrible Sally called me "The Maltese Curse"? The level of my anxiety jumped several degrees and I had to talk myself down again, a process which easily consumed the remaining waiting time.

The rain had diminished to a fine mist, making headlamps glow impressionistically, as I darted across Ebury Street and walked the two short blocks to Chester Square. Fiona's house was third on the right and my finger hit the doorbell at seven-thirty on the dot. For several moments nothing happened, then the door was flung open and there she was. Fiona. Black pants, a white silk blouse, pearls around her neck turned pink by the glorious red reflection of her hair. I felt myself begin to swell.

"Mickey," she smiled. "So nice to see you. I've been wondering where you were at. Have you come from Rome?"

"Yesterday," I grinned and nodded, my eyes devouring her face.

"How's your Pa?" she asked.

My Pa. How exquisite. How perfectly Fionesque. I was skewered by three words and still standing in the doorway. Why should Fiona ask about my father? This was hardly a common topic of our conversation. In fact, he hadn't even attended our wedding, since I had secretly destroyed the invitation, then sent some small gift from Asprey with his name attached to cover my tracks, and as a result was forced to destroy Fiona's "thank you" note as well.

"I haven't seen him" (or spoken to him in years). "Why do you ask?"

"Here, let me take your coat," Fiona said after she had guided me inside. "Then we'll go upstairs to the drawing room."

Still bewildered by Fiona's totally unexpected inquiry about my father, I handed over my damp Burberry and followed her up the steps, my eyes automatically fixing on the soft and graceful motion of her bottom tenderly ascending. There was always something special about the way Fiona climbed stairs.

"Oh, stop gawking at my bum," she laughed without turning. "God knows you've seen it before."

Yes, and in my dreams as well, but that familiarity only increased the fascination. To become bored at the song of Sirens would be far easier than even feigning indifference at the sight of Fiona's rear on a flight of stairs.

"I saw your Pa about six weeks ago," Fiona succeeded in distracting me at last. "He came into the gallery."

"You didn't buy anything from him, did you?" I tried to sound casual, but the question came out worried.

"No," Fiona reached the landing, then waited for me, her eyes spotting the lump in my trousers. "For heaven's sake, Mickey, can't you control that thing?"

Obviously not.

"What did he want?"

"Who? Your Pa?"

Fiona was playing games. Of course my Pa. We both knew what my roger wanted.

"Yes," I said.

"He was looking for you," Fiona led me into the drawing room.

It had been beautifully decorated, matching floral couches separated by an oak and leaded glass coffee table, muted yellow walls with paintings perfectly positioned. Real art, no naïve paintings here.

"Are you sure?" I asked.

"Of course, I'm sure. He asked if you were in town and I told him that I thought you were in Rome and he said he'd find you there."

"I mean, are you sure it was my father? You never met him before, so it could have been anybody," I added hopefully, trying to wish it away. "What did he look like?"

"Mickey, what's the matter with you?" Fiona eyed me strangely. "It was your Pa."

"Describe him to me. Please."

"Oh," Fiona sighed. "All right, he was tall, good features, gray hair, but well trimmed. Distinguished, I mean there was a quality of refinement and he said his name was Amour Maltese, but that I should call him Maury. Satisfied?"

"Yes," I admitted. "That's him. Why was he looking for me?"

"Well, how would I know?" Fiona was a bit exasperated now.

"A father has the right to look for his son, doesn't he?"

Not necessarily. My father, sometimes referred to as "The Notorious Maury Maltese," belongs to that exclusive group of people who often create havoc in my life and who generally regard me with suspicion and hostility because they can only profit by my mistakes and wish me ill at every turn of the road. They are crooks, which is to say they are Art Dealers. Well, that may be too broad a statement, but some of them are not altogether honest in their dealings, more intent on a quick profit than a truthful provenance.

My father, however, is a crook, a man who had specialized in selling Chagalls created by Lothar Malskat and, naturally, Vermeers by Hans van Meegeren, to name only two examples. He claimed, of course, to have been taken in by the expertise of the forgeries and, while once indicted, he was never convicted. After that unpleasant episode, which somehow instead of besmirching his reputation gave him an aura of mysterious glamour, he watched his step for a while and actually came up with several genuine finds. But the number of forgeries placed by my father and now hanging in museums and private collections has got to be in the hundreds. When, as occasionally happens, one of these frauds is revealed, Maury Maltese is always shocked and surprised in a most convincing way. I know better.

"Campari?" Fiona asked.

"Lovely," I answered.

But why was he looking for me, or why would he tell Fiona he was? And why didn't he find me in Rome, where I could have been easily tracked down with a couple of phone calls? Troublesome questions. But everything about my father was troublesome, particularly since I exposed the Paul Klee he was in the process of selling as a reasonably good Josef Jenniches imitation, an act which I felt he considered cowardly filial betrayal. There had been cruel words and reminders of all he had done for me—not so much actually, since it had been my grandfather, Mellos "Mightly Mel" Maltese, who had set up the generous trust fund which paid my way through both boarding school and New Haven. Besides, since beauty was in the eye of the beholder, if the painting pleased, why did I place such importance on the identity of the painter. After all, didn't the great Bernard

Berenson himself purchase (and sell, for that matter) a number of forgeries, at least one of which, "St. Catherine," falsely attributed to Simone Martini, remains on display with the other venerated paintings at *I Tatti?*

"Cheers," Fiona said, handing me my Campari.

"Cheers," I replied automatically and slugged the whole thing down without thinking.

After Fiona pounded my back and succeeded in ending my coughing fit, she seated herself on the floral couch opposite. She instinctively found the spot where the lighting was perfect, making her peach complexion radiate with beauty, adding sparkle to her already sparkling eyes and the illusion of moistness to her lips. She sighed and shook her head.

"Oh, Mickey, you are impossible."

"Me?"

"Why did you keep him hidden all these years?"

"Keep who hidden?"

"Your Pa, silly. The way you acted, I thought he was some dreadful embarrassment, but I have never met a more charming, cultured man."

Oh God. Maury had turned it on.

"Are you sure he didn't try to sell you anything?" I had to ask.

"He doesn't deal in naïve paintings, but he thought they were all very nice. In fact, he knows quite a lot about the field. In fact, he even told me some details about the artists that I'd never heard before."

I'll bet.

"Then," Fiona went on, "he took me out to dinner at Le Gavroche and got us a table instantly without a reservation. Do you know what that means, Mickey? A table at Le Gavroche *without* a reservation. It's impossible."

But not for the man who could sell a Frans Hals with the paint still wet. Yet this was the kind of thing that impressed Fiona, something I could never do. I couldn't even get a reservation at Le Gavroche or if I could, the table would be next to the kitchen door.

"And," Fiona gushed ahead, "he didn't even bother to look at the menu, ordering *Poulet an Lentils* and *Tournedos au Bandol* and, Mickey, not everyone knows that at Le Gavroche those are *the* dishes."

"What did he want?" I interrupted, trying to break the enchanted spell.

"Want?"

"Who paid the bill?" I shifted to a different tactic.

"Your Pa, of course," she said. "He just signed it, so he must have an account there."

Well, I suppose that's possible. My father enjoys the elegant life and the fact that he is not always able to afford it has never been much of a restraint. But why put on the act for Fiona?

"Well, what did the two of you talk about during this lovely meal?" I asked with a dog-like smile.

"As a matter of fact," Fiona was getting serious now, "we talked mainly about you."

About me?

"Your Pa thinks very highly of you, Mickey. He's very, very proud of you."

Amour, it was quite evident now, desired something from Amicus, and since we were not on speaking terms, my father had seized upon Fiona as the intermediary, knowing that, sooner or later, the message would get through. It was an old family trick, as long stretches of non-communication were practically a Maltese tradition, my grandfather, the Mighty Mel, having maintained a stony silence with his own son for months at a time. At the end of these periods, I was usually the messenger of reconciliation, but Mel, ancient but still fierce, had died peacefully in his sleep many years ago, leaving me and my father without an interlocutor. Now Maury had chosen Fiona as his bridge over our troubled water. From my point of view, he couldn't have made a worse choice, because, unfortunately, it would work to perfection.

"Darling," Fiona was rising to her feet as gracefully as any portrait of the Ascension. "Come with me."

"Where?" I lurched up.

"I have a little surprise for you," she smiled.

5

"Promise that you'll never tell," Fiona fingered the small package in her hand.

"I promise," I responded eagerly.

"I mean really, really promise."

"I really, really promise."

Fiona opened the small package and took out a clear plastic shower cap, then put it on, sweeping her flame colored hair under the elastic band.

"Don't laugh," she said sternly.

Laugh? No one in history has been more beautiful wearing a plastic shower cap. I sat on one of the counter stools in the large, white, country-style kitchen and watched in admiration as Fiona dumped the sliced potatoes into the pot of hot oil. A chicken was browning aromatically in the oven and the *mange-tout* were waiting to be steamed. Fiona was cooking my favorite meal. This was a portrait of domestic bliss and I wanted to make it last forever. Cherishing my warm inner glow, I glanced at the now empty shower cap package. It was from the Hotel George V in Paris.

"Open the wine, sweetheart," Fiona was absorbed in her cooking. "It's in the fridge."

One darling and one sweetheart. Obviously, I was getting to her. I nimbly plucked the bottle—a Louis Latour Puligny Montrachet—out of the refrigerator and uncorked it with surprising expertise, then filled two glasses, holding them both in one hand, without spilling a drop.

"Oh, lovely," Fiona said after taking a sip, her eyes fixed on the frying chips.

The first time I had seen Fiona do her shower cap trick was shortly after we were married and still living in her parents' Belgravia flat. I had just had (a familiar American flaw) a sudden craving for McDonald's french fries and was trying to persuade

Fiona to come with me. "Oh, darling," she had laughed, "I can make better chips than those." Then out came the shower cap, that time from the bathroom, rather than the George V. The George V? Why would Fiona be at the George V? And with whom? The answer, of course, that swept through my mind was unthinkable. Unbearable. Unmentionable. Not even Maury Maltese could be that heartless.

"Well," Fiona plucked out one french fry and examined it critically, "aren't you going to tell me about Rome?"

I would have preferred to ask her about Paris, but being on the tender edge with Fiona that didn't seem a sensible question, so I began telling the tale of my long and persistent adventure with the *professore* and the *faux* Michelangelo sketchbook, making myself seem as modestly brilliant as I could without actually bragging. I was only six months into the story when dinner was ready and finished the report between bites. Fiona's roast chicken, chips (much better than McDonald's) and lightly steamed *mange-tout* were all delicious, reminding me of all the meals we had enjoyed together and how much I missed them. After Fiona, eating other food was only a bland, spiceless ritual.

"But, Mickey, how could you have possibly known," Fiona's beautiful green eyes filled with soft admiration.

"You have to go by your feelings," I said.

Now that I was on emotional ground, I was just about to slide into the subject of reconciliation, but Fiona spotted my expression and rose to clear the table, cleverly heading off my pass. She was always, somehow, ahead of me, a fact which once amused her. "Mickey, you are so transparent," she had laughed. "You'd make a simply awful spy."

Still, there had to be some way that, little by little, I could creep back into her life without her noticing before I was firmly in place. Then, like a pair of old and comfortable shoes, I could sit in the closet and be taken out on rainy days, which, in London, would be most of the time. Not, I realized, that this made a great deal of sense, but a lot of things in life didn't make sense, like when Maurice Vlaminck forged a Cezanne and Cezanne, for some reason, then certified it as his own work.

"Sweets," Fiona announced on her return, then plunked down strawberries and Double Devon cream, which we ate in a heavy silence.

I could tell that Fiona had something on her mind, but I was content to wait, thrilled by the wonderful way she licked the cream from her lips, her perfectly pink tongue darting as gracefully as any cat's. Fiona could never quite grasp the immensity of my love for her, but on those occasions when she sensed the heat, it made her uncomfortable, which, naturally, made me even more uncomfortable, resulting in long, awkward pauses in our otherwise flowing communication.

"So," she said finally, asking the question as if she wasn't sure whether or not she wanted to hear the answer, "what brings you to London?"

"Just a job," I shrugged it off, then couldn't resist. "Actually a very unusual job."

"How so?" Fiona nibbled at the bait.

My solemn assurance, in the Farrow & Farrow conference room earlier in the day, of absolute confidentiality fell like a rock, but my urgent need to impress Fiona assumed instant priority and I told her everything, casting myself in the best possible light, but not in too heavy-handed a way. And, in fact, it was true that the fate of *Sakura* was resting on my provenance if not my shoulders.

"Oliver Godolphin!" Fiona brightened suddenly. "He's wonderful. I've read all his books. He's my absolute favorite. Oh, Mickey, how exciting. Do you realize how important this is? I mean, if Oliver Godolphin really wrote the book. God, I can't wait to read it. What's it about?"

"Well, it's sort of a love story," I admitted, withholding the fact that I hadn't yet finished reading Mrs. Bettina Sachs's less-than-gripping synopsis.

"And it's so strange," Fiona said excitedly. "So coincidental."

"What is?"

"I know Sheffy Eccleston. She's a very important agent now, but she used to be Oliver Godolphin's secretary years ago."

Oliver Godolphin's secretary? Fiona had topped me again.

"Sheffy Eccleston?" This was as unlikely as a long lost painting showing up at an exhibit in Newcastle, but that had actually once happened. "How well do you know her?"

"Not all that well, but I see her all the time at parties,

openings, things like that." Fiona thought about it. "And she's been to the gallery once or twice. Never bought anything, though."

Obviously, Sheffy Eccleston and I shared the same opinion about naïve art.

"Then how do you know she was Godolphin's secretary?"

"She told me, silly. How else would I know? This is just the wildest coincidence. And a missing Oliver Godolphin novel. That's so mysterious." Fiona was getting interested again. "And with his editor saying he wrote it and his daughter saying he didn't, Mickey, how are you going to find out?"

I had for years tried to impress upon Fiona that provenance was a highly exciting and even glamorous field, but she always regarded it as a fairly dull occupation, hanging around dusty old libraries and museums. Until now. A possibly fraudulent Michelangelo was nothing compared to a possibly fraudulent Godolphin. Well, I had to admit that you didn't find a lot of Michelangelo's work in airport book shops, nor had he ever won the Nobel Prize.

"Maybe I won't," I went fishing again. "There's always that possibility."

"Of course, you will." Fiona delivered the sought-after compliment. "Everyone knows that a Maltese provenance is the absolute best."

"Oh, not everyone." I was positively glowing. "But this one is going to be very difficult."

"You'll do it." Fiona was my coach now. "I know you'll do it."

Once, purely as a matter of curiosity, I started to casually investigate the famous bust of Flora, which had once been hailed as a newly discovered masterpiece by Leonardo da Vinci, as it possessed a Gioconda smile, and had been enthusiastically pursued by various museums and collectors. Flora finally wound up in the Prussian Art Collection in Berlin at the staggering cost (at the 1909 exchange rate) of 160,000 marks, whereupon it was immediately attacked as a forgery, beginning a dispute which attracted considerable publicity.

The general manager of the Berlin Collection, of course, defended his purchase vigorously, but the controversy did not go away. In fact, it was made even more controversial by the announcement that the Leonardo Flora had been manufactured by the English sculptor Richard Cockle Lucas, who could personally neither confirm nor deny the attribution, since he was, unfortunately, dead at the time of the revelation.

His son, however, then well into his eighties, claimed to remember his father working on Flora, but, believing Lucas Jr. to be in his dotage, his word was not taken as definitive, at which point another German expert examined the statue and pronounced the work as being that of the great Bastianini. That it was a forgery was no longer in question, but who was the forger? I was fascinated and, as always, shared this conundrum with Fiona, who found the entire topic quite boring. "If it's not by da Vinci, what difference does it make?" she had announced with a shrug. But Fiona was not deeply involved in the art world then.

"Could you introduce me to Sheffy Eccleston?" I asked.

"I suppose," Fiona said, hesitating.

"It might be important," I told her. "Vital."

"Oh, all right. I'll ring her tomorrow," Fiona gave in unenthusiastically.

For some reason, Fiona has not been exactly eager for me to meet her friends and, I suspect, does not include the fact that we were once husband and wife, albeit briefly, in whatever personal history she chooses to reveal in her social circle. I have always respected this decision on her part and maintained a discrete position in my constant pursuit of her affections, though I did happen to meet her other two now ex-husbands on occasion.

"But just to talk about Oliver Godolphin," she added.

"Of course. What else would we talk about?"

"Mickey," Fiona took a deep breath, then let it out slowly. "There's something I have to say to you."

"There are so many things I want to tell you, Fiona."

"No, you don't understand."

"I understand that I love you, that I have always loved you, that I will always love you," I had to say it.

"Jesus, you make things difficult," she seemed irritated.

"Fiona, you and I . . ."

"Stop it," she said, then held out her hands. "Take my hand."

It was clearly an invitation that I could not resist. I took them both, holding them tightly as Fiona stared deeply and seriously into my admiring eyes. I could feel the pulse of her life travel through her hands into mine and tried to send back my love in return.

"Mickey," she said softly. "Mickey, I want a divorce."

6

Another May London morning, another day of rain. Even the sight, seen through the window of my room at the Rembrandt Hotel, of the V & A, did nothing to lift my spirits. I was suddenly desperate to get out of town. But to do so I would have to force my body, which had turned to lead, to move. Earlier, I had placed my call to Pierre Rougemont in Geneva and now I was trapped waiting for the return, incapable of preventing myself from replaying again and again last night's trauma with Fiona.

"Mickey, I want a divorce," her voice had been echoing in my head all night.

"But, Fiona, you already have one," I had answered. "Three, in fact."

"No." We were still holding hands, but by now my palms had become clammy. "I mean a real divorce. Not just that legal thing. I want you out of my life."

"Never!" I had blurted out.

"Forever."

That's when I became sick and had to dash for the loo (the toilet, the bathroom—it has been said that I am one of those Americans who have spent too much time abroad), as even Fiona's splendid meal was determined to part from me as well. Later, lying on the floral couch with a cold cloth on my forehead, I still couldn't believe what I had heard. How could she want me out of her life? Forever? There was nothing I had done to deserve this.

"I've been seeing someone." Fiona clearly felt no sympathy for my pathetic condition. "Someone who is very important to me. It's become serious."

What could be more serious than my feelings for Fiona? Who else in the world could care for her more than I did? Whose love could possibly be greater? It simply wasn't possible. Fiona had become the victim of an emotional fraud.

"Who?" I asked weakly.

"It doesn't matter."

"Fiona, you have to tell me who it is." I started to push myself up from the floral couch, then felt the room spin and collapsed. "You have to."

"All right," Fiona's voice was cold and crisp. "It's Roddy Startle, but if you ever go near him, I swear I'll kill you."

Go near him? There was no way I could get even vaguely close to him.

"Roddy Startle? The rock star? The one with the concerts with all those screaming people? The one with those tight silver pants and all the hair? Good God, Fiona," was all I managed to say.

The man's photograph was everywhere, his every song an enormous hit. He must be worth millions. Perhaps Fiona was tempted by the money.

"He's the most wonderful and sensitive man I've ever met," she said. "Neither of us expected this to happen so quickly, but last weekend in Paris, it just did."

That finally explained the George V shower cap, but I could take little solace in the realization that at least Fiona hadn't fried chips for Roddy Startle in the meantime. First Fiona and my father at Le Gavroche and then Fiona and Roddy Startle at the George V. I felt a sudden wave of Francophobia. After all, Fiona hadn't expelled me so violently from her life when she married the City man, Clive Price (my first successor) or the stocky oil-man, John Lipscomb (my second), so why was she attempting it now. What had changed?

"Fiona, don't you think you're overreacting?" I sounded very reasonable.

"Mickey, there's no point in continuing this conversation." Fiona plucked the cold cloth off my forehead. "And I know you're not feeling well, but I want you to leave."

Rejection in love is like a Spanish song. It tears at the heart.

And, thus wounded, I couldn't think of any way to stall, so I pried myself off the floral couch and followed Fiona down the stairs. Without meeting my eyes, she handed me my coat, then simply opened the front door, and somehow my feet carried me out into the rain. After a few stumbling steps, I turned back for one last look.

"Good-bye," Fiona said and closed the door.

Stunned and even weeping, I found my way to Elizabeth Street and headed blindly right, somehow managing to navigate my way back to the Rembrandt as I relived the scene over and over again with no lessening of pain. How could this have happened? And why? Had my father said anything to make her veer off so abruptly?

Or could it have been that awful Mrs. Gorse, the psychic from Shoreditch. Fiona not only believed in psychics, she swore by them. "She sees into the future, Mickey. She really does," I remember her telling me time and time again. After all, hadn't Mrs. Gorse told her that she would meet the man she would marry on the bridge in St. James's Park? Or at least this is what Fiona had claimed as absolute proof of Mrs. Gorse's powers.

And I would make fun of it all, wrapping a towel around my head and becoming Gypsy Petulengro, the fortune teller, which always made Fiona collapse with laughter. Once there had been a lot of laughter.

The loud ring of the phone made me jump.

"Hello?"

"Mr. Maltese, I have Mr. Rougemont for you."

A pause.

"*Allo?*"

"Mr. Rougemont, this is Amicus Maltese. I called you earlier because we have a mutual concern which I cannot discuss over the telephone. However, if you can arrange some time, I can be in Geneva tomorrow."

"How large is this mutual concern?"

"Seven figures."

"In which currency?"

"In any currency."

"Then I shall look forward to seeing you at three-fifteen."

Click.

I like that about the gnomes. No unnecessary chit-chat. Not that I was on intimate terms with many Swiss bankers, but I knew Geneva as well as Switzerland is a common transit point for many questionable dealings in the art trade, being so conveniently located between Italy and France. Also the claim that the *objet* for sale was from the collection of a private party in Switzerland was usually the clincher in the deal, since, after all, anything from the careful Swiss was practically as good as gold. Now, that is a laugh. Some of the greatest connivers I have ever met were Swiss, no reflection on Pierre Rougemont, of course.

Actually, our brief conversation had made me feel much better, taking my thoughts away from Fiona and steering them back to Oliver Godolphin. Suddenly, I was filled with a sense of determination, which, however, wasn't strong enough to move me into finishing Mrs. Bettina Sachs's turgid synopsis. Instead, I pulled on my coat and hurried out the door. Destiny would resolve my temporary problem with Fiona and I knew that destiny was on my side.

After instructing the Rembrandt hall porter to book me on tomorrow's morning flight to Geneva and reserve me a nice room at the Hotel Richemond, I managed to flag down a taxi and went speeding off to Great Russell Street to bury myself in the great domed reading room of the British Library. Here, I was confident, I would learn all there was to know about the late Oliver Godolphin, because if it isn't in the British Library with its many millions of books, it wouldn't be anywhere, particularly about a best selling author and Nobel Prize winner.

Two hours later, I was both seriously disappointed and totally intrigued. Oliver Godolphin, it seemed, simply appeared from nowhere in 1955 in Marseille after having served *("avec honneur et fidelité")* in the French Foreign Legion, which entitled him to become a citizen of France. Before then, there was no information available, not even in the British Library. He spoke English and French with equal fluency and no trace of a regional accent in either language.

A number of sources raised the question of his original nationality (assumed to be English, since he wrote exclusively in that language, but so did Joseph Conrad and he, there is no question of this, was Polish). These sources also questioned the name

that Oliver Godolphin was purportedly born with, since genealogical researchers were unable to trace a missing male Godolphin in
any branch of all the families by that name. The Foreign Legion,
of course, refused all inquiries as was their duty, until the pressure mounted after Godolphin became a Laureate and he was
claimed as a son of France. The Legion then announced that all
their records had been destroyed, which may have not been true,
but which preserved their honor.

Oliver Godolphin himself, in countless interviews, rejected all
questions that dealt with events prior to his emergence from Fort
Saint Nicolas ("Were you at Dien Bien Phu?", for example, was
sufficient cause for terminating the interview and leaving the
room). But it was widely noted that when *Le Boudin*, the traditional march of the Legion, was played, Godolphin would always
snap to attention.

By comparison, the post-1955 years were an open book. He
was married to Alexandra Whitfield (b. London, 1933) that same
year, but there is no indication of a prior relationship, just a
whirlwind courtship and a quick civil marriage. Their only child,
Alexis (b. Paris, 1956) arrived eleven months after the nuptials,
so it obviously wasn't a shotgun wedding. Both of Alexandra's
parents had perished in a traffic accident, leaving her, an only
child, with a small inheritance, which brought her to Paris and
which apparently supported the Godolphin family while Oliver
scribbled away at his first novel.

The rest is history. Success followed by success followed by
even more success. The first book was snapped up by MGM and
the Godolphins moved to Hollywood for a year, but this was not
a happy experience, as Oliver did not approve of the way his
novel was translated onto celluloid and publicly disowned the
film, which was an enormous box office hit anyway. They then
moved to London, where best seller number two was written,
then finally, after an absence of four years, back to France. All
subsequent offers from the Hollywood moguls were ignored,
which explains why there is only one Godolphin-based movie,
although that is a question that had not previously occurred to
me.

Other than writing prolifically and amassing millions, Oliver
Godolphin appeared to have no outside interests other than flying

helicopters (something he picked up as a Legionnaire?) and was considered to be an excellent pilot, obviously an unfortunate hobby. The fatal crash took place in the Mediterranean, while the three Godolphins were cruising on the famous yacht, *Al-Bakhîl*, owned by Ali Habibi, the well-known Arabian playboy and darling of the Riviera at the time. Habibi, who had even more money than Oliver Godolphin was later revealed to have been the middle-man in a lot of shady deals in the arms trade. *Al-Bakhîl*, it seems, means The Miser in Arabic, so Mr. Habibi clearly had a sense of humor. Unhappily, it was one of his helicopters (the *Al-Bakhîl* had room for two) that carried Oliver and Alexandra Godolphin to their deaths, while young Alexis and Mr. Habibi were engaged elsewhere in a hot game of backgammon.

And that was it. The British Library had the transcript of Oliver Godolphin's Nobel acceptance speech, which I found less than fascinating, but not a single connecting reference to Salzburg, Vienna or even Austria. From the information available, there was no evidence that Godolphin had even visited the country, so why does the character of Jordan Leander, the American journalist, become so "filled with a deep and abiding detestation" for all things Austrian? And what inspired the creation of the beautiful Lulu von Hofmannsthal? One of the constant dangers of research is that it often confuses before it illuminates. I would have to finish reading Mrs. Bettina Sachs's synopsis.

It had taken me several hours to accumulate this surprisingly small pile of information and I was just about to leave when another avenue opened up. The Foreign Legion. Didn't Legionnaires, these comrades in arms, form strong bonds of friendship and vow to, for example, meet at the *Manneken Pis* in Brussels on New Year's Eve to share a bottle of *marc* and remember the fallen? Perhaps another former Legionnaire had written the exciting memoirs of his youth and included a fellow *combattant* who went on to become a world famous author. No such luck. There are fewer contemporary Foreign Legion memoirs than one would think and most of them were written by former officers who were still outraged over the loss of Algeria, the F.L.N. and the *fellagha*. Many God damns, but no Godolphins.

The rain had stopped, the sky actually clearing by the time I left the great neo-classical building that houses the British

Museum as well as the British Library and headed toward Totten-ham Court Road and beyond to the Third World Country known as Oxford Street. My mind still buzzed with the growing mystery called Oliver Godolphin. The surrounding babble of (it seemed) fifty-two different languages (none of them English) filtered through and disturbed my thought process, so I quickly left Oxford Street behind and walked toward Piccadilly, trying to pre-tend that I hadn't already determined my destination, which was, of course, St. James's Park. Twenty minutes later I sat on a bench, sharing my bag of sandwiches with the always ravenous geese and staring at the bridge where Fiona and I first met so many years ago. Did Jordan Leander ever return to that cafe on the hill overlooking Salzburg where he first saw Lulu von Hof-mannsthal? I definitely had to finish reading the synopsis.

7

The law offices of Putnam, Dick and Thurston (why do lawyers always run in threesomes?) were conveniently located on Wig-more Street, just off Portman Square, which meant that I practi-cally had to retrace my steps and cross Oxford Street again, not that I had planned on coming here. I had decided, out of cour-tesy, to phone Rupert Farrow and inform him of my imminent departure for Geneva and my three-fifteen appointment with Pierre Rougemont, but instead of putting me through, the Farrow & Farrow receptionist had instructed me to communicate with Stephen J. Thurston, with whom I would be dealing from this point on. I generally prefer conducting my business with princi-pals rather than intermediaries.

Nevertheless I phoned Thurston dutifully, as my information was not so complex that it was in danger of becoming garbled in the retransmission. The Putnam, Dick and Thurston secretary was obviously expecting my call. Since Mr. Thurston was not avail-able at this precise moment, he would appreciate seeing me in his office at four p.m. promptly. It sounded ominously like a summons. But for what reason? I had only been hired yesterday and had done nothing to demonstrate a lack of alacrity. In fact, from my point of view, I had accomplished quite a lot, even if I still hadn't finished reading the synopsis, provenance being as it is a slow and painstaking process.

"Mr. Thurston will see you now," said the secretary—actually a very attractive young woman in a provocative blouse—indicating one of the three doors that led off the reception room. "Just go right in."

I opened the door to find Thurston sitting grimly at his desk in the small, cluttered room. The atmosphere was clearly troubled. Perhaps there had been an unexpected revelation on the case.

"Ah, Maltese," Thurston did not stand up or offer to shake hands. "Come in and close the door. Have a seat."

I followed the triple instructions and waited silently. Thurston sucked at his cheeks, fiddled with his fingers, then finally met my eyes warily.

"Look, old man," he said. "We had just better have this out in the open. Get right to the pudding, if you know what I mean. Is there anything you want to say?"

"About what?"

"You bloody well know about what!" Thurston's sudden anger seemed a bit contrived. "Rupert is damned upset and I can't say that I blame him."

"About what?" I asked again.

"About you bonking his wife, that's what!" Thurston shouted.

"Bonking his wife?" was all I could manage in my stunned condition. "I don't even know his wife."

"There's no point in trying to cover up now. Rupert was so upset after lunch yesterday that he went straight home and accused Fiona of having an affair and she admitted it."

"Fiona?"

"What you do with your fannybanger is your affair, but good Lord, man, there's no earthly reason to inform the husband." Thurston had to pause for a moment to control his outrage. "Since the publication of the new Oliver Godolphin novel is so important to Farrow & Farrow, Rupert has agreed, and I can't say I would do the same, to overlook this disgusting indiscretion on your part and continue your employment on the condition that you never see his wife again. Do I make myself clear?"

This was very strange. In the past twenty-four hours, I had been forbidden to see two Fionas, one of whom I've never met. I was aware that I had unconsciously verbalized a few of my thoughts during lunch at Les A, but for it to come to this was beyond my wildest dreams. Now to unravel the confusion and explain the basis of the misunderstanding would be a Herculean task. Besides, I'd been through too much already.

"I agree," I said.

"I want it in writing," Thurston opened his drawer and pulled out a piece of paper. "Sign this."

"I, the undersigned," the statement read, "agree to immediately terminate forever my relationship with Fiona (Mrs. Rupert) Farrow and state emphatically that I shall never attempt to see or contact her again."

I signed it. If it had been the other Fiona, a pistol to my head would not have produced a signature. Thurston snatched the declaration and shoved it back into the safety of the drawer, his mood seeming to improve now that this ugly issue had been settled. After I informed him of my travel plans, he walked me to the door and actually gave my back a pat as I went out.

"Heaven may smile upon fools, but good God, you like to live dangerously," was his farewell.

Live dangerously? Hardly. Other than my passionate obsession for Fiona, how could anyone live more cautiously? My concept of adventure was removing my seat belt and rushing to the lavatory on an airplane. My father was the one who had spent his life living dangerously and growing up around him was a sure cure against risk taking. What he, I assume, considered to be parenting was something to be dreaded.

To this day I can easily recall the terror of those occasional weekend afternoons when Maury would be inspired to teach me to perform some feat of athleticism by simply placing me on whatever instrument (roller skates, bicycle, etc.). With an unannounced push or shove, he would then send me careening into inevitable disaster. I think I was four or five by the time I discovered that my father was a dangerous person to be around, something which my sister, Elisa, already knew, although she was only ten months older.

"Daddy is crazy," I remember her whispering to me tearfully once after, in a particularly ebullient mood, he had thrown her practically up to the ceiling over and over, catching her each time an instant before she would hit the floor on her flailing descent.

Our mother, Mary Frances (nee Smith) never objected to these exuberant forms of child torture. Then she never objected to anything Maury did. I have no recollection whatsoever of a single disagreement, much less argument or fight, between my parents, something which I then took to be normal but later realized was quite unusual. That Mary Frances (not Mom or Mother or even Mary, but always Mary Frances) loved Maury exceptionally was never in question, but how she tolerated him was something Elisa and I could never understand, which probably accounts for the fact that we were so close as children. Very close, exceedingly close, as there was no one else with whom we could share our secrets, though Elisa did have a much closer relationship with Mary Frances than I ever had. I never knew what they talked about.

During my father's long, regular absences, he was seldom mentioned—except privately by Elisa, who hoped each time that he would never return. Our grandfather, the Mighty Mel, would then appear to fill the male role in our household, coming over for dinner two or three times a week, which he never did when Maury was in residence. They were seldom on speaking terms, something I was still too young to understand. We were only told Maury was in Europe on business, though the exact nature of that business was not explained until much later, and even then not totally. But these were reasonably calm periods, as Mary Frances and Mel had a warm, friendly relationship and even Elisa liked her grandfather. Then Maury would return and so would the fear. At least my fear. Maury, it seemed to me, was not afraid of anything.

"Daddy steals paintings," Elisa confided to me once, just having gotten an inkling of the family business.

"No, sweetheart," Mary Frances had overheard. "Daddy sells paintings."

Elisa was not convinced and remained constant in her character assessment of our father. It wasn't until I was eleven that the

museum visits began, Maury having decided to begin my real
education. Elisa refused to go. I, however, had no choice and, in
fact, was enormously relieved that my father's attentions had
changed from the athletic to the artistic. It was much less painful,
but it still made me nervous. It seemed Maury, who was not
afraid of anything, knew everything. It wasn't good enough just
to look at paintings. Maury made me touch them.

"Feel the texture," he would command. "Feel it!"

And I would, my fingers numb with fear, terrified by the
guards and the "Do *Not* Touch" signs, both of which Maury
ignored. Though I was thoroughly convinced I would go to jail,
the fact is we were never questioned, much less stopped, all due,
I am sure, to Maury's imperious attitude. The guards saw what
was happening, but they were afraid to talk to him. So was I.

"What's good about this painting?" my private tour guide
would demand. "What's different about these two paintings? What
do you see? Now close your eyes and describe it. What? Don't
whisper."

I was in agony. But the visits continued. Even when Maury
was in Europe on business, every Saturday morning I would follow the instructions he left behind, the museums to visit, which
paintings to study ("Don't forget to feel the texture," was the one
command I couldn't obey, too intimidated to break the law
without Maury's protective presence). I would then report to Maltese Antique Silver, Mighty Mel's elegant store on Lexington, in
time for lunch with my grandfather, which also included yet
another lecture about the three Pauls, Lamerie, Storr and Revere,
the masters of smithing.

"I hate art. I hate paintings. I hate Daddy," Elisa would hiss in
the night. "I'm going to medical school. I'm going to become a
doctor and cut people open."

The next five years were difficult emotionally. Maury's indictment for dealing in forged paintings made the front page of *The
New York Times*, complete with photograph ("See, I told you!"
Elisa crowed victoriously). Then Mighty Mel died and I went to
boarding school to experience a new variety of suffering. It was
in my senior year when I was summoned out of class and taken to
the headmaster's office where Maury was waiting for me. Mary
Frances, he told me, was dead. A cerebral hemorrhage. There

had been no pain. I started to cry, as I had cried on the news of my grandfather's death, and Maury hugged me, holding me tightly until I stopped. Mary Frances was buried (for some unknown reason) in New Jersey, in a private ceremony marred only by my sister's outburst.

"You killed her, you cocksucker! You killed her, you fucking crook!" Elisa had shouted across the coffin, these being the last words she has ever spoken to my father.

Maury was shaken, but since Elisa (again thanks to Mighty Mel's munificence) was already away at Radcliffe, there was no forced contact and Elisa's name simply vanished from my father's vocabulary. The prediction that Elisa made about her choice of profession turned out to be correct, as she went from Radcliffe to the Harvard Medical School. But she does not (at least literally) "cut people open." She is a psychiatrist, practicing in Boston. I haven't talked to her for more than ten years and there are no current plans for a reunion.

8

Morgan the Organ turned to glare at me furiously as I entered the Gallerie Naif, then switched her smile back on as she refocused her attention on the well-dressed couple admiring a painting on the wall, a colorful, yet primitive attempt to reproduce a group of people standing in front of what was supposed to resemble a house. At least it had windows and a door, if not perspective.

After my odd meeting at Putnam, Dick and Thurston, I had gone directly from Wigmore Street to the Rembrandt, determined to finish reading Mrs. Bettina Sachs's prosaic synopsis of *Sakura* with the hope that my newly acquired knowledge about the life of Oliver Godolphin would gain me some insight into the story. The Rembrandt hall porter handed me a slip of paper with my room key. A telephone message to please call the Gallerie Naif as soon as possible immediately altered the direction of my intent.

Foolishly convinced that Fiona had had a change of heart and had phoned to recant her impulsive rejection of last night, I handed my room key back to the hall porter and ran to find a taxi to rush me to Ebury Street. Even if my assumption was wrong, at least I would have a chance to see Fiona again, an opportunity that had seemed out of reach, which if nothing else could replace the hurtful memories of those events which led to my despondent retreat from Chester Square.

After some further discussion, hinging on interior decoration rather than artistic merit, the well-dressed couple decided that the colors wouldn't fit in and departed without making a purchase. The Organ somehow maintained her poise until the gallery door closed, then she revealed her true malevolence.

"What are you doing here, asshole?" was her greeting.

"There was a message. Fiona called," I answered, already aware of my mistake.

"Fiona didn't call, I did," salacious Sally responded. "And the message was for you to phone. It wasn't an invitation and you fucking well know that, so why don't you just get the fuck out."

"Oh, Sally, Sally, Sally," I smiled. "You do have a way with the English language. Have you ever considered committing it to paper? Write the story of your life, perhaps. That shouldn't take long. And you know all the right words."

"Give it up, Mickey," the Organ tried to sound human. "Can't you realize that you and Fiona are over? Didn't she make that clear last night when she told you to piss off?"

"A temporary setback," I admitted.

"Fuck temporary," the Organ returned to form. "Fiona never wants to see you again. She wants you out of her life."

"She may change her mind," I held fast.

"Don't be an absolute shit. You've already screwed up two of her marriages. Isn't that enough?" the Organ turned and walked to the desk.

"Me?" it was, for some reason, a pleasing thought, "I was only involved in one of Fiona's divorces."

"You don't know fuck all." The Organ held out what I instantly recognized as a sheet of Fiona's stationery. "Here."

I rushed to seize it, but the Miserable Morgan pulled it back at the last second.

"No," she said. "You'll put it under your fucking pillow. It says meet Sheffy Eccleston for a drink at the Athenaeum bar at seven-thirty. It's not even signed."

Before I had a chance to intervene, the Organ shredded the page and dropped the pieces in the dustbin, then backed away as if anxious about my reaction to her reprehensible behavior. I was too overjoyed to respond. Despite everything else, Fiona had remembered.

"Oh, shit," the Organ said in soft defeat, recognizing the rapture in my eyes. "Go away, Mickey. Just go away."

Of course, arranging a meeting with Oliver Godolphin's former secretary could have been explained as an act of friendship on Fiona's part, the decent and responsible thing to do. But somehow I felt it was more significant than that. Just how to interpret that significance preoccupied me sufficiently that, after my return to the Rembrandt, I couldn't concentrate on the synopsis and gave up after reading the same page three times without comprehending any of it.

In addition to Fiona not forgetting, there was also the Organ's remark about my playing some role in Fiona's divorces from first Clive Price and then John Lipscomb which demanded further thought. How could I have been involved? Was my effect on Fiona so strong that it still held some part of her emotions outside the range of total commitment to other men? Would this, might this, possibly, apply to Fiona's relationship with Roddy Startle? Was there, however small, still hope? I remained lost in these questions, until I realized that it was time to leave for my drink with Sheffy Eccleston.

The Athenaeum Hotel on Piccadilly sits just across from Green Park which is just above St. James's Park where my bridge of dreams is located. Known as a show business hotel, the Athenaeum attracted quite a few guests from Hollywood, which is probably the reason I had never had the occasion to visit it before. Museum directors, curators, dealers and wealthy collectors generally prefer the more staid atmosphere of the Ritz, Claridges or the Savoy. To my slight disappointment, there were no film stars in the lobby, but there was an astonishing collection of whiskey bottles, displayed like works of art, in the crowded, cheerful bar.

"I'm meeting Miss Eccleston," I said to the barman.

"Oh, yes, sir. Right this way," he seemed very happy about it.

With an unflagging smile, he led me to a corner table where what appeared to be an accident victim was waiting, one eye purple and swollen and an awful scrape down one side of her nose.

"Miss Eccleston," the barman announced felicitously, "your guest is here."

"I was mugged at Cannes," Sheffy Eccleston explained, seeing my reaction. "Right outside the *Palais des Festivals*. What would you like to drink? I'm having a vodka on the rocks."

"I'll have the same," I said, then sat next to her while the barman smiled as if this were the most wonderful idea, then rushed to carry out his delightful task. "Cannes?"

"The film festival. Crikey, what a zoo," she added.

"Well, it's very nice of you to see me on such short notice," I smiled. "Particularly under the circumstances."

"What circumstances? Oh, you mean my face," she laughed. "If I'd had to make a living on my face, I'd still be rinsing glasses in a pub. Besides, I have a client, a marvelous young American actor, staying in the hotel and we're going out for dinner in half an hour, so I was going to be here anyway. Now what did you want to ask me about? Fiona said something about confidential research. That sounds interesting."

Faithful Fiona. Not only had she remembered, but she hadn't blabbed. Fabulous Fiona.

"It concerns Oliver Godolphin." I lowered my voice, leaning closer. "I understand that you used to be his secretary, Miss Eccleston."

"Sheffy, please. Oliver Godolphin? Crikey, that was almost twenty-five years ago."

"You must have been very young," I said.

"Aren't you sweet," Sheffy parried the compliment. "Actually, I was twenty when Oliver hired me and twenty-three when the family moved back to France. What are you working on, a biography?"

"Not exactly." It's always difficult for me to deal with direct questions. "But it's confidential."

"Darling, I'm an agent. Everything I do is confidential," she explained. "Now if you actually want my help, you have to tell me what it is exactly that you're doing. Otherwise we're both wasting our time."

"Here we are. God bless you." The happy barman returned with our drinks.

It was clear that I had no choice. Sheffy was the only person I knew with an actual connection to Oliver Godolphin, and, though I had just met her, I felt that confiding in her would be safe. Maybe it was her personality, her strength of character. Any woman who would appear, and without embarrassment, in public with a battered face had to be strong. So, after a sip of vodka, I let it come out, my assignment and what I had discovered so far. I only omitted irrelevant details, such as my signing a false confession at Putnam, Dick and Thurston and related confusions. Sheffy was an extraordinary listener, reacting in all the right places, interest sparking in her eyes. As a result I found myself speaking with an unfamiliar eloquence and, I suppose, making it all sound a mysteriously dramatic adventure rather than just a search for provenance.

"I like it a lot," Sheffy announced when I wound down. "Of course, you'll have to come up with a powerful ending, but, and I never say this lightly, I think it has serious potential."

Potential for what? Before I could ask, the barman hurried over to inform Sheffy that she had a phone call, which gave me more time to mull. And what did she mean by a powerful ending? The ending of provenance was, hopefully, truth. It was sometimes interesting, often surprising, either satisfactory or disappointing, but never powerful. Or perhaps she meant if *Sakura* had a powerful ending it would have serious potential. I rejected that possibility instantly (though I still didn't know, via synopsis, how the novel would eventually end), because any newly found work by Oliver Godolphin would have much more than that.

"That son of a bitch doesn't want to be seen with me in public," Sheffy had returned. "Oh, he claims he has a headache, but when he suggested room service, that was the giveaway. And after everything I've done for him. What a nerve."

Obviously, this marvelous young American actor's potential had suddenly become less serious.

"What are you doing tonight?" she asked.

"I don't have any plans," other, I said to myself, than going back to the Rembrandt and Mrs. Bettina Sachs's captivating prose.

"Good. You've just won a free dinner at Braganza. Let's go." Sheffy got to her feet.

Events happen much faster in show business than in the art world, but I was determined to keep pace, following on Sheffy's heels out of the bar and the hotel and into a taxi to Frith Street. The restaurant entrance was bright and full of chrome, with a plaster dummy (I hope they don't consider it a statue) indicating the stairs. Sheffy stopped to greet half the other diners and it wasn't until we were finally seated in the second floor dining room that her full attention returned to me.

"Mickey," she said.

"Yes?"

"Is it short for Michael?"

"Well, actually, it's Amicus."

"Amicus?" it made her giggle. "Amicus Maltese. It's cute."

The waiter came to my rescue by delivering the menus, which were printed on clear lucite and impossible to read unless held flat on the white table cloth. Sheffy ordered assorted seafood on a bed of crisp stir-fried fresh vegetables. I followed suit. Then, after I politely deferred the choice, she ordered a bottle of Australian Chardonnay, which arrived before the meal and was quite good, if a little fruity.

"All right, Amicus." Sheffy lowered her wine glass and gave me a warm smile. "Here's the deal. In exchange for my helping you, you let me represent the story, packaging included, which means I'll have to split everything with an agency on the coast."

"Represent what story?" I was completely out of my element.

"Don't be daft. Your story."

"But I don't have a story."

"The story of how you find the long lost last novel of Oliver Godolphin," Sheffy explained the obvious.

"But it's already been found," I protested. "I'm just supposed to establish the provenance."

"I know," Sheffy said. "That's the great mystery. And with his old editor saying that he wrote it and Alexis saying that he didn't, the whole story is a natural. I love it. I simply love it."

If only Fiona had felt like this about my work. Perhaps, in a subtle way, of course, Sheffy could mention it to her, share her wonderful enthusiasm. I had another sip of the Australian Chardonnay. Somehow, the taste had improved remarkably.

"Let's see. What do I remember?" Sheffy turned reflective. "The family had just moved here from Hollywood, and Oliver was rather bitter about MGM. We were working out of this little office on Ebury Street."

"Ebury Street?" I involuntarily interrupted.

"Yes. Why? Oh, Fiona's gallery is there. That's a coincidence." Sheffy didn't know half of it. "In any event, even though Oliver hated the studio, he stayed in touch with Danny Speers. I remember they used to speak on the phone regularly."

"Danny Speers?"

"The producer. He was the one who bought the rights to the book, optioned it actually, then layed the deal off at MGM."

"What did they talk about?"

"God, I haven't the foggiest."

"When you were working for him, what exactly did you do?" I finally began my interrogatory.

"Actually, most of it was running the household accounts." Sheffy made a moue. "And he used to send me off to research odds and ends, old newspaper clippings, nothing too exotic. The story of the book took place in London, so he had everything available. Then I used to proofread the chapters. God, do I know that book. I still think it's the best thing he ever wrote."

"No typing?"

"Oliver always typed for himself."

"What was he like?" I glided nimbly to the point.

"What was he like?" Sheffy repeated my question thoughtfully. "He was friendly, very serious about his work. Oh, and he never discussed it, figuring everything out in his head. He was very devoted to Alexandra and the little girl. In fact, Oliver dedicated all his books to her, I think."

"The little girl?"

"No, Alexandra."

"He never mentioned the Foreign Legion?"

"Never. That was definitely a no trespass area." She waggled a finger. "In fact, Oliver was the kind of man who managed to discourage any questions. If he wanted to volunteer something, you listened and took note. If not, forget about it. I remember he used to vanish from time to time and I never once asked where he'd been. But I wouldn't be surprised if he was out fooling around. Everyone was in those days."

The waiter arrived with our meal before I could pursue that line of questioning, determined to file away every scrap of information available, as in my mind determining the provenance of Oliver Godolphin was the key to determining the provenance of *Sakura*. There had to be a connection. Who he was would reveal what he did and why he did it.

"So, how do you know Fiona?" Sheffy asked after testing her assorted seafood. "Mm, this is quite good."

How do I know Fiona? In what sense?

"Didn't she tell you?" I tried the crisp stir-fried fresh vegetables.

"She only said that she'd known you for a long time."

"Oh, yes."

Since Fiona hadn't chosen to reveal our true relationship, I felt constrained to silence on the subject. There would be no breach of confidence here.

"She's so pretty, with that incredible copper hair," Sheffy went on. "And she and Roddy make a beautiful couple. In fact, when she rang me about meeting you, she was just on her way to Heathrow, flying back to Paris to be with him during the last rehearsals. It seems they can't stay apart."

Copper hair? I never thought Fiona's hair was copper. It was the color of a beautiful sunset.

"Rehearsals?" I asked.

"For Roddy's concert at Roland Garros. It's been sold out for weeks. The tickets are worth their weight in diamonds. And he timed it so cleverly, just before the French Open."

"Oh?" I wasn't sure what she was talking about.

"Nabbing Roddy Startle's not bad for one of Jimmy Fitzhugh's old party girls," Sheffy said pointedly.

"Who?"

"Jimmy Fitzhugh. The club owner. He had that place on Finchley Road years ago when they had that enormous scandal. You must have heard of him."

"Actually, I haven't."

"Oh, it's a wonderful story. He's Jewish, you know, Jimmy Fitzhugh. His father's name was Morris Fine and he was a tailor in North London and his advertising line was "A Suit From Morris Fits You Fine," and then he became known as Fits You Fine. Jimmy just dropped the Fine and changed the spelling and everyone thought he was a proper Englishman until the scandal."

"The scandal?"

"With all the underage girls. Jimmy used to give these wild parties and invite all these terribly important men, Lords, MP's, people with a lot of money, and they would have these orgies. Cocaine and God knows what."

Underage Fiona? Orgies and cocaine? My mind was on fire, my heart wrapped in briars. Though Sheffy was still speaking, my ears refused to hear any more of these appalling words. I would somehow have to warn Fiona about the vicious, unfounded gossip this woman was spreading. Though it had never occurred to me to question Fiona intimately about her life before that crucial moment on the bridge at St. James's Park, I knew that this frightful tale could have no basis in truth. And if, by chance, there had been a Fiona involved, then it was another Fiona. Perhaps Rupert Farrow's wife. She had, after all, confessed to an affair. But then so had I.

"Coffee?" the waiter was asking.

Sheffy shook her head, so I declined as well, allowing my hearing to cautiously recrudesce.

"I'll draw up the papers and in the meantime I'll try to dig up some more about Oliver," she had thankfully returned to the intended topic. "Where can I get in touch with you?"

"I'm going out of town tomorrow, but you can always leave a message at the gallery," I responded immediately.

Sheffy and I parted on Frith Street, taking separate taxis as we were going in different directions. Not an altogether satisfying evening, but in the search for provenance, one takes what one gets. I had heard too little about Oliver Godolphin and too much about Fiona.

And I had an agent.

GENEVA

1

Le Richemond is just down the street from Sotheby's and I had collapsed on the bed in the Directoire style room immediately upon arrival, already exhausted by the events of the day. First it was the headline of the tabloid left by a previous passenger in the taxi that transported me from the Rembrandt to Heathrow for my early flight to Cointrin, "Jimmy Fitzhugh Named in Mayfair Sex Scandal." The story revived memories of my dinner with Sheffy at Braganza and those discommoding tales about Fiona that I had blocked by my self-inflicted surdity, but that were, I knew, lurking dangerously in the dark cave of my mind.

Once safely inside the terminal, I succeeded in distracting myself by going into the bookshop and examining the row of Oliver Godolphins, every single novel dedicated "For Alexandra." The Alexandra Dedications. I thought it sounded like something by Elgar, something beginning with a kettle-drum, and marching to the soft roll of this imaginary timpani I proceeded to the gate, boarded the plane and, after strapping myself down, plunged once again into Mrs. Bettina Sachs's synopsis.

By the time we crossed the Channel, I had discovered that the beautiful red-haired Lulu von Hofmannsthal had a husband, the wealthy but older Baron Hugo, a ruthless industrialist, and that Jordan Leander had a red Alfa convertible, in which he drove Lulu, after an afternoon of Mozart at the *Festspielhaus*, back toward Vienna, stopping at Schloss Fuschl for a drink at her suggestion.

"*Ich Möchte bitte einen Kirschlikör,*" Luly says enticingly, explaining that she wants her breath to smell of cherries. ("Sakura" means cherry blossom, I made a mental note.)

Then there is a long conversation in German ("The use of language here too beautiful to lessen by translation," Mrs. Bettina Sachs remarks parenthetically) in which Lulu describes Jordan Leander to himself, painting a word picture of his lined face and weary eyes and how when she first saw him she had known that they would meet. Then, suddenly, Lulu tells Jordan Leander to close those weary eyes, and he does, but when he opens them Lulu has vanished. Despite all his worldly journalistic experience, Jordan Leander is overwhelmed by a sense of loss greater than anything he had ever experienced. But the feeling lasts only a moment as Lulu returns with the key to a turret bedroom, the Baron, obviously, keeping her on a long leash.

An offer of coffee from the cabin hostess allowed me to pull myself away from this gripping tale. The two English businessmen seated alongside were in a deep discussion about American overheating and liquidity gushers, so I looked out the window and down at France, remembering how Sheffy told me that Fiona had returned to Paris. That cracked my mental block and the echo of Sheffy's voice slipped through.

"With this television presenter who everyone knew was rather kinky," it began in mid-sentence, "rubber and leather and bondage. I can't imagine what those people do to each other. Apparently, the story goes, he was seen driving his red Aston Martin around Hyde Park Corner with Fiona all trussed up in a clothesline in the seat next to him."

Absolutely not. I forced Sheffy's voice away, then realized that the two English businessmen were staring at me, and for a terrible moment I thought that they had heard Sheffy, too.

"Were you speaking to us?" the closest businessman asked.

"Me?"

"Yes. You said absolutely not."

"Oh, sorry."

"No problem," he smiled, then turned back to his companion, and picked up at the point where I had evidently interrupted.

I tried to continue my attack on Mrs. Bettina Sachs's prose, but my concentration seemed to be consumed by my effort to keep Sheffy silent and once again the thread of the story slipped away.

So I marked the spot and traveled the rest of the way to Geneva listening to a discussion of currency fluidity, which was far preferable than my own thoughts. By the time we arrived, I was up to date on marks and yen.

Some people have said that Swiss taxi drivers are dishonest, but I have never found this to be true. So it was not suspicion that kept my eyes focused on the meter during the three mile trip from the airport into the city. Watching the numbers click over and counting with my inner voice was all that I could do to block Sheffy out, knowing the moment I relaxed that she would speak again and again it would be dreadful. Driving around Hyde Park Corner, tied up in a red Aston Martin with a deviate television presenter? Why would Fiona do something like that? It couldn't be. And now Roddy Startle, a man whose jaded wants were probably beyond the norm.

Had my relationship with Fiona been too dull, too boring? Was that the reason for our sexual problem? It definitely couldn't be. Fiona and I had, of course, experimented a bit, but she had never encouraged me to bind her, and if she had found that concept exciting, she certainly would have suggested it as a possible solution. What were Fiona and Roddy doing to each other at the George V?

The telephone rang before I could contemplate further, the concierge inquiring if everything was satisfactory. Of course, it was, at least in so far as the hotel was concerned. Not yet feeling up to making a public appearance, I rang room service and ordered lunch. Then, washing down my *croque monsieur* with a bottle of Feldschlosschen (the Swiss make great watches, but their beer is watery), I began making my mental preparations for my meeting with Pierre Rougemont, who, in all likelihood, would tell me no more than he told Thurston. Still, the effort had to be made. People who simply accept "No" do not go far in the field of provenance. Besides, dealing with rejection had become the specialty of my life.

Allowing myself ample time, I left the Richemond, coming out into the Jardin Brunswick, I turned left, passed Sotheby's without a glance and headed directly for the Pont de la Machine, where the Rhône River on one side becomes Lake Léman on the other. Halfway across, I forced myself to stop and become a tourist for a few seconds, watching the water flow from the dam beneath the bridge. The lake beyond was fantastically blue, the perimeters dotted with graceful swans and bobbing ducks. It was restful, I told myself. In the end, though I wasn't quite sure how, everything would work out, the mystery of Oliver Godolphin, Fiona and I, life in general. Things certainly couldn't continue this way forever.

Choosing the more positive attitude, I crossed the bridge to the south shore and then wandered through the crowded, lively streets for a few blocks before finding my destination. Rue de Monnaie. On what better street could a bank be located? Rougemont & Cie, had its own building, a modest gray structure with a small brass plaque beside the entrance to announce its identity, clearly a low profile establishment. I entered, identified myself to the elderly guard inside and was directed up the stairs, my footsteps the only sound audible in the hushed building. I decided that people didn't come here to cash checks. That is, except very large ones.

"Mr. Maltese?" a serious, unsmiling woman in conservative wardrobe waited at the top of the stairs. "Would you come this way, please?"

It was not a question designed to be answered, so I simply followed her down the silent corridor, framed engravings of old Geneva on the wall, to the door at the far end. Here she stopped to look at her Rolex. I glanced at my Seiko. It was exactly three-fifteen. She rapped softly on the door, then opened it, moving aside for me to enter. It was a solemn moment.

"Come in, Mr. Maltese," Pierre Rougemont was smiling at me. "Come in."

He seemed about forty, mostly bald, his friendly and amused eyes instantly dispelling the gravity. He was wearing a corduroy jacket and a checked shirt. This was not my idea of a Swiss banker.

"Mr. Rougemont?" I asked in case there had been a mistake. "Pierre Rougemont?"

"The one and only," he laughed. "Now sit down and tell me of our mutual concern. I believe you mentioned seven figures in any currency. Is that correct?"

He leaned back and put his tasseled Gucci loafers up on what appeared to be a Louis XV *bureau,* the amusement never leaving his eyes. I didn't understand the humor, but Rougemont's happy spirits were contagious and by the time I had taken the chair across from him, I found that I was grinning.

"Here." I took out my letter of authorization from Farrow & Farrow and handed it to him, trying not to giggle. "I believe this will explain my purpose."

"Mmm. Oliver Godolphin," the contents of the brief letter did not dampen his mirth. "Are you a lawyer, Mr. Maltese?"

Rather than answering, I gave him my business card which seemed to delight him.

"Provenance," his eyes stayed on the card. "How very interesting. May I keep this?"

"Of course." No one had ever asked before.

"So the seven figures which concerns us mutually are the advance fees for the book?" He didn't seem at all disappointed.

"Precisely." I nodded. "But a book which may never be published, because Oliver Godolphin's daughter claims it is a forgery and has threatened to sue Farrow and Farrow if they proceed."

"Oh dear."

"And since the instructions were for all monies concerned to be paid directly to Rougemont and Company, it appears to me that it is in your best interest to aid me in attempting to establish provenance of the authorship of the novel."

"My best interest."

"It appears to me."

"Mmm."

"On top of which, if the novel is truly the last work of Oliver Godolphin, withholding it from publication would be a literary crime," I added for some reason.

"And what is in your best interest, Mr. Maltese?" Rougemont swung the Guccis off the Louis XV and leaned forward to study my expression.

"Simply to do the job I have been paid to do regardless of the results. Provenance is not done on a contingency basis. Whether the book is published or not, I have no further financial involvement."

"I presume you know that I have spoken with the Farrow and Farrow lawyer," he said.

"And you told him that you had been instructed not to say anything."

"Then, since you are aware of my constraints, how can I help you?"

That we would eventually reach this point, I knew, was inevitable. In provenance, frustration occupies many rungs on the long ladder to truth, but this was a new variation on obstruction. Rougemont knew, or had access to, the answers to many of my questions, but he was constrained not to tell me, which was very different from outmaneuvering a deceitful, avaricious art dealer. But I hadn't come to Geneva to be thwarted.

"Have you examined the manuscript?" I asked casually.

"Very briefly." Rougemont seemed amused again.

"Under the title page, there is another page on which are written two words, 'Page Missing,' which could only be the page containing the book's dedication." I let my deduction hang there for a moment before I popped the question. "Do you have that page?"

"Very good, Mr. Maltese," Rougemont clapped his hands together.

"Can I take that for a yes?"

"You may."

"Then may I also assume," I was hot now, "that you were instructed to send that page to Farrow and Farrow on receipt of the advance fee?"

"I think that is a reasonable assumption." Rougemont was smiling.

"Would it be permissible under the restrictions for me to see that page?" I had, at last, arrived at the crossroad.

"Why do you want to see it?"

"All of Oliver Godolphin's novels were dedicated to his wife, Alexandra." I didn't think it was necessary to explain that I had only verified that fact a few hours ago. "If this book is also dedicated to her, that would indicate, partially, that Oliver Godolphin is indeed the author."

"And if not, what would that partially indicate?"

"Another avenue of investigation."

"Yes, you are quite good at this, Mr. Maltese." Rougemont had obviously enjoyed the show. "Provenance. Quite fascinating. Have you done many of these investigations?"

"Well, this is my first literary one," I admitted. "Usually I do paintings and sculpture."

"And have you discovered many forgeries?"

"There've been a few."

"Mmm. My father was an art collector, in a small way, of course, and in fact, among a few other pieces I inherited, is a Corot."

It would have to be a Corot. I tried not to wince.

"Really?" I said.

"If you're free this evening, why don't you come to my house and have a look at it. My wife, unfortunately, is out of town. But I can promise you a decent meal."

"I'd be delighted." I had no choice.

"Which hotel are you at?"

"The Richemond."

"Would eight o'clock be convenient? My driver will pick you up. I live in Versoix. It's not too far out of the city."

"Perfect."

"In the meantime, I shall review the instructions and determine whether or not I can fulfill your request." Rougemont got to his feet, signaling an end to our happy encounter.

Still bubbling with Pierre Rougemont's infectious good spirits, and with Sheffy safely locked away, I strolled along the Promenade du Lac to stare off at the famous Jet d'Eau, that mighty stream of water soaring up next to the harbor beacon and, as far as I knew, the world's highest fountain. This was a liquidity gusher I could understand. After completing my observation of the saturating spectacle, I promenaded back toward the Richemond, pleasantly anticipating the evening ahead. How could any man, much less a Swiss banker, be so jolly? Pierre Rougemont, obviously, knew more about life than I did, but probably much less about Corot.

2

As Sepp Schüller quotes in his seminal *Fälscher, Handler und Experten* (roughly), *"Von den etwa siebenhundert bewährten Originalen von Corot, findet man acht tausend von ihnen allein in Amerika,"* which translates (roughly) as "Of the seven hundred odd proven originals by Corot, eight thousand of them are in America alone."

Plus one in Switzerland.

Jean-Baptiste-Camille Corot is considered to be one of the great artists of the 19th century, a man whose style influenced the work of many painters, from Degas to Renoir to Picasso, a man whose pictures have been in demand since his death in 1875. He is a nightmare to provenance. Aside from the fact that he would sometimes copy his own paintings, he actually encouraged his students to forge as well, occasionally correcting their work and even signing his name to them.

Immediately after the master died, an entire industry was born. Within a few years counterfeit Corots were everywhere. I suspected every legitimate collection had at least one fake, though I had yet to see Rougemont's inherited Corot, I thought it best to explain the background over an excellent meal of *pied de porc au madère*, washed down with a lovely bottle of St-Saphorin.

"Remarkable." Pierre Rougemont was as jovial in his fine, old 18th century house in Versoix as he had been in his office. "Tell me more."

With that encouragement, I began rattling off the familiar anecdotes that everyone knows about forgery in the art world, all of which Rougemont appeared to enjoy enormously, finally finishing with the famous story about how Maurice Utrillo was once unable to determine in a Paris courtroom whether a number of paintings, all bearing his signature, were actually by his hand or that of Mme. Claude Latour, his admitted fabricator. By that time, we were on the cheese plate, with which we polished off the St-Saphorin. There had been no mention of whether the instructions would allow Rougemont to let me see the "Page Missing." But we were having such a pleasant time that I felt it would be intrusive to bring up the subject without shifting gears.

"I'm sorry your wife is out of town." I began to weave. "I'm sure I would enjoy meeting her."

"No," Rougemont smiled. "I am afraid that you would not."

"Oh," the response threw me off stride.

"My wife is a schizophrenic," Rougemont continued pleasantly. "She is in a psychiatric hospital in Berne. I visit her on weekends and sometimes she recognizes me and sometimes she does not. The doctors do not believe that she shall ever recover."

"That's terrible." I meant it.

"Yes, it is," he agreed. "Particularly since we have no children and, since I am an only child, that shall end the family line. Do you have children, Mr. Maltese?"

"No. I'm divorced."

"Recently?"

"Two days ago," I answered to my own surprise. "But I'm hoping for a reconciliation."

"Then I wish you well." Rougemont pushed his chair back. "Now shall we have a look at my Corot?"

How could this man be so cheerful? Compared to his life, my problems with Fiona seemed insignificant. Yet I was miserable and he was happy. The last image of Fiona closing the door to her house on Chester Square two nights ago flashed through my mind. Did she really mean it when she said good-bye?

"You're not leaving?" Rougemont turned to look at me as we walked down the hall.

"Leaving?" I didn't understand.

"I thought you said goodbye."

"Oh." I had to dissemble. "I meant that I hope the Corot was a good buy."

"It was a gift, actually," Rougemont smiled, as we continued walking.

The Corot was alone on the rear wall of the warmly furnished study, well framed and with its own light, and unfortunately I recognized it instantly. It was one of "The Artist's Studio" variations, where Corot used the background of his studio on Rue Paradis Poissonière for a number of paintings of melancholy young women. In fact, Corot had painted two almost identical versions, one hanging in the Louvre and the other at the National Gallery in Washington, D.C. Now here was a third in Versoix. It was, I suppose, possible.

"May I?" I reached my open hand toward the Corot.

"Please," Rougemont gestured for me to proceed.

I let my fingers touch the canvas lightly, closing my eyes as I felt the texture, then opening my eyes to stare at a corner of the painting. Finally, I stepped back to look at the whole work again. In the portrait, the woman was seated at an easel holding a small unfinished landscape, her left hand touching the lower corner of the piece in progress, gazing at it, her face turned, her right hand holding the neck of a mandolin. There was a stove, the flue pipe horizontal then angled up to the top of the frame. On the studio wall beyond were six small paintings, three very small sculpted figures and what appeared to be two larger ones.

"Well, what do you think?" Rougemont asked softly.

"The texture is correct." I wanted to be gentle about it. "And the brush strokes are historically accurate. In his earlier work Corot used a fairly short, firm stroke. The transformation of his technique began when he was about fifty-five. Then his hand became broader and more flexible. The "Studio" series were done after he was sixty. If it is a copy, then it's certainly a very good one. The signature is perfect."

"Thank you." Rougemont's eyes were very amused. "But what I intended to ask is if you like it."

"It's beautiful," I responded quickly.

"Yes, I think so, too." Rougemont stared at the painting for a moment. "It gave my father many years of pleasure and now it does the same for me."

"If you like," how could I not make the offer? "I'd be happy to look over the documentation."

"That is very kind of you, but there is no need," Rougemont said with his happy smile. "I enjoy the painting and that is all that matters, isn't it?"

"Of course." It was time to back off.

"And if you," Rougemont hadn't finished, "with your expertise, were to find some small flaw in its provenance, would I enjoy the painting less?"

"An authenticated, genuine Corot is very valuable." I was in retreat.

"I have no plans to sell it," Rougemont was no less pleasant.

"Why should you?" I grinned then looked away, trying to find a path that would lead us off the troublesome Corot.

On a side table a silver plate was displayed, propped up in a wooden holder. Without asking permission I walked over to it and took the plate in my hands, flipping it over to glance at the hallmark. I couldn't believe my eyes. It had all four, the crowned leopard's head, the letter F, the lion passant and, unbelievably, the silversmith's personal hallmark, a crown over the letters LA with a small cross beneath. Still slack-jawed, I turned back to Rougemont, who was watching me curiously.

"Do you know what this is?" I asked stupidly.

"Of course. Do you?" Rougemont's eyes were practically twinkling.

"Paul Lamerie, London, 1722." I simply translated the hallmarks.

"*Formidable!*" Rougemont exploded with laughter. "How could you possibly know that?"

After my many hours with Mighty Mel, how could I possibly not know that? The crowned leopard's head and the lion passant were simple because they were more or less constant. The date letters changed faces at the end of the alphabet (which only went as far as V, though usually U preceded a new style) and each London maker's mark, registered at Goldsmith's Hall, was different. I could only identify three, the three Pauls, Lamerie, Storr and (the really easy one) Revere. Mighty Mel knew so many that he read silver the way other people read the newspaper.

"My grandfather was in the silver trade," I said. "When I was young he tried to teach me about it, but I'm afraid I wasn't a very good pupil."

"But that was very impressive," Rougemont protested.

"Just lucky," I declined the compliment. "Nothing more than that."

An original Paul Lamerie plate belonged in a museum and I couldn't even begin to calculate its value, so little Georgian silver remaining. Throughout history, no other art form has been so totally decimated, the substance being more valued than the style, resulting in vast numbers of beautifully crafted works getting tossed into the melting pot and becoming silver bars or coins, which the masses and the misers could more easily appreciate. Carefully, I returned the Lamerie plate to its display position, noticing the center design for the first time and bending over to study it.

"The family crest," Rougemont said. "A gift to one of my ancestors."

"You have a popular family," I meant it to be courteous, but it sounded wrong.

"It is a family of bankers, Mr. Maltese." Rougemont didn't seem at all offended. "Gifts have come from people seeking favors or in gratitude for having received them. What is your schedule tomorrow?"

"I'm flying to Nice to meet Alexis Godolphin," I answered, though I hadn't yet made an appointment.

"Then come to the bank before you leave. Anytime will do." Rougemont gestured gracefully at the door. "Let me give you a glass of Kirsch. It comes from the north, in Zug. I find it has an excellent quality."

The evening ended with my being driven back to the Richemond with the taste of cherries in my mouth, just like Lulu von Hofmannsthal, and contemplating the coincidences that were piling up. Fiona knowing Sheffy, the Ebury Street connections (Did Oliver Godolphin ever go to the local pub for a pint? Was he ever known as Ted, the writer fellow?), Corot, who was one of my father's favorites since forgeries were in such easy supply, and, finally, Paul Lamerie.

"When he was fifteen, this Paul was apprenticed to Peter Platel," I remember my grandfather telling me over a Saturday lunch, "and learned the craft in only seven years. Seven years, Amicus, think of that."

I wasn't too impressed at the time, and, as much as I cared for my grandfather, I could never develop much of an interest in silver, which I know disappointed him. My father had shown no inclination to share his father's passion either, leaving Mighty Mel alone in his consuming appreciation of the art. That Mel was called Mighty I knew was because, or so the legend had it, he was so powerful that he could bend a silver coin with his fingers, a feat that I never personally witnessed.

Other than that, I had very little information about my grandfather. I knew that he had arrived in New York when he was thirty-five with a trunk full of European silver with which he set himself up in business, married my grandmother (whose name was Alice and who died before I was born) and was over forty when my father arrived. But where Mighty Mel had come from originally was something that was never discussed.

Once, though, I accidentally overheard Mel and Maury in a violent quarrel in some totally unrecognizable language. When I asked what they were speaking, they both replied "Maltese" and then both erupted into laughter, their argument forgotten for the moment. For a long time after that I assumed that Mighty Mel had come from Malta, which, of course, made sense, but when I mentioned it to my father, he said, "Don't be ridiculous," and discouraged any further genealogical inquiries. So there was another coincidence. Both my grandfather and Oliver Godolphin had no past history.

These thoughts kept me busy until I tumbled into bed, my mouth still tasting of cherries, but too tired to delve into Mrs. Bettina Sachs's soggy summary to find out what was going to happen to Lulu von Hofmannsthal and Jordan Leander in that turrent bedroom. Besides, I thought I could guess.

3

It was a terrible nightmare. I was in the Foreign Legion, stationed at Fort von Hier, and there was a fire that no one seemed to notice except me. Though I tried as hard as I could, I was unable to put out the flames. The fire spread and still no one noticed.

Terrified, I panicked. Then my father and my sister Elisa (as a child) somehow walked in through the front door, talking about what they were going to have for lunch, without paying any attention to the inferno. I yelled at them to help me.

"Immer schlimmer," my father said.

The scene shifted to a cafe. There were Legionnaires and Sheffy, wearing robes and lots of jewelry, was leading me toward a curtain.

"Anything," Sheffy was whispering in my ear. "She'll let you do anything you want. She doesn't care. She was one of Jimmy Fitzhugh's party girls."

Sheffy pushed the curtain aside and there was Fiona, all tied up in a red Aston Martin.

I bolted awake, completely shaken, my mouth dry, my head throbbing painfully. It must have been that Kirsh of excellent quality from Zug. After a long, hot shower and several cups of room service coffee, it being still too early to do anything else, I seized the synopsis with determination. Maybe it was the hangover, but Mrs. Bettina Sachs's peculiar prose seemed even more difficult to penetrate.

Once inside the turret bedroom, the lamp romantically dimmed, the beautiful red-haired Lulu von Hofmannsthal lets the kimono fall and leads the stunned Jordan Leander into the bed of prurient ecstasy, although there are no anatomical descriptions of what transpires—either Mrs. Bettina Sachs being reticent or Oliver Godolphin, if he were indeed the author, leaving it to the imagination. In the morning, not only is Lulu gone (surprise, surprise), but so is his red Alfa, and Jordan Leander is left to make it back to Vienna the hard way.

And there in front of his house is his car, with a package of cherries on the seat. Wryly amused and madly in love, Jordan Leander goes in search of the mysterious and enticing Lulu von Hofmannsthal. After several desperate days, Jordan Leander takes the most dangerous step and goes to see Baron Hugo, the ruthless industrialist husband, who appears to have been expecting him.

"Ah, the latest fool," says the Baron.

Lulu, it becomes clear, has pulled this stunt before, leaving a heap of love-stricken men in her wake. No man can possess the beautiful Lulu, not even Baron Hugo. He, however, owns her.

Actually, the Baron is rather melancholy about this whole situation, being in love with her himself. But Lulu is a free spirit and there is no way to tie her down. Jordan Leander, however, obsessed with love, remains determined. He must have Lulu and, like a man, he informs Baron Hugo of his intentions. The Baron doesn't think he has a chance. Only he, Baron Hugo, has been able to maintain some tenuous hold on her, and that at great cost, both emotional and financial. Still, Jordan Leander refuses to yield.

"You don't understand Lulu," the Baron warns him sadly. "Tie her down and she will die."

I didn't like where this was going and put Mrs. Bettina Sachs away quickly, but Baron Hugo's phrase, "Tie her down" made me remember Fiona's ligation in the red Aston Martin, both in Sheffy's awful story and my terrible dream. A red Aston Martin and a red Alfa. Another coincidence. I wondered suddenly, was Lulu into bondage?

I could see my mind was heading into hazardous territory so I phoned down to the concierge and instructed him to book me on the afternoon flight to Nice and make a reservation for me at the Negresco, then concentrated on packing until I was suddenly distracted by the realization that Cannes was much closer to Cap d'Antibes than Nice.

Why had I chosen the Negresco instead of the Carlton? It couldn't have been because of Sheffy's mugging, could it? Still, some unconscious force had made my choice and I decided not to call the concierge back and change hotels. It would be a longer drive, and that would give me more time to think over how I would approach Alexis Godolphin.

That Alexis had threatened to sue Farrow & Farrow, her father's original publisher and loyal friend, certainly indicated that she was taking this possible Oliver Godolphin forgery seriously, unlike most painters who considered imitation as an act of flattery. Even Pablo Picasso, it is said, claimed that he would gladly sign a counterfeit if he ever came across a good one.

Had Alexis Godolphin read the manuscript of *Sakura*? That was a question I had neglected to ask. And if she hadn't, would she? And if she did and liked it, would she, in effect, sign her father's name to the piece? It seemed quite evident now, this was a very fertile field. And, if I succeed, I would be making history. There have been spurious memoirs, but no one, as far as I knew, had ever done provenance on a best-selling novelist, and Nobel Laureate to boot. And if Sheffy happened to be right and sold my story to the movies, could I become famous? Well, not as famous as Roddy Startle, but just a little bit famous, famous enough to impress Fiona?

Buoyed by this fancy, I strutted out of the Richemond and set out for Rue de Monnaie with a chipper and confident step until I was halfway across the Pont de la Machine. In a lightning flash of percipience, I suddenly apprehended that when Pierre Rougemont had declined my offer to examine the provenance of his Corot he had reflected my father's point of view. If the painting pleases, why place any importance on the identity of the artist?

"Truth!" I answered, causing several other pedestrians to turn and stare.

What could be more important than the truth? If the provenance of Pierre Rougemont's Corot was shaky, as I was certain, would he enjoy it less? I could neither answer that question nor ask it. And if *Sakura* turned out to be the product of a hand other than Oliver Godolphin's, would Mrs. Bettina Sachs find it less of a masterpiece? Was the purpose of provenance purely financial? And, if so, what did that make me? An insurance man. Was that it, was that all there was?

When I was married to Fiona, I was sure of everything, sure of myself, confident, content, as if somehow all things had become right in the world, my world at least. Wherever we went, I knew who I was simply because she was with me. No intimidation, no unanswerable philosophical questions, no uncertainty. I just knew. I was Fiona's husband.

Now, here I was, halfway across the Pont de la Machine, filled with self-doubt, personally and professionally. My buoyancy floated down the Rhône. Was I having an identity crisis?

"Art is still," I suddenly remembered my father saying to me one afternoon at the Met. "The viewer moves."

He was so sure, so confidently certain about everything. I tried to imagine Maury Maltese being frightened, paralyzed with hesitation, but I couldn't even conjure up a vision of him faltering for any reason. Of course, he had been shaken at my mother's funeral, particularly after my sister's outburst. But how had he reacted at Mighty Mel's burial? I didn't know, as neither Elisa nor I were taken to that sad event.

"Amigo," my father would say, using the Spanish version of my name as he always did. "Amigo, you worry too much."

Of course, I did. He was the one with nerves of steel, the man with the audacity to sell fraudulent works of art, the man who could get a table at Le Gavroche without a reservation. And I was afraid to tell an outright lie for fear of being caught. Was I using my quest for truth as the shield behind which I could hide my cowardice? God. No wonder Fiona left me.

The thought made me dizzy and I leaned forward against the bridge railing, staring down into the calming flow until the sounds of a commotion made me turn. Two gendarmes were racing toward me. An instant later they had seized me, hauling me back from the railing.

"Non, monsieur," a gendarme said sternly. *"C'est interdit. Defense de statuer."*

What was prohibited? What was against the law?

"Se donner la mort."

Suicide?

Despite my protests that they were totally mistaken, I was escorted to the *Poste de Police*, where it turned out they had received several complaints about a dangerous foreigner babbling out loud on the Pont de la Machine. Apparently I had been verbalizing my thoughts again and it was when I became dizzy and reached for the railing that they jumped to their suicidal conclusion. After considerable explanation and convincing persuasion on my part, and after they had verified with the concierge at the Richemond the fact that I was leaving Switzerland that same afternoon, the Brigadier decided that there indeed had been a misunderstanding. His decision was an enormous relief because the only person I could have called for help in Geneva was Pierre Rougemont, which, while it would have been effective, would have been too embarrassing.

Because of this unfortunate delay, I was forced to take a taxi to Rue de Monnaie, but strangely grateful for the experience, as the shock of the whole episode drove my negative thoughts away. Now I was eagerly looking forward to my meeting with

Rougemont, a man I had come to admire in so short a time, regardless of the outcome. If his instructions allowed him to show me the "Page Missing," it would either answer one question or ask another. If his constraints were too strong, so be it. I would find a different way.

The taxi let me off in front of Rougemont & Cie and I entered the building with a smile, identified myself to the elderly guard and went tripping lightly up the stairs. The same serious, unsmiling woman was waiting for me at the top. She had changed her wardrobe, but this one was equally conservative.

"Bon jour, Madame," I greeted her. *"Comment allez-vous?"*

"Would you come this way, please?" was her response.

Again I followed her down the silent corridor. Instead of leading me to Rougemont's office at the end, she ushered me into the empty conference room and left without an explanation, closing the door behind her. Evidently, this was going to be a large meeting. There were twelve chairs around the long table. Perhaps Rougemont had decided to give me the opportunity to state my case. But to whom? Besides, I had the definite impression that he would make the decision himself. I could only wait. I walked to the window and stared down at the traffic on Rue de Monnaie.

After five minutes, no one else had come and I had the feeling that something was wrong. The Swiss are a solid, punctual people. Why would they leave me in this room by myself? What had Rougemont said when he asked me to come to his office? No, he had said, "come to the bank." Anytime would do. What was he telling me?

I turned away from the window and saw the answer immediately. A thin folder rested on the table. I rushed to it. "Please Do Not Remove" was written on the cover and inside there was a single page.

"For L.W."

So much for the Alexandra Dedications.

NICE

1

The first time I had visited Nice (or, anywhere, for that matter) I had turned eighteen, having completed my freshman year at Yale. It was not my own idea. My father was summering on the Riviera and he had summoned me for reasons that were never made clear. Somehow Maury had acquired the use of an apartment on the Boulevard Victor Hugo, a lovely tree-lined street not far from the Promenade des Anglais.

The apprehension I had suffered since learning that I was due to travel was dispelled by my father's warm greeting at the airport. He was tanned, fit and elegant and filled with enthusiasm about the wonderful summer he and I were about to share, though he did mention that some of his time would be occupied with business.

Despite the fact that I was drowzy from the trip, Maury insisted that we go out for dinner and he took me to a restaurant on Rue Beaumont. The restaurant was run by a rather strange woman who seemed to know my father well and who actually pinched my cheek when he introduced me, then sent over a bottle of wine. After two glasses, I was practically unconscious. I do not remember what we ate, though I still have a dim recollection that there were two old cars parked right in the dining room, but that was probably an alcoholic hallucination.

The next morning, Maury had a client coming over so he suggested I go to the beach, which was only a short walk. He instructed me to return to the apartment at lunchtime, after which we would have "a tour." Then when he saw the disappointed expression on my face, he laughed and said, "No, Amigo, not a museum. I'm taking you to Monte Carlo."

Monte Carlo. It sounded so romantic and exciting and I set off for the beach probably as happy as I had ever been in my whole life. Probably happier. This was a new side to my father, a definite improvement, compared with the intimidating, overwhelming parent I carried in my head. Something had changed and, while I didn't understand it, I was too euphoric to question the motivation.

The sight of the sparkling waterfront ahead made me hurry and I crossed the Promenade des Anglais, then scampered down to spread my towel on the pebbly beach almost in a state of bliss, only peripherally aware of my immediate surroundings. I settled myself on the towel, inhaled and exhaled a deep breath of contentment. Then I looked around.

The girls were practically naked, their breasts and bottoms exposed and only tiny cloth triangles covering them in front. I experienced an immediate, enormous erection, my monster rocketing up to rip its way free of the flimsy restraint of my bathing suit, determined to expose itself in all its deformity. In a panic, I rolled over onto my belly, trying to crush this creature into limp submission. But the turgid mammoth would not surrender, and I had to cling to the beach with all my strength to prevent being catapulted onto my back. Finally, furtively, I hollowed out a pit in the rough sand and managed to maneuver the traitor into it.

I fixed my eyes on the towel, blocking out everything except the cheerful yellow, red and blue pattern, trying to concentrate my will power. But still the leviathan refused to comply, needing only the knowledge that we were beset with naked breasts and bottoms and limbs to keep the arousal intact.

I tried thinking about death, about maggots, about God, even about my sister who, up to that point, had been the only female I had seen nude and never with any stimulation. Nothing worked, not even the frantic awareness that the hot sun had passed its zenith and that I was late for lunch with my father. I was a prisoner of the *plage*.

When, at dusk, having been the last person to leave the beach, I returned to the apartment, my father was furious, rejecting my feeble excuse of having fallen asleep and demanding to know the truth. There was no way that I could tell him the real reason for my delay, so I stuck to my pitiful story, which made him even angrier.

"Jesus Christ, Amigo. I thought you had grown up!" he shouted.

The miracle had ended, and even later, when he took me to the emergency hospital for my sunburned and blistered back, I knew that there was rage beneath the concern. For the next two days, I was confined to my bed and then sulked around the apartment for the next two weeks, leaving only when Maury had a business meeting, but never going anywhere near the beach.

It was clear that we were not sharing a wonderful summer, and when my father announced that I was to return to New York, the news filled me with relief. But since I was already in France there was no point in wasting the trip entirely, so he and I went to Paris to visit the Louvre. We had adjoining rooms at the Bristol on Rue du Faubourg-St. Honoré and spent three days touring the museum with Maury back at his hectoring best.

It was a horrendous experience, my mind blanking on every question, my speech reduced to a stammer, my eyes glazed and idiotic. I was a great disappointment to my father, and I knew that when he put me on the plane at Paris Orly, my deliverance was only slightly greater than his. The rest of the hot and sticky New York summer was spent with my sister, who had deigned to return to the apartment since Maury was not in residence, but Elisa kept his presence alive with her running commentary of hate. I'm afraid that I did not stick up for my father once.

After leaving Rougemont & Cie, I dashed back to the Richemond, wrote a quick thank you note (for the dinner and the conversation, but no mention of the favor) to my favorite banker and raced to the airport just in time to catch my flight. From Cointrin to Nice-Cote d'Azur was just a short hop and I was still silently repeating "For L.W." when we arrived. I found my suitcase easily on the carousel, as everything else was Louis Vuitton, then picked up my Mercedes at Le Sporting Car Rental *("Pour how long, monsieur?" "Pour le weekend.")* and swung right onto the N7, the bumper-to-bumper traffic not diminishing my excitement.

L.W. I kept playing it. L.W. L. as in Lulu. And Mrs. Bettina

Sachs had said that *Sakura* was Oliver Godolphin's most personal book. Personal? Autobiographical? Could it be that in the character of Jordan Leander, Oliver Godolphin was writing about himself and that the fictional Lulu was the factual L.W.? Was this what drove him to join the Foreign Legion? My mind, though not the traffic, was racing. This was a definite breakthrough.

When I finally left my Le Sporting Mercedes with the Negresco doorman in front of the merange-like hotel, I registered and, paying no attention to the Edwardian splendor, hurried to my Napoleon III style room to seize the telephone.

"*Allo, allo,*" a woman answered.

"Good afternoon. My name is Amicus Maltese and I must speak to Miss Alexis Godolphin on a matter of utmost urgency," it sounded good.

"*Ne quittez pas,*" she said.

There was a long silence, but I knew I was on the scent. I waited confidently.

"Hello, who is this?" a French-accented male voice spoke.

"My name is Amicus Maltese and I have some urgent news for Miss Godolphin." I spoke with authority. "Very urgent."

"She is not available," the man said and hung up.

Not available? Did that mean not home or that she wasn't taking calls? I dialed again.

"Hello?" It was the same man.

"Hello, this is Amicus Maltese again." I tried to be warm and sincere. "I'm sorry to trouble you, but could I please leave a message for Miss Godolphin?"

"Miss Godolphin does not accept messages," he hung up again.

So Miss Godolphin was at home, though obviously her privacy was well guarded. As I unpacked, I decided that would not present much of an obstacle. It was still early, so I would simply drive over to Cap d'Antibes, knock on the door and talk my way in. If Mrs. Bettina Sachs was right (and why shouldn't she be?) and Oliver Godolphin authored this novel, there had to be a very good reason for Alexis Godolphin's denial of the fact.

From what I had read of the synopsis so far, the story, while perhaps trivial, was hardly offensive. And even if my previous conjecture was wrong and the L.W. affair came after the Foreign Legion period, would the fact that her father had lapsed into marital infidelity be so gruesome that Alexis Godolphin would prevent the publication of the book? This was something that happened a long time ago, so what possible difference could it make now? Or was it the money?

Too many questions and too little time for me to just wait this one out, as I had done in the past. Besides, if *Sakura* turned out to be a forgery, its creator wouldn't step forward to claim authorship as that would destroy his purpose. What was the purpose?

I ransomed my Le Sporting Mercedes from the Negresco doorman, and just as I was about to head for Cap d'Antibes, something told me not to do it, that the blitz-kreig approach wouldn't work. Since I was already in the car, I might as well go somewhere while I thought it out again. Turning left, away from Cap d'Antibes, I nosed my way into the heavy traffic and crept along with no particular destination in mind until I saw the direction sign. Monte Carlo. I would, at long last, take that trip that circumstances had prevented years ago, a decision that pulled away my useful thoughts about Alexis Godolphin and thrust them suspiciously onto my father.

Why did Maury go out of his way to impress Fiona? And why did he tell her that he was looking for me? Was there something Fiona didn't tell me, some important detail she left out, distracted in what was obviously only preamble to her Roddy Startle revelation?

Since I was now in France, making it practically a local call, I could phone Fiona at the George V in Paris and ask her, but she would undoubtedly misinterpret my intent. By the time I was able to shunt these useless speculations aside. I was already well past Beaulieu and fast approaching Monte Carlo.

Of course, there was no place to park. After circling three times I realized I was being penalized for my adolescent stupidity, not the part about not leaving the beach on schedule, but for not telling the truth about the reason for my tardiness. My father, I think, might have understood. He might have even laughed and we might have had that wonderful summer together, instead of the awful thing that happened in New York, which I try never to think about.

I had walked back from the Met and was dripping with sweat by the time I got home, so I took a quick shower and was towelling off when I again remembered all those naked bodies on the beach at Nice, which, as it always did, created a condition of instant tumescence. I grabbed the thing and was about to hold it under the cold water tap when the bathroom door opened and my sister walked in, having also come from the heat outside and intending to shower, which explained why she, too, was naked. Seeing me with my erection in my hand, she smiled.

"Christ, it's huge." She came forward. "Let me do that."

She grasped it with her hand and began to stroke it gently.

"Touch my breasts," she whispered.

I know I wanted to run, to flee, but I couldn't move. Elisa took my hand and put it on her breast, still stroking. I closed my eyes, my body trembling.

"Now feel me here," Elisa whispered and put my hand between her legs, stroking faster.

I ejaculated instantly, both gratified and filled with shame. Then I heard Elisa's laughter and opened my eyes to see her expression of vicious satisfaction.

"If Dad could see us now," she said. "That son of a bitch, it serves him right."

"Oh God, you're not going to tell him," was all I could manage.

"Only because I won't speak to that motherfucker," she said and stepped into the shower.

I spent the next two months worrying if Elisa's vow of silence was greater than her need to hurt our father by revealing what we had done, though my sister seemed to forget about the incident almost immediately. Still, from that day on, I undressed and dressed in the bathroom with the door securely locked, knowing that my lie to Maury was the only reason it had happened, which saddled me with a second and far worse secret. If not being able to park in Monte Carlo was the only punishment, it would be a very light sentence.

Sunset was approaching when I reached Beaulieu on the return trip. Needing a drink to calm myself, I drove down to the port— there was plenty of parking here—and sat at one of the little cafes to sip a white Lillet and then another, steering my thinking process back toward its proper direction. How to approach Alexis Godolphin. Then how would I make her talk to me? I couldn't think of an answer and it wasn't until I was having a solitary *soupe de poissons* at an unpretentious little restaurant in Villefranche (not feeling up to the grandeur of the Negresco) that it suddenly came to me. How would Maury do it? I started to laugh and it must have been the release of laughter that jarred my mind-set asunder.

"Dressed in short pants and wearing a little schoolboy cap and then taking it up the bum," Sheffy's voice continued her horrible tale. "And holding a cricket bat as well."

Fortunately, I must have reacted very fast, but apparently I was holding onto the tablecloth at that instant, because the tureen of *soupe de poissons* was in my lap and the ensuing commotion drowned out the rest of the story, not that what I had already heard wasn't bad enough. Up the bum? Impossible. It was clearly a case of mistaken identity. And who was wearing the short pants and schoolboy cap? Besides, the cricket bat revealed that Sheffy's version was totally wrong, as I knew for an absolute fact that Fiona detested the game.

2

The Negresco concierge assured me that the five dozen yellow roses, along with my intriguing note, would be delivered by noon. Then I let him see that it was 200 Francs I was pressing into his waiting fingers before I made my next request. Could he make an 8:30 dinner reservation for three at the Eden Roc? The corners of his mouth began to twist downward, but I was still holding the money in his hand to prevent him from returning the bribe.

"But, *cher Monsieur,*" he began to protest, "the Eden Roc at this time of year and with such short notice, *c'est impossible.* Perhaps I could suggest Chez Marinette in Cannes or La Terrasse in Juan-les-Pins?"

"Oh, I'm sure it won't be a problem," I said with a nonchalant smile. "I'm dining with Warren Beatty and he said if there was any difficulty to use his name."

"Of course, *monsieur,*" The concierge was smiling, too, and I released his hand. "Forgive me for not understanding. Eight-thirty at the Eden Roc. I will deal with it personally."

"I'd appreciate it." I started to turn away.

"Pardon, Monsieur," the concierge caught me. "But I know that *Monsieur* Beatty is not staying with us. Is he at the Carlton?"

"He's on the yacht," I sauntered away.

Under different circumstances I would not have gone to this extreme, but dinner at the Eden Roc was essential to my plan. Besides, though I had never actually met Warren Beatty, there was some distant connection. Fiona told me shortly after we met that Warren Beatty had once pursued her after a chance encounter at a party and that he had, in fact, come to the Chelsea flat that she and Sally Morgan were sharing. Morgan the Organ was thrilled by the visit, but Fiona knew that he was expecting more than a drink. After rejecting his advances, she left the flat in a dither, hardly the reaction of a Jimmy Fitzhugh party girl, which explains the awful Morgan's motto and her self-professed tattoo.

Still, this was a bold move, perhaps bolder than anything I had ever done other than the way I first met Fiona on the bridge in St. James's Park. But there was an enormous difference, as I had thought out my plan to approach Alexis Godolphin carefully. With Fiona, it had just happened.

"Will you marry me?" were my first words to her.

"When?" She had laughed, her green eyes merry.

"Right now, if that's possible." Her response had encouraged me.

"I'm afraid that might be a little too sudden." Fiona started to walk away.

"Wait," I cried. "I'm serious."

"You're an American," she said. "And Americans are never serious."

"How many Americans do you know?" I persisted.

"More than I need to." Her amusement had faded. "Look, you're beginning to be a bit of a nuisance."

"I can't help it. I've fallen in love with you." I was in earnest.

"Really? And how often does that happen to you? Every five

minutes or just every time you try picking up a girl?" Fiona's expression had grown cold.

"It's never happened to me before in my life. It never will again."

Fiona must have heard the sincerity in my voice because her beautiful eyes softened and she glanced down shyly, the hint of a blush on her cheeks. We stood there on the bridge silently for several moments. Then Fiona looked up, her eyes searching mine.

"Really?" she asked softly.

"I swear on my life." I placed my hand over my heart.

"My God." She ran a hand nervously through her flame red hair. "Then you had better take me to tea and tell me who you are."

We walked all the way to South Audley Street and had tea at Richoux where I presented myself in the most favorable light, relating the de Castagno affair with some braggadocio perhaps, but with enough humor to keep Fiona amused. I even provoked her laughter on several occasions, having to remind myself constantly that this was really happening. Fiona, incredibly, became more beautiful by the instant which kept that part of my brain that was engraving her image on my soul very busy.

"You have the happiest eyes I have ever seen," Fiona interrupted my monologue.

"Because they're looking at you," my response was right there.

"And you are absolutely mad," she laughed.

After tea, we continued walking up South Audley Street to Grosvenor Square and the sight of the huge U.S. Embassy somehow provoked me, in my cloud of joy, to sing "God Bless America" at the top of my lungs, overcome with the need to thank someone for my good fortune, an act which gave Fiona a fit of uncontrollable giggles. She finally ended my performance, which was attracting some attention, by placing her hand over my mouth. It was our first physical contact.

"Ask me again," she said. "If you really mean it, ask me again."

"Ask you what?" I was a little slow.

"The question you asked me on the bridge, silly," Fiona poked me in the ribs.

"Will you marry me?" I spoke the words clearly.

"You had better be careful, Mickey Maltese." Fiona's eyes sparkled with green mischief. "Because I just may take you up on that."

"Heiraten in Eile," the German saying goes, *"Bereut man mit Weile."* Fiona and I were married in haste, but I have never repented, nor would I ever have, had the marriage lasted long enough to afford time for that leisure. Some relationships were just meant to be, mine with Fiona, though, for now, not hers with me. Destiny, I told myself, cleave to destiny.

The Marc Chagall National Museum on Avenue Docteur Ménard is a glorious place, if you like Chagall. The museum houses the most complete collection of the artist's work, including the large canvases of the "Biblical Message" series that he painted between the ages of sixty-seven and eighty. After my thrust and parry with the concierge, there was no way that I could loiter around the Negresco so, rather than fighting the traffic in my Le Sporting Mercedes, I took a taxi to visit the Chagalls out of curiosity, as few other contemporary artists have been so widely forged, intentionally or otherwise.

Since Chagall, a Russian Jew who lived in France, used religious subjects and occasionally included Hebrew letters in his paintings, any painting by a less known Russian Jew could become a valuable Chagall with a few additions and a simple alteration of the signature, which, of course, was performed by the dealer involved, not the original artist.

Then, to create further confusion, there were the actual forgers turning out mock-Chagalls when there was a market for them and since Chagall lived to ninety-seven, he had over his long career done so many paintings that he couldn't remember all of them. As with Utrillo, the artist was not always able to denounce the forgeries. Unlike Corot, however, he did not aid and abet these counterfeiters, with one possible exception, as it has been claimed that Chagall did verify a particularly good imitation by Lothar Malskat, one of Maury's favorites.

I did not fully comprehend the extent to which my father was involved in selling fraudulent art, despite the story of his indictment in *The New York Times*, until I began to work at the Met for the first time and then the revelation came about by Maury just coming out and telling me. I was, understandably, horrified, and then became outraged when he made it clear that he was trying to involve me in his shady business, which was the beginning of our current estrangement. It was, perhaps, a slight overreaction on my part, something which I would not admit at the time.

After touring the galleries and admiring the large exterior mosaic of the Biblical prophet Elias flying up to heaven in his chariot of fire, I left the lovely museum and wandered slowly back toward the Negresco. I stopped for lunch at a *brasserie*, where, in a moment of New York nostalgia, I had *Le Super Hot Dog sur Toast Garni*, which was a definite mistake. Still reluctant to return to my hotel room, I meandered for another hour, trying to walk off my indigestion and feeling anxious about Alexis Godolphin's reaction.

It had seemed a very good idea at the time. Now I was having second thoughts, which were instantly distracted by the color photograph on the cover of *Paris Match*, displayed prominently at a newsstand. Blonde tresses flying, wearing gold spangled tights, microphone in hand, Roddy Startle had been captured by the photographer in, judging by his expression, a moment of triumph. I didn't really need the reminder, but I bought the magazine and, folding it over to conceal the cover, scurried back to the Negresco, hoping to discover some useful information in the article.

Fortunately, as I was not up to any further probing about Warren Beatty, it was another concierge who handed me my room key and, to my great relief, no messages. As planned, I then requested that all my incoming telephone calls be screened and only female callers put through, which concierge number two assured me would be done, accepting my 100 Francs with a Gallic twinkle in his eyes. Weaving my way through the bellboys, all oddly attired in red breeches and white gloves, I carried my *Paris Match* to the elevator and then to my room. On the writing desk, neatly positioned by the maid, was the draft of my note.

Dear Alexis Godolphin,
Please accept these roses and my invitation for dinner this evening at the Eden Roc. It is essential that I talk to you about the manuscript currently in Farrow and Farrow's possession which is being attributed to your father. I have some information which you will find to

be quite significant. If I do not hear from you, I will assume that you
accept and will pick you up at eight o'clock.

Cordially,

Other than a few minor improvements and changing the Cordially to Sincerely when I copied the message on Negresco stationery in my neatest handwriting, my brief letter, I reassured
myself, would produce the desired result. Even if Alexis Godolphin declined, she would have to phone me personally, as my
screen would deflect her surly friend who had hung up on me so
rudely. Once I had her on the telephone, I knew I could make
some progress. Either way I would take a step forward, but
dinner with her was by far the preferable option. So far she
hadn't called. If she were to decline, she would have done so
immediately.

Not bad, I thought, and settled myself in the comfortable
armchair to open *Paris Match*. There were a dozen photographs
of Roddy Startle, all glamorous and none with Fiona, for which I
was grateful, and the lengthy article was, naturally, in French.
This created a slight problem. Despite my many visits to the con-
tinent, my speaking knowledge of the language was only fair, but
better than my ability to read with adequate comprehension,
romance languages not being one of my strengths. My German,
however, was fairly fluent, thanks to my father's insistence that I
study the language, starting at an early age and continuing right
through Yale.

Maury had even shipped me off to Munich for my twentieth
summer, having arranged for intensive language lessons, many of
which were conducted in bed with my attractive instructor, an
older (I thought then) woman of thirty-three whose name was
Monika *("Der Schwanz ist sehr gross!")* Brentano, an arrange-
ment which I suspected my father had also organized. But why
German? Maury didn't speak the language and he never
explained why he decided it was so important that I did. But it
resulted in my having a linguistic ability for which I have little
use and the only time I have ever been to Germany was that single, rutting summer in Munich. Another family mystery.

In the middle of the Roddy Startle article, my eye hit upon the words, *"une belle demoiselle Anglais aux cheveux roux, a vrai dire, cuivré,"* and knew I had found the painful paydirt. A young English woman with red hair? Who else could it be? But what was *cuivré?* Just as I reached for the telephone to request a French-English dictionary from the concierge, the phone rang, stopping my hand in mid-air. I knew it was Alexis Godolphin calling to refuse, and since I had been so distracted by the *Paris Match* article, I wasn't as verbally prepared as I should have been if I were to succeed in making the right impression. Another ring and I considered not answering, but realized instantly that would be foolish and picked up the receiver, ready to improvise to my best ability.

"Hello?"

"Amicus? First let me say I feel an absolute fool for what I said the other night. I had no idea that you were once married to Fiona. Crikey, why didn't you tell me?"

"Sheffy?"

"Now I know you're probably upset with me, but I have something very important to tell you."

"How did you find me?"

"I phoned the gallery and spoke to that horrible woman Sally something and she told me that you had been staying at the Rembrandt. I phoned the hall porter and he told me you were at the Richemond in Geneva and the concierge there told me you were at the Negresco. I simply adore that hotel. What are you doing there?"

"I'm going to talk to Alexis Godolphin."

"Well, it will have to be tonight because you must leave for Rome on the early flight. My secretary has already made the reservations. Tomorrow is your only chance to catch Danny Speers. I've spoken to him and he's agreed to meet you in the bar at the Grand, but he doesn't have much time. I gave him my word that you would be there at noon."

"Danny Speers?"

"He's only doing this as a personal favor to me because he's about to begin production on his new film. Once that starts he'll have his hands full. Crikey, both of his stars are absolute alcoholics and his director is a well-known lunatic, so the only chance you have is at the Grand tomorrow."

"At noon?"

"Ring me afterwards. Bye."

3

For yet another 100 Francs, concierge number two was kind enough to show me on his map how to find Chemin de la Garoupe in Cap d'Antibes, inquiring saucily if I had received the anticipated phone call. I gave him a leer for an answer, which provoked a hearty chuckle, then went out to redeem my Le Sporting Mercedes and creep along with the traffic on the N7 toward Cannes. Sheffy's unexpected phone call had accelerated my plans and confused my emotions while she hadn't retracted the nettling untruths about Fiona, she had at least apologized. She was right that I should have spoken out immediately despite the fact that Fiona had withheld the details of our relationship.

My agent was certainly doing her job though, as an interview with Danny Speers, particularly during this hectic period, was a rare opportunity. Here was someone who had known Oliver Godolphin well during the early years and a man who had maintained their relationship notwithstanding Oliver Godolphin's hostility for Hollywood, perhaps even Godolphin's confidant. And all this was due to Sheffy's diligence, which dissipated any negative feelings I might have had about her personally.

After our telephone conversation, I requested the concierge to have my ticket to Rome picked up and ordered a French-English dictionary at the same time, both of which were shortly delivered by a bellboy. *Cuivré*, I quickly discovered, meant copper colored. Copper colored? To my eyes Fiona's hair was the red of glowing embers, of tropical sunsets, not a lack-luster copper. The author of the article obviously did not have the keenest perception, but, with the help of the dictionary, I struggled through the remaining pages. I was relieved to find that there were no further references to *"une belle demoiselle Anglais,"* though the information that

Roddy Startle was handsome, rich, talented, charming and deeply involved in charitable causes and the struggles for human rights sounded a little too good to be true. There had to be a dark side to the man, which I hoped for Fiona's sake was not too unpleasant.

Because of the traffic, it was already after eight by the time I turned left at Antibes and, worried about arriving late, I drove through the city without taking the time to appreciate the sights. Since Sheffy had been my only phone call, I knew that my floral approach to Alexis Godolphin had worked, but there was no way of knowing how open she would be about her father's past, as I certainly was reluctant to discuss mine.

I finally reached the coastal route around the Cap, the pine forest above, and went searching for Chemin de la Garoupe, then discovered that the road climbed up onto the peninsula. I was twenty minutes behind schedule, far more than what could be considered fashionable. This was not a very good system for beginning a helpful relationship. When, at last, I arrived at the large villa I had already conceived a variety of excuses and rejected all of them.

Then on seeing a dozen cars parked along the circular gravel driveway, an even greater anxiety appeared. Alexis Godolphin was having a party, so how could she go out to dinner with me? Perhaps the flowers and my note had never been delivered and that was the reason she hadn't phoned to decline my invitation. Still, having come this far, I was not about to retreat and left my shabby Le Sporting Mercedes parked behind a gleaming, sleek Ferrari.

I crunched my way up the driveway to the front door, rang the bell, checked that my regimental tie was straight down the front of my Turnbull and Asser shirt, and waited. The door opened and I found myself facing the second most beautiful woman I had ever seen, her dark hair and eyes making her fair skin pale by comparison. She was dressed in an elegant pale blue jacket and skirt, a single tear-drop diamond hanging at the base of her perfect throat, suspended by a gold chain around her neck.

"Mr. Maltese?" She spoke finally.

"Yes." I nodded.

"I was afraid you weren't coming, but I guessed that you were caught in traffic on the N7. It's just impossible to get anywhere this time of year." Her accent was mid-Atlantic and her lips moved gracefully around the words.

"Alexis Godolphin?" It was hard to believe.

"Come in, please. Give me a minute to say good-bye, collect my purse and then we'll go." Then she turned and walked back inside the house.

The foyer led directly to the living room, where the whiteness of the Mediterranean decor contrasted only with the large display of yellow roses in a vase on the coffee table. The far wall consisted mostly of glass. Doors opened onto the wide terrace where about twenty people, very chic, held cocktails and appeared to be talking enthusiastically all at the same time. There seemed to be no need for anyone to listen. I watched from a distance as Alexis Godolphin moved through the crowd, kissing cheeks and making little waves with her fingers. Just observing her took my breath away. How could Oliver Godolphin's daughter be so incredibly beautiful? And she had said she was afraid I wasn't coming. Why should she be troubled about that? I was the interloper here, yet she had welcomed me. Was it the roses? As if in a dream, I watched her come in through the terrace doors, pick up an exquisite white beaded handbag and approach with a smile that revealed her flawless teeth.

"Ready?" she had to ask, art in motion and the viewer still.

We walked to my Le Sporting Mercedes and drove off, Alexis Godolphin providing the directions to the Hotel Cap d'Antibes. She guided me perfectly to Boulevard Kennedy at the tip of the peninsula and appeared not to notice that I was incapable of speech. It wasn't until we were about to arrive at the cream-colored palace that I remembered what I had done and realized that I would have to explain my deceit before the fact.

"By the way, I have a small confession," was the best entrance I could think of.

"Oh?"

"You see, in order to get a table at the Eden Roc, I made the reservation in Warren Beatty's name."

"You didn't."

"Well." I chewed on my lower lip. "It seems I did."

"Then Rupert was right about you," she laughed. "He said you were a dangerous man."

"You talked to Rupert Farrow?" My signed confession leapt to mind.

"Bon soir, Madam. Bon soir, Monsieur." The doors to my Le Sporting Mercedes were pulled open the instant I stopped the car in front of Eden Roc. Alexis Godolphin stepped out before she answered, forcing me to race around the bumper to catch up with her.

"Of course, I did," she said as we walked toward the restaurant entrance, the building overlooking the shimmering sea at the bottom of the hotel's garden. "After your mysterious letter, what else would I do?"

It was too complicated to explain standing up, so I didn't try to prevent Alexis Godolphin from entering the Eden Roc, where the maitre d' seemed to be waiting for our arrival.

"We are supposed to be meeting Warren Beatty," I said as softly as I could.

"Yes, sir," the maitre d' smiled. "Mr. Beatty is already here."

Oh? I hadn't figured on that possibility. Instantly, my mind began dancing the tango, as I tried to think of a way to extricate us from this situation without too embarrassing a scene, then Alexis Godolphin breezed past me, saying something in rapid fire French which I couldn't understand.

"Certainement, Mademoiselle," the maitre d' responded and led us smartly to a table along the terrace railing.

"What did you do?" I asked after we were seated.

"I simply requested my usual table." She looked at me and laughed. "I can't believe you really did that. What would you have done if I hadn't said anything?"

"Probably fallen to my knees and begged forgiveness."

"Well, I'm glad I didn't have to witness that." She was absolutely beautiful. "But why didn't you just tell Marcel on the phone that you were from Farrow and Farrow instead of all that urgent confidential nonsense?"

"Marcel? Oh, the man who kept hanging up on me. He never gave me a chance to finish." The waiter arrived with the menus, providing the moment to switch topics. "Would you like a drink?"

"Evian," she said. "I don't take anything alcoholic. But don't let that stop you."

"*Deux Evian, s'il vous plait,*" I told the waiter, then looked back at Alexis Godolphin. "Excuse me for saying this, but you are an amazingly beautiful woman. I know you must hear that all the time, but I just had to add my voice to the chorus."

"Why, thank you, Mr. Maltese." She knew how to accept a compliment. "And your yellow roses are gorgeous."

"Call me Mickey."

"Mickey? As in Mickey Mouse?" She laughed. "I think that suits you."

"Without the mouse, please." Another request.

"Well, Mickey without the mouse," Alexis Godolphin obviously had a sense of humor, "all this is very nice, dinner at the Eden Roc, the huge bundle of flowers, but it was all totally unnecessary. Did you think I wouldn't speak to you otherwise?"

"I sometimes suffer from paranoia," I admitted. "But that is often helpful in my work."

"What exactly is your work?" she asked.

I gave her my card, then explained the details briefly, adding that this assignment was my first in the field of literature and that, as far as I knew, I was breaking new ground. Alexis Godolphin listened seriously, then she picked up her menu.

"Let's order," she said, and at her signal the waiter hurried over with pad in hand. "Salade Niçoise."

"I'll have the same," I told the waiter, then waited until he left. "So while I am employed by Farrow and Farrow, who obviously want to publish the book with your father's name on it, I nevertheless remain impartial. Impartiality is essential to good provenance."

"My father did not write that book," she said firmly.

"Then, Miss Godolphin . . ."

"Alexis."

"Then, Alexis," I went on smoothly, "proving that he did not write it accomplishes my objective just as well. All I want is to determine the truth. That places me on your side as much as it places me on the side of Farrow and Farrow. Do you understand?"

"Go on." Alexis wasn't smiling now.

"According to your father's former editor, Mrs. Bettina Sachs, the style and the language of the manuscript have Oliver Godolphin stamped on every page."

"That woman doesn't know anything. My father always edited his own novels and he thought Bettina was an idiot." Alexis slammed the door on that.

"But in any event, she is very familiar with your father's work."

"I suppose she is."

"And the last published book of your father's came out almost three years before his death, so theoretically there was time for him to write another novel. Was he working on something during that period?"

"I don't know. My father never discussed his work in progress. We never even knew what he was writing about until the book was finished." Alexis was getting angry.

"What happened then?" I asked anyway.

"He would give the book to my mother. She would read it and then they would discuss it. My father would make changes sometimes because of my mother's comments."

"And all his books are dedicated to her."

"Yes."

I leaned forward to stare into her wonderous dark eyes.

"This one isn't," I said.

"Then that proves it's a forgery!" her dark eyes were furious.

"How do you think your mother would have reacted if your father had dedicated a book to someone else?" I knew this was a dangerous question.

"She probably would have been relieved. All those dedications were becoming silly. She didn't even want the second one, much less the rest, but my father insisted."

Two waiters arrived, each bearing a Salade Niçoise. Alexis's answer was not the one I expected. In my mind, Alexandra Godolphin should have been outraged by this betrayal, infuriated by this infidelity. Another theory shattered against the stone wall of truth. I waited for Alexis to pick up her fork. Then we began to eat.

"Delicious," I said, which made Alexis laugh. "What's so funny?"

"You are," she pointed a finger at me. "The whole scenario to

get me to meet with you, making the reservation in Warren
Beatty's name—he's sitting just behind you, by the way—
beginning your little interrogation moving methodically from one
step to the next. Then your eyes just go blank because you don't
hear what you expect. I could see your mind scurrying around,
looking for another approach. You even move your lips while
you think, and then you taste this rather ordinary Salade Niçoise
and say, 'Delicious.' It's all so obvious that it's like a cartoon.
You are Mickey Mouse."

"This is not good for my ego," I told her.

"Take it as a compliment," she reached over to pat my hand,
"because that's how I intended it. Most people are so closed and
inwardly secretive and your face and eyes and expression reveal
everything. I think it's wonderful. Now let's go on with the questions."

Move my lips when I think? Did I really? Is that why Fiona
said I was so transparent? This was humiliating. Alexis was still
observing me and I knew that from this point on I would have to
watch my step. I asked the first question that came to mind.

"Who is Marcel?"

"My fiancé." She was clearly surprised. "Why?"

"What does he do?"

"His family owns vineyards in Bordeaux," Alexis said
defiantly. "But what does that have to do with my father?"

"How well did your father speak German?" I pounced.

"German?" Now I had her confused. "My father didn't speak a
word of German."

"Are you sure? Perhaps he learned it in the Foreign Legion.
There were a lot of Germans there."

"My father, as you well know, never spoke about the Legion."
She was cold again. "And I never heard him speak anything but
French or English. What are you getting at?"

"The truth, I hope, and I'm sorry if my little interrogation
offends you." I paused to let that sink in. "But there are reasons
behind my questions."

"Oh, I did offend you. I'm very sorry." Alexis sounded sincere. "I told you I meant it as a compliment."

"When I said you were an amazingly beautiful woman, that
was a compliment," I said. "Mickey Mouse is not a

compliment."

"I really hurt your feelings." She stared at me.

"Yes, you did."

Alexis placed her napkin on the table and got to her feet gracefully. At first I thought she was leaving, but she walked around the table, put her hands on my shoulders and, in front of the entire restaurant, kissed me softly on the lips. Maybe it was because it was the first kiss I had received in many years or possibly because it was Alexis who was kissing me, but instantly the monster raised his horrible head and came rigidly to life. I almost fainted.

"Forgive me," Alexis whispered, her face still close to mine.

"Yes," I whispered back. "Yes."

How was I going to be able to leave? Was I doomed to repeat the agonizing experience at the beach in Nice at the Eden Roc? Would I wind up sitting in the darkened restaurant, the other diners long since gone, the staff waiting impatiently for my departure? Could fate really be that cruel?

"Are you all right?" Alexis had returned to her chair and was looking at me.

"That was very stimulating." I seemed to be breathless.

"That was my very best apology," she said. "Now why were you asking if my father spoke German?"

"Because in the questionable manuscript, the story takes place in Austria and the use of the German language is quite extensive." I forced myself to concentrate.

"How do you know? Have you read it?"

"Only the synopsis."

"What's the story about?"

"It's the story of Jordan Leander, a burnt-out American journalist in Vienna," I began and then went on to describe his subsequent adventure and obsession with the beautiful red-haired Lulu von Hofmannsthal up to his encounter with Baron Hugo.

"What happens then?" Alexis asked.

"That's as far as I've gotten."

"Have you read my father's books?"

"I've been meaning to."

"Well, this doesn't sound like one of them."

"Mrs. Bettina Sachs said it was your father's most personal

book."

"Hardly an opinion that I value," Alexis tossed it aside. "Rupert told me that you had gone to see this banker in Geneva, the one who submitted the manuscript."

"Yes, but his restrictions didn't allow him to tell me much." I reached into my jacket pocket and brought out the envelope. "I have copies of two pages of the manuscript. Would you look at them?"

Alexis hesitated, her shoulders stiffening, her body language indicating refusal. I took out the pages and unfolded them, but she leaned away, still silent.

"These pages could be compared to your father's other manuscripts, the typing method, even the typewriter." I didn't want it to appear threatening.

"No, they can't," she said. "Because I have the manuscripts."

"But if I fail to establish provenance and this becomes a legal matter, the court can force you to provide the manuscripts for comparison." I wasn't sure of this point but it sounded convincing. "So it's in everyone's best interest for me to determine the authorship of the manuscript rather than a pack of hungry lawyers. This way it keeps the whole affair private and free of any potential scandal."

It wasn't until I spoke the words that I remembered my deal with Sheffy, but this didn't seem an appropriate moment to bring that up. Still, I realized that I had just created a serious conflict of interests. Alexis suddenly reached for the pages, then studied each of them carefully before her eyes returned to mine.

"I'm trusting you, Mickey," she said.

"You can." My heart was pounding with guilt.

"These pages are very similar to my father's other manuscripts," Alexis handed them back to me. "Now I don't know what to think."

"Yes, it is very confusing," I agreed. "Particularly since the book suddenly appeared seven years after your father's death."

"Both my parents died that day," Alexis corrected me.

"I'm sorry. I didn't mean to be insensitive." I bowed my head.

"Don't overdo it," Alexis sounded suddenly amused. "Look, I know you're working up to something, so why don't you just come out and ask me."

"Are you still in contact with Ali Habibi?"

"Of course I am. I see Baby whenever he comes to the South of France and I usually go to Marbella at least once a year."

"Who's Baby?" I thought Alexis had misunderstood my question.

"Baby Habibi," she explained. "No one calls him Ali. Why did you ask?"

"Because I want you to introduce me to him."

"What for?"

"He was there when your parents died."

"So was I."

"But perhaps there is something he knows that you don't," I said. "And since there are too many unknowns for me to work backwards from here, I want to try working forward from there."

"Baby feels very badly about the accident." I could hear the emotion in Alexis's voice. "He blames himself for having allowed my father to fly the helicopter, though my father was an excellent pilot. And he worries that it was something wrong with the helicopter, something mechanical, that caused the crash. He still carries the burden of that responsibility and I doubt very much if he will agree to talk to you or anyone about it."

"Will you ask him?" I persisted, then went on when she didn't answer. "Under the circumstances, you have only three choices. One, you allow Farrow and Farrow to publish the book. Two, you go to court. Or, three, you help me."

"And if Baby refuses to see you, what then?"

"I continue with whatever resources are available, though the chances of my success diminish with each piece of information that is withheld." I was not being altogether straightforward with Alexis, but that was in the nature of provenance investigation.

"All right," she said finally. "I'll phone Baby and ask him, but I want your solemn promise that if you discover anything about my father that will in any way damage his name or reputation, you will never reveal that information."

"You have my word." I meant it, though I wasn't sure how I would keep this promise.

Alexis looked into my eyes and I stared back unblinkingly, Mickey Mouse dead and buried, and my expression as transparent as a concrete wall. Abruptly, Alexis got to her feet and I found myself hoping for another kiss.

"I'm sorry, but I have to leave. Marcel is waiting for me in front." She tried to smile, but I could see that she was wounded. "Call me tomorrow afternoon."

She walked away and I knew that if it hadn't been for Fiona, I would already have fallen in love with Alexis Godolphin, totally even if unrequitedly. With that disturbing thought revolving, I finished my Salade Niçoise, called for the check, paid it. Then, since the giant was again safely sleeping, I got up from the table as casually as I could and turned.

Warren Beatty was gone.

ROME

1

Without question, Alceo Dossena was the most prolific sculptor of the Renaissance and his work, costly to acquire, was displayed with pride at almost every major museum in Europe and America. Like the great Giovanni Bastianini, who died at thirty-seven, Dossena's life came to a relatively early end, as he was only fifty-nine at the time of his death. In 1937. Perhaps the greatest forger of this century, at least in the area of sculpture, Dossena never considered his art to be fraudulent and would even add his name or initials to his work, which was, of course, removed by the dealers before selling the piece.

One of his most famous works was the Mino da Fiesole tomb which brought the astonishing price, in 1924, of $100,000 and remains in the possession of the Boston Museum of Fine Arts despite the continuing controversy over its provenance (the familiar old story of it having been discovered in a long hidden church in Tuscany which had been buried by an earthquake. Hah!).

Dossena's genius with marble was balanced by his financial gullibility, the enormous profits from the sale of his work staying almost entirely in the dealer's pocket. In fact, of the $100,000 paid by the Boston Museum for the Mino da Fiesole tomb, he received only $420.00 and spent his entire working life desperate for money, which, of course, made him sculpt all the harder.

Over the next several years, Dossena produced a prodigious amount of work that made the dealers even richer, but they still refused to share the wealth, knowing that the artist's dire finances would keep him at the hammer and chisel. Finally, one dealer, Alfredo Fasoli, went too far, turning Dossena away without paying him anything. Dossena took him to court, revealing his whole story to the Magistrate.

The resulting scandal shook the entire art world. The Met, the Cleveland, the Frick Collection and even the British Museum were among the hallowed galleries forced to admit that they had been deceived, banishing their Dossenas as if they had the plague. Most of these works vanished quietly into private collections or were returned to their dealers. But Dossena's massive output more than indicates that many of his pieces remain undetected and are still on display, including the three Florentine terracotta reliefs, all Madonna and Child, but these bearing Dossena's name, in Room 46 at the V & A. Personally, I don't consider them to be representative of his best work.

After my unremarkable exit from the Eden Roc, I drove slowly back to the Negresco, packed, left a wake-up call and fell into bed, my dinner conversation with Alexis somehow having exhausted me. The next morning, I returned the Mercedes to Le Sporting (*"Mais le weekend is not finished."* *"Oui, mais j'ai un change of plans."*) and thirty minutes later was lifted off Nice-Cote d'Azur and carried south across the blue Mediterranean toward the chaos that was Rome.

Fiona and Alexis or Alexis and Fiona, both equally beyond reach, both equally perfect and both totally different. It was not that my love and desire for Fiona had lessened in any way or that I had fallen in love with Alexis. But my emotional reflections which had played the same solo note for all these years now seemed to have become a duet. I tried thinking of Oliver Godolphin. I tried preparing for my meeting with Danny Speers. I tried reading Mrs. Bettina Sachs's synopsis. But Fiona and Alexis would not be denied. Not even forced recollections of Monika (*"Schneller, Schneller mein Pferd!"*) Brentano could drive them from my mind.

At least with Fiona I had a past to remember. With Alexis I had only last night, so why should she expropriate so much of my mental territory? And, other than being scion to vineyards in Bordeaux, who was Marcel? Did, I wondered, Alexis leave the door open when she went to the bathroom?

When I was married to Fiona, the sound of her tinkling became an important part of my life, as Fiona never closed the bathroom door and, in fact, she would plop herself down on the toilet while I was brushing my teeth, peeing with aplomb and chatting at the same time. Her casual attitude about urination astounded me since I was seldom able to pass water with anyone present, which gave me a great deal of difficulty in boarding school and continues to this present day.

There have been many times that I have stepped up to a public urinal in privacy only to have my flow stop with the arrival of another pilgrim sharing the same urgent need. Even in the isolation of a public restroom cabinet, the footsteps of a stranger entering the men's room could cause an involuntary stricture which would reduce my stream to a sputtering trickle.

Only with Fiona had I been able to relieve myself without anxiety, and even that had taken a lot of doing. It had been a lazy Sunday on Ebury Street, reading the papers, nibbling leftovers and making love, and after I had rolled out of bed, padded to the loo and was contentedly experiencing a necessary relief when Fiona just opened the door and walked naked into the bathroom, her hair all rumped and beautiful. My plumbing shut down instantly.

"I'm finished," I announced quickly.

"You are not." She came up behind me. "You just started and I want to hold it whilst you pee."

"Fiona."

"Shush," she said and took the loppy creature in her hand, pointing Cyclops toward the bowl. "I've always wanted to do this. Tell me if I'm aiming right."

"Fiona, I can't," I complained.

"Pee!" she commanded.

And, somehow, I did, which was only the beginning of our adventures in mutual micturition, culminating in her finally holding back until I could join her. Then she would sit on the toilet with her legs spread and direct my rush carefully between them to create an intimate confluence, a bond that, frankly, Fiona found more meaningful than I did. Is this what was happening in Paris?

So it was with no sense of accomplishment that I disembarked

at Fiumincino, finally retrieved my bag from the erratic carousel
and hailed a taxi into Rome, to Via Margutta, in the center of the
city, where I had been living in a small pensione (the Met not
being exactly generous with expenses) on and off for the past year
while hounding the *professore*. Since I had been given no guarantee of employment before my meeting at Farrow & Farrow, I had
kept my room and therefore had no need of a hotel. Under other
circumstances, following in the tradition of the Richemond and
the Negresco, I would have selected Le Grand, where Danny
Speers was staying, over the Hassler. But since my expenses had
been running rather high, a modest bill from the Via Margutta
pensione would offer some compensation.

When, some 30,000 lire later, the taxi carried me into the rau-
cous city, it all seemed vividly familiar. I realized that I had been
gone for less than a week and that I had been so caught up in the
Oliver Godolphin provenance that I had lost track of time, which
returning to Rome made all the more confusing. This city had an
odd effect on me, as if my life here continued whether or not I
was actually in residence, a feeling I first experienced on only my
second visit. Returning now, having spent so many lonely months
uncovering the truth about the *faux* Michelangelo sketchbook, I
almost expected to glimpse myself walking down the street and
anticipated the combining of my two lives into one, at least for
the duration of my stay. When I would leave, this Roman
Doppelgänger would remain. How strange. But how strange that
Danny Speers should be in Rome and how strange that Oliver
Godolphin did not speak German and that I did.

And how strange that it wasn't until after I had first moved into
the pensione that I learned Alceo Dossena's last studio had been
just down the street at Via Margutta 54, and what bitter years
those must have been. From the moment the fraud had been
revealed, Dossena's genius was denied, critics attacked his work
as inadequate and demanded to know how these mediocre pieces
could have deceived anyone and his signature on a statue actually
decreased its value, the V & A having paid only 12 pounds apiece
for the three Madonnas. Dossena, naturally, was crushed. There
is little doubt that this depression contributed greatly to his
premature death. It was a very sad story.

My room at the pensione was just as I had left it, again

creating the feeling that I had only been out for five minutes to buy a newspaper, rather than the peripatetic adventures I had actually experienced. No one had been surprised to see me arrive, nor did they take any particular notice of my departure a few minutes later, having decided that the somewhat long walk to the Grand would give me time to, at last, prepare my interrogation of Danny Speers.

Walking in Rome I found to be conducive to thought and I had composed some of my best impassioned, articulate imaginary letters to Fiona, trying to convince her to explore with me how and why our relationship had gone wrong. Once I had gone on at eloquent length about how deeply she had hurt me when she told me that she had sold the bracelets.

When I was married to Fiona, my first gift to her was an antique bracelet made of 16 carat gold that I found in a little shop near Sloane Square, a reddish gold to match Fiona's glorious hair. She thought it was beautiful and this appreciation set me off in search of more, scouring jewelry stores all over London in my determination to increase her collection. Over the next eighteen months I had only managed to discover four others in glowing 16 carat gold that I thought were at least the equal of the original. Fiona had greeted each new find with genuine joy, always wearing one or another and sometimes even all the bracelets on her slender wrist.

I felt that I had given her something almost as precious as she had given me. Every so often I would find Fiona at her dressing table, gently rubbing the bracelets with her fingertips, trying them on and looking at them or simply holding them. I would then tip-toe away, not wanting to disturb her reverie and feeling almost overcome with rapture. It wasn't until Fiona was married to John Lipscomb that, not having seen the bracelets for a very long time, I asked about them.

"I sold them," Fiona had answered and I thought I saw some little discomfort in her expression. "It made me so sad to look at them."

"Oh, well," was all I could manage.

The bracelets were, after all, hers and she was free to do with them whatever she wanted, but I was hurt and in my heart I cried. Even thinking of it, instead of thinking about Danny Speers as I walked to the Grand, brought tears to my eyes.

Two sad stories. Alceo Dossena and Fiona's bracelets.

2

"Let me tell you about Godolphin," Danny Speers gestured with what was obviously not his first scotch on the rocks of the day, though I had arrived promptly at noon. "He was the cheapest son of a bitch I ever met in my life. And when I say cheap, Ollie Godolphin gave new meaning to that word. That prick never spent a nickel of his own money, and God knows he had enough. He just got everybody else to pick up his tab, like it was some small price to pay for the privilege of being in his company. What a pain in the ass."

"I thought you were friends," I prompted.

"Of course we were friends." Speers drained the scotch, then waved the glass over his head. "I fucking discovered him, didn't I? I'm the guy who brought him to Hollywood and, let me tell you, if that picture hadn't been a smash, nobody would've ever heard of him again. Just another flash in the pan, the world's full of 'em."

The waiter arrived to rescue Speers's glass just before the ice cubes went flying across the plushly appointed bar. Danny Speers was a man who was obviously accustomed to instantaneous service. He was in his mid-fifties and not at all what I imagined a Hollywood producer to look like. Far more a bearded aging hippie than a businessman, he was smoking a large cigar, the ashes of which were distributed over both his worn bush jacket and faded blue jeans.

"Now what's this book you're writing about Ollie?" Speers peered at me through his dark glasses. "Sheffy promised me first refusal so I'd talk to you."

First refusal? What was first refusal, and was there a second refusal? And what book was I writing? Fortunately, the waiter returned with another glass of scotch, which gave me time to come up with an answer.

"Well," I tried to be interestingly evasive, "It's still in the early stages. But I would greatly appreciate it if you would just tell me the story from your point of view."

"My point of view about Ollie Godolphin. Now that's funny." Speers chuckled, then banged down his drink. "I was this young kid in Hollywood, you see, thirty-one, thirty-two, and I read this book and I say this book is a hell of a movie. So I track down the writer and I tell him I want to option it. And he says that he'll give me an option for one dollar. I couldn't believe my fucking ears. So I go to Metro and I make a deal, just like that.

"Except now, all of a sudden, Ollie wants to be involved. So I arranged for him and his wife and their kid to come to the Coast, find him a nice house with a pool, get him all set up and what does he do? He pisses on everything. Sure, we had to make some basic changes in the story and we had to compromise here and there on the casting, but that's the nature of the business. Try to explain that to fucking Ollie. No fucking way.

"Still, I get the picture off the ground and what does he do? He shits on everyone. The script is no good, the director's an idiot, the actors stink, the costumes are wrong. You name it. The man was creating a serious problem. The studio is not happy, so they come to me and they say you get this son of a bitch out of here or you're fired. They're going to fucking fire me because Ollie won't keep his fucking mouth shut."

Speers finished the rest of the scotch and began waving the glass again. This time the waiter was ready, seizing the glass before there was even a chance of an accident. I waited for Speers to continue, but he was involved in relighting his cigar.

"What did you do?" I encouraged him to go on after he blew out a cloud of smoke.

"What do you think I did? I went to Ollie and I told him."

"What did he say?"

"He said they were a bunch of Jews, fucking anti-semite bastard." Speers looked around impatiently for the waiter, then belted down half the fresh drink as soon as it arrived. "I mean, he knew I was Jewish. I even told him my real name was Abramowitz. In fact, he used to ask me about my past, about when I was Danny Abramowitz growing up in the Bronx, about the old neighborhood, about going to N.Y.U., about how I got to Hollywood, all that shit, like he was going to use it sometime, but he never did."

"Did he ever talk to you about the Foreign Legion?" I pulled the conversation back to a useful area.

"The Foreign Legion? That's a lot of bullshit. Ollie Godolphin was in the Foreign Legion like I was in the Ku Klux Klan." Speers drained the remaining scotch and banged the glass on the glass-topped table empathically. "Ollie always had to be mysterious about everything, especially himself. The man had an absolute genius for self-promotion. That Foreign Legion gag was just part of it."

"Then who was he?"

"Who the fuck knows." Speers waved at the waiter and pointed at his empty glass. "Listen, I don't have much time, so why don't you cut the crap and get right to the point?"

"Yes." I decided to use a little razzle dazzle. "I understand that you're about to make a new film."

"Yeah, and what a fucking mess that is." Speers went for the bait. "The studio won't approve the budget, after I spent three years putting this picture together, so I have to make this cockamamy co-production deal with the Italians, who don't know shit about American movies, which forces me to use an Italian crew and not one of them speaks a fucking word of English. And this is a submarine movie, for Christ's sake, so there's a lot of talk. On top of which I'm saddled with this multi-lingual production manager, who claims he's Swiss, but ten to one he's still got his Gestapo uniform hidden in the closet. When this fucking picture is over, I'm going to turn his fucking name into the fucking Simon Wiesenthal Center."

"It sounds difficult." I sympathized, as the waiter brought yet another scotch on the rocks.

"Difficult?" Speers seemed outraged at my choice of words and swallowed most of the new drink. "Listen, I'm taking a hell of a chance on this director, used to be a big name until he went nuts and fucking destroyed his career with cocaine. Now he's straight, but he's still crazy and instead of snorting, he eats. The guy must weigh four hundred pounds, and what he doesn't eat, his *meshuggeneh* wife buys. This woman does nothing but shop and she's driving the production office insane. What's the best bargain for this, what's the best bargain for that? And that's the good news, because I'm stuck with these two *shikker* actors who haven't sobered up since they got off the plane."

That thought clearly disturbed Speers so much that he finished his drink and signaled for a refill. I was amazed that he could still talk, but even behind the dark lenses, I could see that his eyes were becoming glassy.

"And where do we have to go to shoot the end of this fucking movie? Fucking Malta, the asshole of the earth." Speers held his head in his hands. "If only they'd let me make this movie in San Diego, Christ, what a difference. Night and fucking day."

Danny Speers puffed morosely on his cigar until the waiter brought, by my count, the fifth scotch to be consumed in my presence. It was astonishing. This time Speers just took a sip, then looked at me.

"Where was I?" He seemed slightly confused.

"I was about to ask how, considering Oliver Godolphin's displeasure with Hollywood, you remained such good friends?" I felt the moment had arrived.

"Friends," Speers repeated. "I stayed in touch with him. To tell you the truth, I figured if anybody had a shot at getting the film rights to another one of his books, it was me."

"But you never did."

"No, and it cost me a fucking fortune, too, flying to Paris, picking up all those fucking restaurant bills, and in the end, that son of a bitch stiffed me good."

"How did he do that, Mr. Speers?"

Speers thought about it for a while. Then he waved to the waiter for another scotch, though the one in front of him was practically untouched. I knew I was about to receive some important information, and instead of pressing the question, I waited.

"What the fuck difference does it make now?" Speers finished off the fifth drink just before the waiter arrived with the sixth. "It was a long time ago."

"Yes?"

"Ollie left Hollywood. It must've been 1960. He moved to London. I knew he was working on a new book, so I used to call him, you know, just keep my finger in. And Ollie, he was always friendly on the phone, so we'd bullshit about this and that, and sometimes he'd call me to ask about some fucking Hollywood scandal that had made the London papers. He liked to know the gossip. This goes on for three or four years, and he keeps dangling the rights to the new book and making jokes like, 'Don't worry, Danny, the new book is yours. I'll send you a copy,' which the cheap son of a bitch never did, by the way. Then he and Alexandra and the kid move back to Paris, and for seven years, I don't hear one fucking word from him."

"What happened then?" I prompted after Speers drifted off.

"Then one day I walk into my office. I was at Paramount and what a bunch of shitheads they turned out to be, and my secretary says that Ollie called. Fuck, did I get excited. Every studio in town had been trying to get the rights to the new books and he wouldn't even talk to them. Now he was calling me. What else could it be? I was going to get an option. Yeah, some fucking option. When I get him on the phone, he says, 'Danny, old chum, I'm in a bit of a jam and, since I know you're rolling in dough, could you please wire $10,000, and I'll get it back to you in a jiffy.' That son of a bitch has made a fortune and he says I'm rolling in dough and hits me for ten grand."

"And did you send the money?"

"What else could I do? And he mails me a check the same day, so right away I know something fishy's going on." Speers made a bitter laugh.

"Did you send the money to Godolphin?" I could feel L.W. waiting in the wings.

"No." Speers seemed to suddenly notice the waiting drink and gulped half of it. "It was some fucking account number at the Credit Lyonnais. And this goes on every six weeks, two months, ten, fifteen grand a pop, and every time he sends me a check. It made my accountants fucking crazy, let me tell you. But I figure I'm on to a good thing here, that I can deal with Ollie from a position of strength.

"So after a year of this, I fly to Paris, out of my own pocket, and I meet with him. 'Come on, Ollie, what's the scoop?' I say and he just smiles, doing his whole fucking mysterious bit. 'What about an option?' I say and he says, 'If anyone gets one, Danny, it'll be you, my old son,' or some bullshit thing like that. 'Can I quote you?' I say. 'Absolutely,' he says.

"So I go back to Hollywood and I sure as hell quote him, which gets me a three-year deal at Warners, where I let everybody know that I'm on the phone with Ollie regularly. But do we talk about options? Fuck no. He just tells me when to send the money. Why the fuck am I telling you all this?"

"Because, Mr. Speers," I gave the words great meaning, "because you play a major role in literary history."

"Yeah." Speers considered the idea. "Yeah, I guess I do. Fuck, I was there and nobody else knows this. Make sure you get it right, but leave out the part about Abramowitz. I want to go down in history as Danny Speers. It'll be easier for my kids."

"You have my word."

"So after about a year, Warners is getting a little impatient, and they send me back to Paris. I've got to make Ollie shit or get off the pot, fat fucking chance. But there's this studio executive who comes with me, so I've got to make it look good. I call Ollie and I lay it out for him and he says he'll take care of it and invites us to dinner at the fucking Tour d'Argent. He does this whole number about how great I am and impresses the hell out of this schmuck from Burbank. But do we fly back to Hollywood with an option? Fuck no. So what happens? They don't pick up the last year on my deal. And guess who got stuck with the fucking bill at the Tour d'Argent?"

"This is a fascinating story," I encouraged when Speers appeared, not surprisingly, to lose focus. "What happened after that?"

"Well, I figured there was no way I was ever going to get another one of Ollie's books, so I let it go," Speers sighed and finished the drink. "But fucking Ollie, he didn't let go, and I kept sending the money and he kept sending me checks, right up until the time he died."

"And you never found out who the money was going to?"

"I tried to figure it out, maybe it was blackmail, maybe he was keeping some fucking broad, but I never knew, which is really too fucking bad. Ten years it went on, fifty, sixty grand a year. You know what that adds up to?"

"But you said that Oliver Godolphin always repaid you."

"Yeah, he repaid me, that son of a bitch, but he put every fucking check down as a loan, so when he dies I get a letter from his fucking lawyers saying I owe his fucking estate over half a million dollars."

"What did you do?"

"What the fuck could I do? The account at the fucking Credit Lyonnais was closed and my lawyer couldn't tie Ollie into it, so I settled." Speers turned and shouted toward the bar. "Hey! What the fuck do you have to do to get a fucking drink in this fucking place?"

If Danny Speers ever came to London, I would have to introduce him to Sally Morgan. They spoke the same language.

3

There are one hundred and thirty-seven steps leading down from Trinità de Monti to the Piazza di Spagna, one of Rome's most famous landmarks, all of which I had once counted carefully on that long ago September night with Maury. My father had me join him in Rome for a few days on my way back to New York after my Munich summer education with Monika (*"Je länger je lieber!"*) Brentano, an experience which had left me feeling very confident and quite full of myself. The experience resulted in my drinking too much wine during dinner at the Hassler, where we had adjoining rooms, and the subsequent dizziness compelled Maury to take me for a walk to sober up.

But, dizzy as I was, I was still silly and insisted on counting the Spanish Steps out loud as I lurched down them. Maury's hand firmly gripped my elbow to prevent a dangerous fall. He found my drunken behavior only vaguely amusing, which is understandable as, apparently, halfway through the second bottle of Soave Bertani, I had insisted on speaking only in German and, I'm afraid, in a rather loud voice as well.

The next morning, my father insisted that I swallow a foul

smelling and tasting substance called Fernet Branca. Thirty minutes later I felt miraculously healed and even looked forward to accompanying Maury on a tour. I was eager to boast about my exploits with Monika, with whom I had certainly become infatuated, though the concept of love had never entered the relationship. The arrival of that consuming emotion had to wait until I saw Fiona on the bridge. But my father's mood was somber and he never gave me the opportunity to brag.

We went first to San Pietro in Vincoli where, instead of lecturing, my father had me expound about Michelangelo's great horned Moses and how the artist had captured in divine marble the forever frozen instant of the Lawgiver about to rise to his feet in indignation. The sculpture was an allegorical parallel to Giuliano della Rovere, Pope Julius II, for whose tomb it was intended, a man about whom it had been said, at the time of his election to the throne of St. Peter, had nothing in him of a Pope and very little of a Christian. Michelangelo had known Julius II well and represented the power of the man's personality, rather than his official holiness, in the creation of this monument.

"That's not bad, Amigo," Maury had said without a smile, and we left without viewing St. Peter's chains, for which the church had been named.

The rest of that day and the following two continued in similar fashion, with my father taking me to view the art at the Vatican and various museums and listening seriously as I held forth on various Renaissance artists that he selected, "La Fornarina" by Raphael, "St. Dominic" by Titian, "The Rape of Prosperine" by Bernini, Caravaggio's "Madonna" and so on, choosing only one or two pieces for discussion in each museum before we went on to the next. When at the Capitoline I wanted to take a few minutes to admire Praxiteles' "Faun" and the very moving "The Dying Gaul," Maury objected, saying that I could be a tourist on my own time, which finally made me understand that this whole process was a test, a realization that, naturally, destroyed my confidence.

"You did very well, Amigo. I'm proud of you." My father tried to bolster me out of my sudden emotional slump.

But it was no use, as just the thought of Maury judging me was enough to make me fail. I boarded the flight to New York without any of the sense of well being with which I had arrived in Rome. Again I descended the crowded Spanish Steps accompanied by my Roman *Doppelgänger,* who still carried the insecurity of years ago, while I tried to feel satisfied about my interview with Danny Speers.

Though the identity of L.W. remained unknown, there was sufficient coincidence to leap to the conclusion that the Credit Lyonnais account was somehow connected. Danny Speers, on reflection, didn't have anything good to say about anyone, but, in fact, he had nothing really bad to say about Oliver Godolphin, except for the terrible posthumous joke. By the time the waiter had brought the rudely requested drink, Danny Speers had passed out, so I left, paying his bar bill on my way. The man had been stiffed enough.

But what did it all mean? Half a million dollars, even spread over ten years, was a lot of money, and while Oliver Godolphin could afford it, why did he route the payment through Danny Speers? Was it blackmail, a woman or what? And was Godolphin shielding these payments from (who else could it be?) his wife, Alexandra? But, assuming that Godolphin's air of mystery did not include family finances, a fair assumption since Sheffy had told me that she had taken care of the household accounts during the London years, how could he explain the checks to Danny Speers without creating some suspicion? I had gained information, but I had made no progress.

"You probably won't, either," said my depressed *Doppelgänger.* "You're not good enough."

"Listen," I responded sharply. "I've got enough problems as it is, so I don't need any sandbagging from you."

Several people stopped and turned, making me aware that the words in my mind had, once again, come out of my mouth, but on the Spanish Steps odd behavior is not that unusual. It was still too early to call Alexis, but it was lunchtime and I was hungry enough to increase my pace, turning right to walk through Piazza di Spagna and then heading for the Birreria on Via della Croce, my refuge from the endless plates of pasta which the Italians regard as absolutely essential. I ordered a *Bratwürst* and a Beck's, which was a great improvement over *Le Super Hot Dog sur Toast Garni* that I had foolishly consumed in Nice. My predilection for frankfurters was the result of my many forbidden Sabrett's and Nathan's I grew up eating on the sly, as do so many children in New York City.

Once, Mary Frances caught me by smelling the recently devoured hot dog on my breath which I almost convincingly denied until Elisa walked into the kitchen and announced that I ate the poisonous wieners all the time, causing me to be banished to my room. I really should have recognized my sister's basically treacherous personality at the time, but she was the only ally I had and later she apologized for her indiscretion, promising never to rat on me again. Fortunately, Maury was away on business and, though he was not as concerned about artificial preservatives as was Mary Frances, he would always take her side and his disapproval was far more painful (and far more familiar) than hers. With that in mind, I ordered another *Bratwürst* and a second beer.

Did Alexis know Danny Speers? From the way he spoke, Speers didn't appear to have had any more than a passing, vague social relationship with Alexandra. The only time he referred to Alexis was as "the kid," which did not indicate any relationship at all. But since Godolphin's estate had sued the unlucky Danny Speers for the return of the loan, Alexis must have been advised of the situation. Perhaps I had made a mistake by not bringing up his name during dinner at the Eden Roc. I would mention it to her when I called. If she had any additional information, I could dash back to the Grand and catch Danny Speers before it was too late. Though, based on the amount of scotch he had put away, his hangover might not leave him in a talkative mood. I would recommend a Fernet Branca, I decided.

Feeling that my plan was well thought out, I left the Birreria and headed back toward Via Margutta to make my call, but then decided it was still too early to phone Alexis. I wandered down Via del Babuino toward the architectonic Piazza del Popolo, my mind still searching for both questions and answers. Had Oliver Godolphin really been an anti-Semite, or was that just part of Danny Speers's vitriol? While it appeared that Godolphin created his name along with a new identity, Speers had changed his from Abramowitz and had requested that I omit the fact. What did that make him?

This was an area of speculation where I had little to go on, as the eclecticism in the choice of my own paternal family names was puzzling. Mighty Mel was actually Mellos, which was Greek, and Maury was Amour, which was French, and my own name was Latin. What did that signify? The next time I spoke to my father, which I suspected would not be in the too distant future because of his sudden courting of Fiona, I would have to ask him, which did not guarantee that he would answer.

Since I was already in the Piazza, I decided to revisit the Papal family church, Santa Maria del Popolo. There along the left wall was the tomb of another della Rovere, this one being Cardinal Girolamo Basso, an impressive though somewhat heavy-handed marble monument that I had studied several times in the past, my curiosity provoked by its confused provenance. Depending on the source, the work has been attributed to no less than Mino da Fiesole, Andrea Sansovino or Andrea Bregno. Fortunately, it has been here since the 15th century or by now someone would have certainly blamed the piece on Alceo Dossena and exiled it to the basement.

Poor Dossena. The man certainly had bad luck, and he continued to be vilified years after his death. After the scandal and still in dire need of money, Dossena had created a terracotta figure of "Diana the Huntress" in excellent Etruscan style which he then carefully broke into twenty-one separate pieces and sold, probably for a pittance, though the actual price remains unrecorded to my knowledge.

From that point, the dealers took over, creating a lengthy provenance and shipping the crate of fragments around to confuse the trail until it wound up in the hands of the familiar anonymous "Swiss collector," where, like vintage wine, it was left to age until 1952, the date it was sold to the St. Louis Art Museum in Missouri for $56,000. It took almost a year for the restorer to put the fragments together, as either Dossena or the dealers had removed a number of pieces for authenticity's sake, and in 1953 "Diana" was put on display.

Immediately it was hailed as a masterpiece, one of the finest Etruscan terracottas in existence. Within three years a number of experts had decried it as a fake. The St. Louis officials, of course, defended their marvelous acquisition. But the controversy

continued and finally the Museum agreed to a thermolumines-
cence test, which proved the experts right. After that it did not
take long before "Diana's" origin was traced to Dossena's studio
at Via Margutta 54 and the defamation began again, everyone
forgetting that Dossena had only created the piece and that the
actual swindle had been done by others.

Alceo Dossena and Oliver Godolphin, I thought as I walked
back to the pensione, one man with no success and the other with
nothing but success and both with something to be revealed long
after their death. No matter in which direction I turned, I was
surrounded by coincidence.

"Hello." Alexis answered the phone after I had finally succeeded in getting the call through.

"Good afternoon. It's Mickey Maltese."

"Mickey!" she seemed happy to hear from me. "Where are
you? I called the Negresco and they said you had checked out."

"I changed hotels." I answered truthfully, if not precisely.

"Well, I've spoken with Baby and he's agreed to see you. In
fact, he wants to see you and he's asked me to fly down with you.
So I've booked us on the 9:30 flight tomorrow morning. The sim-
plest thing is to meet at the airport. I'll be there by nine."

"Nine?"

"See you then," Alexis said and hung up.

Not only did I neglect to ask about Danny Speers, I neglected
to mention that I was in Rome. Without the benefit of a concierge
or hall porter, I was left to make my own travel arrangements,
which in Italy are always best done in advance. The Romans may
be very good at improvisation, but they are definitely backwards
when it comes to last minute reservations, throwing up their
hands in dramatic gestures of impossibility.

Since I spoke only enough Italian to read a menu, my usual
powers of persuasion were of no use. There were no available
seats on any available flights that would get me to Nice on time.
After two hours of trying, the best option I was offered was to
come out to the airport and take my chances. Obviously, this
would not do. Admitting defeat, I rushed out of the pensione,
through Piazza di Spagna, up the one hundred and thirty-seven
steps and into the Hotel Hassler, where I thrust 100,000 Lire into
the portiere's hand before I blurted out my breathless request.

"I have to be in Nice by nine o'clock tomorrow morning. And I don't care how."

"Of course, *Signore*. That should be no problem."

After several rapid phone calls, the portiere returned, and he was right. It was not a problem, but it was not exactly what I had in mind. He had booked me a *Carrozze Cuccette* on the midnight train to Milan and a seat on the 7:45 a.m. Milan flight to Nice and since the train arrived at 6:00 a.m., that would give me ample time to get from the station to the airport. The portiere seemed quite happy with this solution. But I was anxious. Suppose the train was late?

The trains in Italy, he assured me, always ran on time.

MARBELLA

1

Alexis nudged me awake as we were landing in Malaga, but I was still exhausted. The Hassler portiere had been right and the train left on the stroke of midnight. But my *Carrozze Cuccette* was already occupied by three young Dutch nuns when I arrived, leaving me the top bunk on the left. Since I had finally vacated my room at the pensione I was traveling with an additional suitcase, which made my entrance all the more awkward. They all smiled and even helped me with my luggage.

But when, shortly after the train had left the station, they began their bedtime preparations I didn't know what to do and rolled on my side to face the wall. One by one the lights went out and soon I heard the sound of their peaceful snores, quickly lulled to sleep by the gentle rocking of the train. By the time, six hours later, we arrived in Milan, they were again fully costumed, rested and brightly cheerful. I, naturally, had never even managed to close my eyes.

At the station in Milan, burdened with my baggage, I Quasimodo'd my way up the platform and into a taxi, actually making it to the airport with time to spare. The Nice flight arrived on schedule and I was able to collect my luggage and stagger out to the departure area a good ten seconds before Alexis arrived.

"You look terrible," she said.

She, however, looked even more beautiful than she had appeared two nights ago. After I had explained the travails of my journey, she again was filled with laughter that carried us through

125

check-in, customs and onto the plane, where, despite the enthrall-
ment of being in her company, I fell sound asleep. I know that I
was dreaming, but the dream evaporated at the instant of awakening and it took several seconds before I realized where I was.

"Who is Fiona?" Alexis asked with some amusement.

"Fiona?"

"You were talking about her in your sleep."

"I was?"

"Who is she?"

"My ex-wife," I admitted. "What did I say?"

"Oh, I didn't really understand anything but the name," Alexis
smiled. "But you seemed very happy. At least, you were smiling.
I've never seen anyone do that before. I mean in their sleep."

What was there to be happy about Fiona? That she was at the
George V in Paris with Roddy Startle? That she had said she
wanted me out of her life forever? Why, while I was with the
breathtaking Alexis, would I dream about Fiona? But evidently I
had, and now that Alexis had asked, how could I explain.

"Your ex-wife," Alexis continued. "I think that's very sweet.
Do you still love her?"

Oh God, it was bad enough that I would occasionally betray
myself when I was conscious, but to do it in my sleep? And in
front of Alexis? It was clearly fortunate that I had remained
awake during my night with the three young Dutch nuns. Who
knows what I might have said?

"Yes," I had to tell the truth. "I am still in love with her, but
she has a different life now."

"Oh, Mickey, that's sad." Alexis touched my hand. Then it
was time to go.

Inside the Malaga Airport, I watched, still groggy, as Alexis
efficiently organized a porter and our luggage was collected
without any difficulty. Then we breezed through customs. Outside, a large, swarthy man in a dark suit and tie waited for us
next to a blue Rolls Royce Silver Cloud.

"Welcome back, Miss Godolphin." He exhibited a lot of white
teeth. "And welcome to you, Mr. Maltese. Mr. Habibi sends his
greetings."

"Thank you, Fahid," Alexis said, and slipped gracefully into
the back of the Rolls.

I turned to watch as Fahid dealt with the porter, loading our luggage personally into the trunk, his suit jacket swinging open to expose a very large gun. Quickly, I joined Alexis in the back seat.

"He's got a gun," I whispered.

"Yes. Fahid is one of Baby's bodyguards." Alexis made it sound quite ordinary.

"Where are we going?" I asked, still thinking about the gun.

"To the Marbella Club Hotel. Baby has put us up there. The ranch is only ten minutes away."

"The ranch?"

"Baby's villa. Everyone calls it the ranch," she explained patiently. "Why do you think he wants to see you?"

"Did you tell him what I wanted to ask him?"

"Of course."

"Then it has to be something about your father," I said, just as Fahid got in behind the wheel. After glancing back to see that we were comfortably settled, he pulled the car away from the curb.

"This is the worst road in the world," Alexis volunteered. "Isn't it, Fahid?"

"Very bad road, Miss," Fahid answered without turning. "The Highway of Death."

The Highway of Death? I didn't like the sound of that. Were there bandits? Was that why Fahid carried a gun? First spending a sleepless night with the three Dutch nuns, cramped on a bunk, and now traveling down the Highway of Death, these were scenes out of a Hieronymus Bosch painting. Then just as we were approaching Torremolinos, a truck swerved right at us and I flinched at the expected impact, but Fahid skillfully maneuvered the Rolls away.

"You see?" Alexis asked, not in the least perturbed.

"Do you remember Danny Speers?" I asked with intentional suddenness.

"No." She was not shaken by the question. "I may have met him as a child, but I don't remember him."

"But you know who he is?"

"Of course. We had to sue him to recover at least part of the money he borrowed from my father."

"Why did your father lend him so much money? Over half a

million dollars?"

Alexis looked at me for a moment, curiously, and I stared back, openly admiring the perfect beauty of her face, trying to dissect it, to figure out how all the pieces fit together with such exquisite symmetry. I was unexpectedly pierced by a pang of jealousy about Marcel. Did he realize how really beautiful Alexis was?

"How do you know about this?" she asked.

"Danny Speers told me."

"That awful man. You know he tried to avoid paying, claiming the money was not a loan."

"Still it was a very large loan. How do you explain that?"

"I can't explain it," Alexis said. "But I remember hearing my father telling my mother that this Danny Speers was down on his luck again."

Down on his luck? Oliver Godolphin obviously knew how to cover his tracks. But if Danny Spears had told the truth and this exchange of funds took place over ten years, that simple answer could hardly be stretched to last a decade. This was, I had no doubt, a definite piece of the puzzle.

"Was your father always so generous?" I asked innocently.

"My father," Alexis was not fooled, "was, as I am sure you already know from your prying, quite stingy."

"I am not prying. I am investigating the true authorship of a book that is being attributed to your father. It's called provenance, not prying," I objected strongly.

"But what does Danny Speers have to do with this book?" Alexis snapped back.

"Possibly quite a lot." I knew I had gone too far. "I like you better when you're laughing."

"Well, I don't find this particularly funny." Alexis turned away.

We drove in silence past Fuengirola, and I admired the way Fahid avoided the rest of the speeding and erratic traffic, as if anticipating each near collision. Finally, the continuing silence made me feel guilty.

"I apologize," I said to the back of Alexis's head.

"For what?" She didn't turn.

"For whatever I did that offended you," I said and then was

suddenly struck by the thought that, this minor argument included, my rapport with Alexis was totally different than my relationship with Fiona, even at the best of times.

"You didn't offend me, Mickey." Alexis turned back and gave me a little smile. "It's just that I'm worried that you are going to find out something about my father that is going to be very painful for me. Maybe too painful. I wish this whole business had never happened."

"Then I wouldn't have met you."

"I'm serious. I loved my parents very much and I truly cherish their memory. And you know as well as I do that there can be no happy ending to this story."

"Do you want me to stop? Would you prefer it if I called Rupert Farrow and quit?" I asked, knowing that if she said yes, I might even possibly do it.

"There's no point in that," Alexis said. "They are determined to publish, and if you quit, they would just find someone else. Besides, I trust you, Mickey. I feel that there's something very special about you."

Something very special about me? I felt myself starting to choke up and had to look away to search frantically for composure. Why was I having such an emotional reaction to this spectacular woman? Had Fiona ever thought there was something very special about me? Had anyone?

"You can trust me." The words came out like a croak. "Now, if you don't mind, I'm going to have a little cry."

And, like a fool, I wept, trying to keep it down as much as possible, until Alexis's hand came over my shoulder with a handkerchief which smelled of the same perfume Mary Frances used. That really did me in, the weeping growing into major sobs. What was the matter with me? Why had I regressed into a child? Particularly in these circumstances where, Alexis being absolutely right, if anyone was going to be hurt by my provenance, it would be her.

Several minutes later, I managed to regain enough control to look back at her with an embarrassed smile, about to make some remark about my ridiculous behavior. But Alexis put her finger to my lips to silence me, her own eyes brimming with tears. Then she held my hand and Fahid drove us the rest of the way to the white stone lion-posted gates and up the driveway to the Marbella Club Hotel without another word spoken.

Baby Habibi was, obviously, a man who knew how to make arrangements, as we were escorted to adjoining suites without the usually required check-in and, despite the lack of that formality, our luggage was already waiting when we arrived.

"What do we do now?" I asked helplessly.

"You take a nap and I'll phone Baby to see what his schedule is," Alexis said. Then she gave me an encouraging smile. "Go on."

I felt a sharp, sudden anxiety about being separated from Alexis, even if it was only next door, but I had no choice and entered my suite. It was exquisite, all pastel and cream, and the large bed, particularly after my sleepless night and my unexplainable nervous breakdown in the car, seemed to beckon me irresistibly. I closed the curtains without even noticing the view outside. I let my clothes fall where they dropped and climbed into the welcoming bed, curling up in a fetal position as sleep descended. Just before I went under, I remembered that I had forgotten to call Sheffy.

When I finally opened my eyes I could see through the crack in the curtains that it was still light, so I was astonished that my trusty Seiko said that it was 7:58 p.m. I had just taken a seven and a half hour nap. Could that be? Perhaps the Seiko had at last malfunctioned and was running wildly fast. I rolled out of the comfortable bed, Godzilla sticking out like an iron rod in tardy matutinal erection, and went to peek out the window.

Alexis was standing on the balcony, her attention attracted by the movement of the curtain, then her gaze dropped to my groin before I could move.

"Nom de Dieu!" I could hear her exclamation through the closed glass door.

I fled into the marble bathroom, locking the door and forcing myself to stand under an icy shower. I was ruined. How could I ever face Alexis again? She had been warm and wonderfully sympathetic about my witless tears, but to have exposed myself to her was a humiliation that I couldn't bear. I would sneak away, go back to America, change my name and find some menial job in some small town in Idaho. I would vanish from history.

Finally, shivering violently, I stepped out of the shower and dried myself with a large, soft towel, keeping my eyes fixed on the wall, too ashamed to even see my own reflection in the mirror. Just as I finished dressing, the telephone rang. But I only stared at the instrument until it was silent. A few moments later, there was a knock at the door and I froze, keeping as still as a statue for five minutes. Then I noticed that someone had slipped some newspapers beneath the door and, figuring that my visitor had left by now, went to retrieve them. There was the *Trib*, the *London Times* and the *News of the World*, a gossipy, sensation-mongering tabloid that I always avoided. I knew that I could not make my escape from Marbella until it was dark. So I sat down and read the *Trib* and then the *Times* and finally opened the tabloid.

There she was. Fiona. Fiona looking radiantly happy, smiling lovingly at Roddy Startle, who had his arm around her. "After his smash concert at Roland Garros Stadium, Roddy Startle and his new love interest, copper-haired Fiona Hazeltine-Taylor head off for a week of fun and sun at the Hotel Cap d'Antibes," the disgusting caption read.

Copper-haired? The photo was in black and white. Whoever had started this copper-hair rumour had no true perception of color. And Cap d'Antibes? The world was getting too small. Would they eat at the Eden Roc, where Alexis, Warren Beatty and I had dinner? But why was I getting upset? Since I had already decided that my life was over, none of this mattered anymore. With that thought I felt a sense of great relief. To hell with Oliver Godolphin. To hell with *Sakura*. Publish and be damned. When I got to Idaho, I wouldn't even read the newspapers. I heard something and turned in time to see an envelope slide under the door. I tiptoed over and picked it up. "Mickey," an unfamiliar hand had written on the envelope. I tore it open.

Dear Mickey,

Forgive me. I know I embarrassed you and I feel miserable about it. I'm sorry. I'm sorry. I'm sorry. Please meet me in the bar at 10:00 p.m. and let's both promise not to mention the accident. You must forgive me.

Alexis

Forgive her? I was convinced that she would never forgive me.
And why was she sorry? I was the one who was sorry. And why
did she feel miserable? This was totally upside down. But what
should I do? I read the letter again. Her handwriting was beautiful, free flowing, every line straight, the perfect handwriting for
Alexis to have. It even expressed her personality. And I was making her miserable. My plans for a life in Idaho dissolved like a
snowflake. Besides, they grow potatoes in Idaho and potatoes
remind me of Fiona. It was a bad choice from the start.

At precisely 10:00 I sat down at the Marbella Club Hotel bar,
calm, composed and even with a hint of confidence. As Alexis
said, we would not mention the accident and I was filled with the
happy anticipation of her presence. What was it about her that
made me long for her company? Part of my earlier desperation
was the thought that I would never see her again and just the
knowledge that she was about to appear brought a smile to my
lips. Out of the corner of my eye, I saw a hand descend toward
my shoulder. A man's hand, a terrifyingly familiar heavy, round
18 carat gold Cartier watch on the wrist.

"Hello, Amigo. We have to talk."

2

Go away, I wanted to say. This is a really bad time, I wanted to
say. Whatever it is you want, I won't do it, I wanted to say.

"You're looking well," I said.

"Am I?" my father inspected me critically for a moment. "You
seem a little weary, Amigo."

"I've been working hard," I shrugged it off. "Fiona told me
you were looking for me. What do you want?"

"She's a very attractive woman, your Fiona."

"She's not my Fiona anymore. What do you want, Maury?"

"Amigo, I don't know why we haven't been close these past

years. I know it's as much my responsibility as yours. You're my son. You're the closest person in the world to me and I want you to be close. I want your company. I want your friendship. I want your love."

My love? After my emotional escapades of the past several hours, this was no time to discuss love, particularly with my father who, as far as I could remember, had never used the word before, at least not in my presence. Maury must have seen the confusion in my eyes, because he smiled warmly.

"I'll tell you what," he said. "Why don't you just give me a hug for now and we'll let that be the beginning."

I got to my feet and found myself in my father's embrace. There was little I could do except hug him in return, each of us patting the other's back in manly fashion. Then, over Maury's shoulder, I saw Alexis walking toward us and pulled away awkwardly.

"Hello, Mickey," she said. "How nice to see you again, Maury."

"You know my father?" It came out before my father had a chance to respond.

"Yes, we met at Baby's this afternoon," Alexis explained.

"You know Baby?" I turned to Maury.

"We've done some business. Baby's an avid collector," my father said casually, then he smiled at Alexis. "Good evening."

"Maury told me that you haven't seen each other for years." Alexis swiveled her focus back to me. "So this is really an astonishing coincidence. And when I saw the two of you embrace, it was very moving."

I smiled, having no choice but to continue the charade. So Maury had done some business with Baby Habibi and just happened to be in Marbella the same time I was. Alexis was right. It was an astonishing coincidence, a little too astonishing for me to buy. This was one sour apple and I was not about to put my teeth into it. Maury had taken Fiona to Le Gavroche seven or eight weeks ago, so that was before the *Sakura* manuscript arrived at Farrow & Farrow. Nowhere in my research was there any reference to Oliver Godolphin being an avid collector. My conspiracy theory started to crumble. But, I could feel it in my toes, something was afoot and while there might be some innocent coincidence involved, not everything was an accident.

"That would be lovely," Alexis was saying.

"What?" I said.

"Your father invited us for dinner," Alexis answered. "Weren't you listening?"

"Oh, yes," I said. "Lovely."

Maury magically organized a corner table in the bar. Alexis and I seated comfortably on the couch while my father perched himself elegantly on the low upholstered corner stool, ordered an Evian for Alexis, an Oloroso sherry for himself, then cocked an eyebrow at me.

"What do you recommend?" I inquired instead of ordering the double vodka I so desperately desired.

"The head barman always recommends the House Special Cocktail," the waiter smiled encouragingly. "Champagne and cassis."

That sounded absolutely awful, but I nodded my approval, determined to maintain my poise for the rest of this dreadful evening, my left hand draped casually over the knee of my crossed leg, until I realized that I had imitated my father's position exactly and then reversed the position to achieve at least a minor variation.

"That's a beautiful watch." Alexis was looking at Maury's wrist. "It's so elegant, but so simple in design."

"Yes," Maury smiled. "It was my father's. He was a great *Aficianado* of precious metals, which isn't surprising since he was a well-known dealer in antique silver."

Aficianado? I could tell that Maury was going into his warmup, and I wondered why he was lying, as I didn't recall ever seeing that massive Cartier on Mighty Mel's wrist. It had always been my father's watch, so why was he giving it a family history? Was he going to try selling it to Alexis? I glanced off and saw the maitre d' approaching with the menus, relieved that we could switch the subject from false heirlooms to food, particularly since I hadn't eaten all day. When I looked back Maury was unstrapping the Cartier.

"Here," my father held out the thick gold timepiece. "It's yours, Amigo."

"What?"

"You take this and give me your watch. We'll switch."

"What are you talking about?" I recoiled.

"I'm giving you this watch," Maury said. "May you wear it for a hundred years."

"No." I wasn't expecting this move. "It's your watch, Maury. You wouldn't be the same without it."

"I want you to have it now," my father said softly.

"Mickey," Alexis whispered.

I was trapped. Why was he doing this to me? Here, in front of Alexis? Too bizarre. I unclipped my Seiko and forked it over, taking the heavy gold Cartier in exchange. The maitre d' watched patiently until this ritual had been completed and each watch secured on a different wrist, before he offered the menus and then recited the specials of the evening, highly recommending the "Filets of Sole a la Prince Alfonso," which Alexis ordered. Maury and I both went for the Entrecote Roque, and a bottle of Marqués de Riscal, with all three of us having Vichyssoise to start. Then, with perfect timing, the waiter returned with our *aperitifs*, making me feel that everything had been rehearsed down to the last detail.

"Cheers." My father raised his tiny glass of Oloroso.

Clink, clink, clink. I tasted my House Special Cocktail, which was truly awful and had a cherry in the bottom. Why had Maury given me his watch and what, besides my inexpensive Seiko, did he want in exchange. My company, my friendship and my love? The Cartier was worth more than that. This was, this had to be a setup, a preamble for disgrace. First, Maury had bedazzled Fiona, not that their evening at Le Gavroche did me any good. Now he was doing it to Alexis. For what? I raised my wrist and looked down at the Cartier. It seemed totally out of place.

"It suits you," Alexis said.

"And I rather like this," my father admired the Seiko.

I gave them each a sickly smile and drifted off again, watching, as if from a great distance, Alexis listened with fascination to whatever Maury was saying. It had to be Baby Habibi, the avid collector. My father was involved in a swindle and now he wanted me to conspire with him in passing off some fake as real. Did he actually believe that I would aid and abet him in a fraud? No. My father knew me too well to even consider such a thought.

But what did Maury want? That was a question I had been trying to answer all my life.

"Your table is ready."

The maitre d' had reappeared and, following him, we trooped off to the Grill Room next door, the waiter bringing up the rear with my still unfinished House Special Cocktail. Since it was only 10:30 (more or less, I was already missing the precise digitalication of my former Seiko), the restaurant was only half full, the truly stylish diners yet to arrive.

"Are you all right?" Alexis asked me as I held her chair.

"Yes. Why?"

"You're so silent."

"I guess I've just been lost in thought."

"I understand," she smiled.

What was there to understand? My thoughts sped around in a circle, a snake biting its tail, but I could find no enlightenment. Had the gold watch, the Cartier that hung so heavily on my wrist, become a bribe? If my father had really wanted to give me his watch, which was hard to believe, why did he do it in front of Alexis? In fact, it wasn't until Alexis commented on the Cartier that my father was overcome with gift giving. But why would he need to impress her?

"All right, Amigo, give me back my watch." I could imagine Maury saying later when we were alone.

The Vichyssoise arrived and I attacked my icy bowl ravenously, finishing the soup before Alexis and Maury had done more than dent theirs. Then I started on the bread and butter, my mouth full with the second piece, when I realized that Alexis was speaking to me.

"At 11:30," she was saying. "He'll send Fahid to pick you up."

"Oh." I tried to pull it together quickly. "Did you have a nice visit?"

"Yes," Alexis looked at me a little strangely. "As I just told you, it was very pleasant."

"Of course," I scraped my empty bowl, then sucked the spoon. "Great soup."

"Amigo was always an eater," my father interjected, distracting her. "As a child he would sneak off to buy hot dogs on the street, which made his mother very upset, as she believed that everything had to be absolutely fresh. But, to be honest, I used to sneak out for a hot dog once in a while myself. That's what happens when you grow up in New York."

My father sneaking out for a hot dog? This had to be another lie. There was no possible way for me to imagine Maury at Nathan's or a Sabrett's stand. Why was he saying this? To rescue me from my obvious lack of attention? Or did he think that he had hooked me with the Cartier and was now slowly reeling me in? The snake bit its tail and went around in more circles.

The *sommelier* arrived with the Marqués de Riscal, popped the cork, then, at Maury's gesture, splashed some into my glass. I took a sip, tasted nothing, and nodded. The wine was poured, the meal arrived and was eaten. I attempted to follow the general conversation as best I could, making an occasional vague remark when my participation was called for. But my mind still raced for some understanding of what was happening. By the time we rejected both the hot chocolate mousse and the orange soufflé, my mental absence had disturbed Alexis sufficiently so that she said good-night and left despite my protests and apologies.

"A striking woman," Maury said. "Beyond beautiful, though you seemed quite bored by her presence."

"My reaction to Alexis could hardly be defined as boredom," I said, then held out my Cartier wrist. "What's this all about?"

"I've been meaning to give it to you."

"Why?"

"For your pleasure. As my father gave it to me."

"Mighty Mel never wore this watch," I declared, not about to be taken in by this ruse. "This was always your watch."

"And now it's yours." Maury smiled. "Look at the date on the back."

I unstrapped the watch and flipped it over. The scalloped back held in place by tiny screws, the inscription worn but the date still legible. 1938. It didn't look that old, but with its classical style it was hard to tell, especially since the pigskin band appeared relatively new. A replacement?

"Mel gave me the watch on the day you were born," my father explained, "with the understanding that someday I would pass it on to you. Tonight seemed like the right moment."

"Why?" I strapped the Cartier back onto my wrist. "What are you after, Maury?"

"Amigo, why are you so suspicious? I'm not after anything."

"No? Then what are you doing here?"

"I've come across a rather exceptional piece and Baby is interested in acquiring it for his collection. It's as simple as that. The fact that you and Alexis arrived was an unexpected bonus. What are you working on, anyway? It seems very mysterious. Or can't you talk about it?"

My work seemed mysterious? My work was clear as starlight compared to the heavy fog that surrounded Maury's. Mine was crystal, his opaque. As if to demonstrate my openness, I told my father the Godolphin saga as it was known to me, omitting only the deal I had made for Sheffy to become my agent and my promise to Alexis to never reveal any damaging information I might discover about her father, as Maury would have been quick to point out that I had created something of a conflict for myself. By the time I finished my tale, the Grill Room had filled with an elegant crowd, all golden tan and with much matching gold jewelry on display. As my father signed the bill, I shot my cuff to flash my golden Cartier, but no one seemed to notice.

Outside, the air remained warm and still while the sound of a far distant breeze added to the languid atmosphere. As Maury and I strolled down the landscaped path toward the sea, my father seemed very thoughtful. I did not want to interrupt, my own thought process trying to keep pace. The story about the watch made sense as, if Mighty Mel had given the Cartier to his son on the day of my birth, it followed that I never would have seen my grandfather having it in his possession, so perhaps I was being overly suspicious.

"What's your gut feeling?" Maury suddenly asked. "Did Godolphin write the book?"

"If I were to bet, I think I'd have a little flutter on that." I sounded suddenly British. "That Godolphin sent Danny Speers over half a million dollars was confirmed by Alexis. I tend to believe Speers's explanation."

"Why do you think this Swiss banker, Pierre Rougemont, allowed you to see the L.W. dedication?" I could sense my father honing in on the details.

"Because it's to his advantage, or his client's advantage, for the book to be published," I knew that wasn't the whole reason, but it was all I had.

"I have the feeling it may be more than that," Maury commented. "How do you explain the seven year delay between Godolphin's death and the delivery of the manuscript?"

"I can't."

"The answer's probably connected to that. I'm sure you'll find it."

"When you met Alexis at Baby Habibi's, did you hear what they were talking about?" I tried to slide the question in effortlessly.

"Bravo, Amigo," my father laughed. "I've been waiting for that one. But, unfortunately, no, I didn't hear a word, though they were both quite serious afterwards."

"Why does Baby Habibi want to see me?" I went for it.

"I didn't know he did," Maury answered easily. "But it may have something to do with the piece. You have managed to make quite a reputation for yourself."

"With your help."

"Oh, I just gave you a start."

It was, to be totally truthful, much more than a start. Maury had made my career. On that day when I took the train down from New Haven to visit the Met, it had been my father who had summoned me and it had also been my father who pointed out the stolen de Castagno and it had been my father who had guided me through my first provenance. And, during my brief glory afterwards, when I tried to thank Maury, he brushed my gratitude aside, saying that I had done the real work and besides he had never liked the dealer involved, much less the Waffen SS. Provenance, he had encouraged me, was obviously my true calling. And now I had a reputation, which meant that I had something to protect.

"What are you selling to Baby Habibi?" I asked anxiously.

"It's a Donatello Madonna," Maury told me evenly. "I had one hell of a time getting it out of Italy."

"Really?" There were no known undiscovered works by Donatello di Niccolò di Betto Bardi, and little chance of one emerging now. "How did you find it?"

"Oh, it was just a stroke of luck," my father said, "not that I actually found it myself. The piece had been owned by the Savelli family in Sienna for four hundred years. I heard about it for the first time three years ago from this dealer in Florence. At first I didn't really believe the story. The family had come upon hard times financially and they knew the only way they could make any serious money was by selling it illegally, as the Italian Government would pay only a fraction of its true value and block any other sale by refusing an export license."

"But you figured out a way." I didn't believe a word of what my father had said, though the story had a certain plausibility.

"Yes, not too pleasant, but effective."

"Tell me."

"When the oldest Savelli relative died about three weeks ago, I had the family request burial in Spain, shipped the Madonna here in the coffin and had the old fellow buried anonymously in Cremona." Maury waggled a hand, gesturing some distaste at the act. "It was the only way I could think of. But that particular detail doesn't need to be spread about."

It was, and my father knew it, particular details like that which made a work's provenance convincing, and I was sure that I had not been let in on some dark secret. But why was Maury spinning this yarn for me? Was I supposed to authenticate the piece? Unlikely. A real Donatello would be priceless and any collector acquiring it would certainly check and double check its provenance very, very carefully, tracing the source back as far as possible. The remaining Savelli family members could not admit, for obvious reasons, to being part of the crime of illegal exportation, but if skillfully questioned regarding the Donatello's provenance, they would have to verify its long existence in their possession if they hoped to reap the rewards.

"Well," I said at last, "there is some information that I hope Baby Habibi can give me about the Godolphin provenance, and if he wants my opinion of the piece, that could put me in an awkward position."

"Why, Amigo?"

"Suppose I find it suspect?"

"Do you really think I'm here to unload a fake?" Maury started to laugh. "Is that what's been buzzing around in your brain all night?"

"If you recall," I felt obligated to bring up the ugly past, "the last time I saw you, we had a very serious disagreement about a fake Paul Klee."

"You had the disagreement, Amigo, not me." My father's good humor did not diminish. "That painting had me completely fooled, but you were convinced that I was doing it on purpose. That's why I got angry, not by what you did, but by the way you did it."

"It didn't seem that way to me at the time," I said. "But maybe you're right. Why did you look up Fiona?"

"Because I wanted to get in touch with you."

"Why?"

"I told you in the bar. I want to be close to you."

"Is the Donatello a fake?" I had to ask.

"Is your Godolphin a fake?" Maury smiled. "Listen, Amigo, you think the book is by Godolphin. I think the Madonna is by Donatello. You could be right or you could be wrong. I could be right or I could be wrong."

"I'm not selling the Godolphin," I objected.

"No, but you are creating the circumstances under which it can be sold. Isn't that right?" My father's eyes sparkled with amusement.

"What's your cut?"

"Seventeen and a half percent and I have to take care of the Florentine dealer out of that," Maury answered without hesitation. "Satisfied?"

"Not entirely."

"Why not?"

"Because it doesn't feel right."

"Suppose I told you the Donatello was a fake, would that make you feel better?"

"No," I said. "I don't know, Maury. I think I'm confused about a lot of things. I keep trying to find out who Oliver Godolphin really was, I mean before the Foreign Legion, and I don't get anywhere. It's like the time I was a kid trying to find out about you and Mighty Mel and where he came from."

"Does it really matter?" My father grasped me by the shoulders. "Think about it, Amigo."

"It has to matter," I insisted.

"Why? The only things that count are who we are and what we do, not where we come from. I'm very proud of you, my son. You may think that you're confused, but we're all confused in one way or another. To my eyes, you're doing well and that makes me very happy."

How could I help but react emotionally to that sentiment. My father and I embraced for the second time that night, standing on the darkened beach, the gentle waves lapping close, and tears in both our eyes.

"By the way," Maury said as we walked back up the path, "when I met Fiona, I was really amazed at the resemblance, except for the hair, of course."

"Resemblance?" I couldn't imagine who he was talking about. "Resemblance to who?"

"To Mary Frances," my father said. "To your mother."

3

The faithful Fahid was waiting with the blue Rolls-Royce Silver Cloud at precisely 11:30 and we started off for the ranch. Actually, I could have arrived much earlier, as I had not slept a wink all night. Fiona didn't resemble Mary Frances in the slightest, but on returning to my room, I rescued the *News of the World* and stared again at the photo of Fiona and Roddy Startle on their way to Cap d'Antibes. With the hotel's pen, I began shading and shaping Fiona's hair. Of course, it did no good, as my memory of Mary Frances's features have been clouded by the passing years, and no matter what I did, it was still a disfigured Fiona in the photo.

But tonight had been one of the very few times that Maury ever mentioned Mary Frances's name, as if, once buried in that New Jersey cemetery, she had been forgotten by him. Apparently not. Then, still mulling the subject, I realized that I had never seen my father with another woman. Not, I'm sure, that there weren't other women, but that I had never seen them.

Maybe Elisa had and perhaps that was the root of her hatred of our father. Asking Elisa would be even more difficult than asking Maury, so I didn't pursue that line of thought. Then I remembered that, after his wife had died, Mighty Mel had also been a man alone. Was there a reason for this, another Maltese mystery? Still, the results of my encounter with Maury the previous night had left me with both warm and confused emotions. Everything he had said, made sense and even the Cartier watch rode more easily on my wrist.

At 10:00 that morning, I had again remembered to phone Sheffy and, when I got through, she took the call immediately.

"Crikey, Amicus, where are you now?"

"In Marbella."

"This is no time for a holiday."

"I'm meeting Ali Habibi."

"Did you meet Danny Speers?"

"Yes. He had a very interesting story."

"I thought he might. Now listen, Amicus, you've got to get back up to London as soon as possible."

"Why?"

"I've got it, Amicus. I've found the missing piece."

"What is it?"

"I'll show you when you get here. Hurry."

Click.

I had myself booked on the afternoon flight, then tried to phone both Alexis and Maury. There was no answer in either room, so I wrote quick notes explaining my unexpected early departure "due to the appearance of important new evidence." I promised to get in touch as soon as possible, then called down to have my luggage collected, I hoped that Fahid could carry me safely down the Highway of Death to Malaga Airport once my Baby Habibi interview was over. I didn't think it would take that long, so I would have plenty of time.

Maybe, I admitted, I was fleeing. Maybe I was using Sheffy as an escape hatch to slide away from both Maury and Alexis, as my emotions about the two of them were very strong, though obviously different. Perhaps it was just too much for me to handle, particularly both at the same time. Well, that was all right, too, I decided. If, for my own sake, I needed to get out, then out I should get.

The ranch was more of an armed camp, with guards carrying automatic weapons at every approach. Even with Fahid driving the blue Rolls Royce Silver Cloud, we had to slow down twice for me to be visually inspected before we could approach the large, white, red-tiled villa. Fahid guided me inside and left me alone in a spacious room that was nicely, but overly, furnished. There was just too much of everything. After a few moments, a short, chubby man with a moustache came bouncing in, wearing a Hawaiian shirt and white slacks.

"So you are Maury's son," he said with more of an odd inflection than an accent.

"Yes, Mr. Habibi, and I really appreciate this opportunity to see you." I wondered whether I should offer to shake hands.

"Baby, Baby, Baby," he slapped me on the shoulder. "Everybody calls me Baby. And you, what does everybody call you?"

"Mickey."

"Mickey and Baby." He stamped one foot. "Okay?"

"Okay, Baby," taking no chances, I stamped my foot, thinking that this might be some strange Arab custom.

"Let's sit and then we'll talk, Mickey."

Baby plopped himself down in an overstuffed chair and I sat on the couch alongside, preferring to avoid a constant face-to-face situation.

"You know what I want to ask you about?" I took the easy way in.

"Yes, Alexis explained to me. These are difficult memories, Mickey. Painful. You understand."

"Yes. I do understand."

"So ask me, Mickey. Alexis said that I should tell you everything. Isn't she a beautiful woman?"

"Very beautiful," I agreed. "Seven years ago, Oliver Godolphin, his wife Alexandra and Alexis were guests on your yacht."

"That stinking boat." Baby shook his head. "I don't have that stinking boat any more. I sold it. I wish I'd never bought it."

"Why were they with you on the boat?"

"He was famous. I like famous people."

"Were you friends?"

"Of course. I am friends with many famous people. Do you want coffee? A drink?"

"No, thank you." I gestured politely.

"Hey," Baby pointed. "You have a Cartier just like your father."

"It's his watch," I said. "He gave it to me last night."

"Why?" Baby leaned forward.

"Because his father had given it to him with the understanding that someday he would give it to me." I gave Maury's explanation.

"What do you think of your father?" Baby asked suddenly.

"I love him," was the first answer that came to mind, but I knew that wouldn't be enough. "And someday I hope to be as wise and to achieve what he's achieved in his life."

"Your father's a crook," Baby laughed. "A big crook. But I love him."

"Well," I shrugged. "Perhaps there have been a few professional misunderstandings."

"And you caught him, Mickey, didn't you?" Baby was enjoying the scene. "You caught him trying to sell a phony Paul Klee. He told me all about it."

"He did?" I was surprised. "Actually it was a very good Josef Jenniches imitation. It would have fooled most people."

"But not you, Mickey. It didn't fool you." Baby was pleased. "I think I want some coffee."

Baby pushed himself up and went to the door to shout something totally unintelligible and instantly there was the patter of running feet. The interview, obviously, was not going the way I intended and I welcomed this little break to regroup my thoughts.

"Was there anything unusual about Oliver Godolphin the last time you saw him?" I asked after Baby was back in his chair.

"On the boat?"

"On the boat."

"He was a very closed man, you know, Oliver. You could never tell what he was thinking. He should have been a poker player."

"But was there anything unusual?" I persisted.

"Not with him," Baby said.

"Then with who. With Alexandra?" I knew I was on to something.

"You can always tell about women. I can always tell." Baby was serious now.

A pretty, young maid entered, a single small cup on a tray. Baby took it, sipped and turned to watch the maid's exit.

"Nice ass," he said.

"What could you tell about Alexandra?" I wasn't going to be distracted.

"She was pissed off." Baby took another sip. "Oh, she was polite and friendly, but I could tell she was pissed off."

"What was she angry about?"

"I didn't say angry. I said pissed off. There's a difference. And she was pissed off at Oliver. You could see it in her eyes when she looked at him."

"Why? What had happened?"

Baby shrugged instead of answering.

"Did Alexis know that her mother was pissed off at her father?"

"I don't think so." Baby thought about it again, then shook his head. "No. She was young. She was having a good time. All the men were after her. Whenever Alexis was there, it was hard to look at anyone else."

"It still is," I digressed accidentally.

"She likes you, too," Baby said.

"She does? How do you know?"

"How else would I know, Mickey? She told me. She tells me everything. I'm like her godfather now, in a way. Because I feel responsible. I never should have allowed Oliver to take the helicopter."

"Everyone said he was an excellent pilot."

"But not excellent enough," Baby sighed. "Only my pilots fly my helicopters and, believe me, they are the best in the world. They check out the helicopter before the flight and they check out the helicopter after the flight. Never an accident, except with Oliver and Alexandra. And that was the only time anyone but one of my pilots flew one of my helicopters."

"What do you think happened?"

"Who knows. Maybe a bolt came off, maybe something

mechanical, but whatever it was, it should not have happened. It's my fault." Baby lowered his head.

"But you can't think about it that way," I said earnestly. "No one blames you. Alexis certainly doesn't."

"I blame me." Baby looked up sharply. "And I'm the only person in the world whose blame I care about."

"Then all I can say is that I'm very sorry."

"So am I."

With that, it seemed that the discussion had come to an end, except I wasn't finished and we sat there in a long silence until I thought of a way to back the conversation up to an earlier point. Still, Baby's silence was intimidating and it took me another few moments to find an angle for that.

"Can I ask some more questions, Baby?" I kept my voice low.

"About what?"

"About the last day. About when Oliver Godolphin and Alexandra took off in the helicopter?"

"You remind me of your father, Mickey," Baby said. "You have the same persistence. All right, ask me."

"Was Alexandra still pissed off?"

"I don't know. I only spoke to Oliver when he asked me if he could use the helicopter. I only saw Alexandra from a distance and she was wearing dark glasses and a scarf."

"Did they say good-bye to Alexis?"

"That's a strange question. What are you thinking?"

"I'm not sure yet. Did they say good-bye to Alexis?"

"No. Alexis and I were playing backgammon and they just waved. I hope you're finished now because I don't like talking about this."

"I'm finished." I had no choice. "And I thank you."

"Okay." Baby got to his feet and I followed suit. "Stay four or five days. Enjoy yourself. Be my guest."

"Thank you, but I have to leave for London on the next plane," I began my request. "And in fact I was wondering if your man, Fahid, could drive me straight to the airport."

"What's so important about London? Take a few days, spend some time with your father, with Alexis. I told you she likes you, didn't I?"

"It's my job," I said. "There's some new information on the

Godolphin book."

"You take this seriously," Baby looked at me.

"It's my profession. Provenance."

"Okay, Mickey. Fahid will take you to the airport. Come on."

I followed Baby out of the room and we turned down the corridor in what I thought was the wrong direction. But it was Baby's house and, obviously, he knew where we were going. Around the next turn, there were two armed guards in front of a doorway and I should have realized then, but I just followed. Baby waved the guards away, opened the door and let me enter first.

The Donatello Madonna was placed in the center of the room, illuminated by the skylight above so that no detail was hidden, the once creamy white marble now aged with the golden patina of years. The artist had worked with great skill, the folds of cloth, the veins in the hands, every fine point done with great care. I knew at once it was by Alceo Dossena, and if I knew, then Maury knew and the complicated Savelli provenance was only a complicated lie, though I didn't doubt that the means of transportation had been a coffin.

I circled the piece slowly and though it was no Donatello, it was a work of genius and, since it was by Dossena, it was also worthless. This is why Baby wanted to see me and this moment was what Maury had been setting me up for, not that he ever suggested that I lie, but moving my emotions around like pieces on a chessboard. Checkmate.

"What do you think?" Baby had been watching me.

"It's beautiful." I told the truth.

"How much you think it's worth?" Baby approached the inevitable point.

"It's priceless," I told the truth again.

"Who do you think made it?"

I turned to face him, my expression serious and thoughtful. I could not lie. But I could not tell the truth. I would have to come in somewhere in the middle.

"If I were to take an uneducated guess, without knowing any of the details or having studied the provenance, I would have to say it was by the disciple, Antonio Rossellino, or possibly even by the master himself." I thought I had hedged that rather well.

"Master? What master?" Baby wasn't satisfied.

"Donatello," I heard myself say.

SALZBURG

1

She was there, sitting at a front table at the Café Winkler on Mönchberg, the panoramic post card view of Salzburg below in the background. Lulu von Hofmannsthal I thought. Lulu. Except that now I knew her name as Lotte Wieland, L.W., her red hair highlighted by the afternoon sun. And, unlike Lulu, she was wearing glasses, but the curved wide frames only made her more attractive. I knew that she was only thirty-eight years old, which must have made her just twenty when she first met Oliver Godolphin. Younger than Fiona when I first met her on the St. James's Park Bridge, and now only a few years older than Alexis. Lotte Wieland.

I had caught the direct Gatwick-to-Salzburg flight and first had gone to the shop on Getreidegasse and from there I had been directed to the Café Winkler, where Jordan Leander had first seen Lulu. I felt that I was in a movie, except that Lotte was not wearing a kimono. It should have been a moment of victory, but now that I had arrived at the moment of truth, I was overcome with sadness.

"Lotte Wieland?" I asked.

She turned and looked at me for several seconds, searching my face, trying to read my expression, her own sadness making a trifle of mine.

"Yes," she said. "Sit down, please."

I took the chair across from her, but she turned back to stare off at the view of Salzburg in the distance. This was not like the book, at least, as synopsized by Mrs. Bettina Sachs. I knew that not only would we not hear Mozart, but we would never go to Schloss Fuschl. I had no red Alfa convertible, and there was no Baron Hugo.

"Have you seen Hans Florian?" she asked without looking at me.

"Yes."

"And how is he?"

"He's all right."

This was not altogether true, but if drugs, mindless sex and rock and roll were all right, then Hans Florian was all right. Barely. After my somewhat dishonest performance with Baby Habibi, Fahid had safely carried me down the Highway of Death to Malaga airport, where I boarded the flight to London Gatwick. After leaving my luggage at the Rembrandt, I had gone directly to Sheffy's agency. On learning of my arrival, she abruptly terminated her ongoing meeting and called me into her large office.

"Crikey, you look awful, Amicus."

"I've been having a rough time."

"On the Godolphin project?"

"The side effects, mostly. What have you got for me?"

"You know, you're not the charming man I took out to dinner the other night."

"I always show my good side to battered women, but you're healing fast."

"All right, after those dreadful things I said about Fiona, you have a right to be angry at me. I understand." Sheffy reached into her desk drawer and pulled out what appeared to be a Sunday newspaper magazine supplement and a pile of typed documents. "These are agency contracts. You sign these and I'll give you this."

Without even glancing at the contents, I signed, affixing my signature to the space above where my name had been typed in and mentally adding these forms to the false confession I had signed at Putnam, Dick and Thurston. I was definitely not in a good mood, angry at my father, at Alexis, at Baby, at Fiona and at Sheffy as well, though not for the reasons she thought. I felt used and abused and the person I was most angry at, the person who was responsible for all these problems, turned out to be myself.

"Oh," Sheffy said. "You have a new watch."

"Just give me the fucking article."

"Crikey, Amicus, I think you may have talent after all." Sheffy handed over the Sunday supplement.

"The Pied Piper of Punk," the magazine article was titled, with a color photograph of a grinning, rather unattractive man with a drooping mustache standing possessively with a very young green-haired girl whose eyes were completely encircled with blue makeup. The article quickly explained that this was Charlie Cunliffe and his fourteen-year-old wife, Angel, and they claimed to be waiting for her to reach a legal age before they consummated their relationship. In the meantime, Charlie Cunliffe's mission in life was to "provide a place for all the many disenfranchised teenagers who, because they had chosen another life-style, were left with nowhere to go." The place that Charlie Cunliffe provided was a bus, on which they would travel around the countryside and have great adventures.

"Keep reading," Sheffy said when I glanced up at her impatiently.

I began skimming until I reached the part where Charlie Cunliffe began expounding on how many young people he had saved, including the children of the rich and famous. "In fact, Oliver Godolphin's son is here with us now," Charlie Cunliffe boasted. Oliver Godolphin's son? I looked back at Sheffy and she smiled.

"This is really hot, Amicus."

"Does it mention his name in the story?"

"No."

"Did you find out?"

"I'm just your agent, darling. You have to do some of the work."

"What the hell do you think I've been doing?"

"Crikey, what are you so angry about?"

"Everything," I told her, then headed for the door.

"Hold on," Sheffy raised her voice and I turned back. "Don't you want to know where the bus leaves from?"

"Where?"

"Battersea Park at ten in the morning," she said smugly. "By the way, what does Alexis look like these days?"

There was no way I could answer that, so I just left, knowing I was rude, but unable to suppress my anger. I had been a fool with everyone, an easy mark, my emotions tipped and swayed by the touch of a feather, manipulated as effortlessly as a child's toy. But I would not be a fool any longer. I would root it all out. L.W., the Godolphin provenance, everything, regardless of signed confessions and contracts and promises. The world would regret making a mockery of Amicus Maltese.

In my fury, I walked blindly, reviewing everything I knew and reciting my vow never to be betrayed again. How could my father have done this to me? How could I have made, however disclaimed, the only false provenance of my life? How could I have allowed Fiona to haunt me all these years? I tried to think of a reason to justify my anger at Alexis and I couldn't, but still the anger remained. I was alone in the world, alone, without friendship, without love.

Had I done this to myself or had it been done to me? Either way, there was nothing left. Except for the Oliver Godolphin provenance. *Sakura* was the thread by which I could hold on to the world. I looked up and found that in my unseeing walk I had directed myself not only to Ebury Street, but that I had almost approached the Gallerie Naïf. I turned and fled, but not before noticing the new display in the window, childlike paintings of boats, all of them pink.

After an early dinner of hot chicken curry and cold lager at the little Indian restaurant on Beauchamp Place, I walked back to the Rembrandt, burning in my belly as well as my mind. There were messages from my father and from Alexis, which I crumpled and handed back, instructing the hall porter not to put through any calls. The next person I would speak to would be Charlie Cunliffe and I would not permit any distractions.

I went to my room and took a hot bath, once again reviewing my mental summary of the past week, turning each incident over in my mind to examine every detail from every possible angle. Nothing made it better. But I persisted, carrying these terrible thoughts from the bath to the bed and finally into my dreams.

I was driving a motorcycle, Fiona riding behind me, both of us dressed in black leather, through what seemed to be Richmond. I was having difficulty in controlling the large motorbike (understandably, as I have never been on one in my life). But Fiona did not appear to notice the technical problems I was experiencing, enjoying herself, her glorious red hair flying in the wind.

Then there was a traffic jam and we had to come to a stop. It was right in front of a pub, the sidewalk crowded with happy people. Suddenly I felt very warm and uncomfortable. Then Maury emerged through the crowd to ask if we would like a drink, which Fiona immediately accepted. I tried to turn and talk to her, but it was impossible as she was sitting behind me. Maury was back with the cool drinks and in that same instant the traffic jam was over, the cars moving in an easy flow. Suddenly, Fiona was standing on the sidewalk, saying that she was going to ride with Maury for a while, then she got behind him on his motorcycle and they left.

At first, I could not get my motorbike started, then had even greater difficulty controlling it as I sped to catch up. Ahead, there was a left turn, almost all of the cars streaming around the corner and I followed in the same direction. Then I saw the road sign. I had missed the turn to Paris. Paris? With that, I awakened in a frothing rage. The Cartier told me that it was more or less 5:00 a.m.

By 6:00 I was out walking, down Sloane Street to Sloane Square, where I detoured to locate the jewelry shop where I had purchased Fiona's first bracelet. But it was no longer there, which only added to my fury, thinking that sometimes life takes everything away, even the memories. I stormed across Chelsea Bridge and into Battersea Park only three hours early, which was just as well as there was a lot of ground to cover and I had no idea where in the large park Charlie Cunliffe had his departure point. Two and a half hours later, I had covered the park thoroughly, but there was no indication, no sign, not even a hint.

Perhaps Sheffy had been wrong. Why had I taken her at her word without the slightest doubt? Why had I believed the magazine article and why would I believe anything that this Charlie Cunliffe said. Oliver Godolphin's son? It could all be a lie. But no, I told myself, this was provenance and I would not be discouraged. I would not yield until I had found the truth.

"Jolly well said," a passing jogger remarked.

I turned angrily to look after him. Then I saw Charlie Cunliffe's bus in the wide parking area near the lake, a small group of people gathered alongside. The aroma of marijuana greeted me as I approached, tunnel visioned on Charlie Cunliffe standing near the open bus door with his green haired child-bride. He saw me and grinned.

"Fifty quid for the ride, guv. If you want to give the girls something later that's up to you."

Fifty quid for the ride? Who was this, the Jimmy Fitzhugh of the punk set?

"Where is Oliver Godolphin's son?" I asked hoarsely.

"Sod you, mate. We don't give out personal information. That's our sacred code." He seemed a little too pleased with his answer.

Without thinking, I brought my right knee up sharply into his crotch and would have done it again if he hadn't fallen writhing to the ground. This was the first time in my life that I had physically attacked anyone and the results were surprising. Charlie Cunliffe was moaning, clutching his groin as he rolled back and forth in pain, but my rage was still building.

"That's for pissing me off," I told him. "Now I'm about to get seriously angry."

I readied my foot to stomp, but the green haired Angel grabbed my arm.

"No! Don't hurt him!" she shrieked in a baby voice, then pointed off. "That's him. That's Florey. The one with the red hair."

I turned to look at the group of Charlie Cunliffe's jolly travelers, all of them staring back at me, too stunned to move. Most of them were adolescent girls, their hair and makeup a rainbow of unnatural colors, the boys' spiked heads with stripes shaved or dyed in equal ugliness, except for the tall boy with the long, tangled, natural red hair that Angel was still fingering, his eyes wide as I walked over to face him.

"What's your name?" I asked.

"Hans Florian," his voice had a tremble in it. "Did my mother send you?"

"What's your mother's name?"

"Lotte Wieland."

Lotte Wieland. L.W. My heart was pounding, my rage subsiding quickly. What had happened to my quiet, gentle life of provenance? I took out a pad and pen and handed them to the boy.

"Would you write down your mother's telephone number, please?" I asked, then gave him a reassuring smile.

2

"I'm sorry to have made you come up here, but after you phoned, I could not stay in the shop, I could not go home," Lotte Wieland said. "I have been waiting for such a long time."

"Seven years," I spoke softly.

"Yes, seven years," she nodded. "You asked me so many questions on the telephone that I am afraid that I have forgotten your name."

"Amicus Maltese. Mickey is easier."

"How did you find my son?"

"It was a lucky break."

"And how did you make him give you my telephone number?"

"I scared him."

"Did you hurt him?" Lotte Wieland looked at me anxiously.

"No," I told her. "But now I think I should have brought him back with me."

"He would only have run away again. Hans Florian is very stubborn, like his father."

"Oliver Godolphin." I wanted to hear her say the name.

"Yes, like Oliver," she tried to smile. "You know he wrote the book for me."

"Yes. Now that we are sitting here I know that."

"Oh, that was just the story. It was not about me and Oliver. None of it really happened the way he wrote it."

"How did it really happen?"

"In Paris," she said. "I had just been there for a few weeks and the only people I knew were the other three models they had brought from Vienna. We had done all the photo sessions and I was planning to return to Vienna after the fashion show at the Hotel Bristol. The lights were very hot and I had stepped outside to catch a breath of air and that is where we met."

"How?"

"He spoke to me in French, and since I did not speak French then I answered him in German, and since he did not speak German he answered me in English. It made us both laugh and we knew right then."

"What?"

"That we would be together. He took a suite at the hotel and I slept with him that night. The next day, Oliver and I went out and we found an apartment on the Left Bank. Two months later, I was pregnant and I did not return to Austria for over ten years."

Lotte Wieland lapsed into silence, but I knew that she would continue when she was ready, when she had decided how much to tell. A fashion show at the Hotel Bristol, the same hotel where I had stayed with my father after my disastrous visit to Nice. The web of coincidence was so thickly woven that it could hold water.

"He told me he was married, so there was no deception about that," she said. "There was no deception about anything, except he never told me he was famous. I discovered that myself. Oliver never thought much of fame, not like a film star. He just had those books to write. The books were all that counted. The books and our son. He loved the boy very much. Oliver chose his name before he was born, but that was after the doctor said he was sure we would have a son. Hans and Florian, they were both Oliver's friends in the Foreign Legion. They were both killed, so it was a remembrance."

"Did he tell you about the time he was in the Foreign Legion?" I didn't want to interrupt, but I had to ask.

"No."

"But he wanted you to have the child?"

"Oh, yes. Oliver was devoted to his daughter and to his wife, but he felt that he must have a son. To have a son was so important."

"Why?"

"I don't know. Oliver was a man who kept many things inside himself and I would never ask questions. I was just happy to be with him, happy to have given him the son he wanted. There was nothing more I needed. When Hans Florian was born, Oliver wanted to hire a nurse, someone to help me, but I refused. I wanted to raise our son myself."

"But he never lived with you?"

"No. That was impossible. He lived with his wife and daughter. Still, he came to see us four or five times a week. After the Nobel Prize, when he became so famous, it was very difficult. We could not go out as a family, because people would always recognize him. But still he would meet us in the Bois de Boulogne and play football with Hans Florian and things like that, when he could. He taught Hans Florian to read in both English and French when the boy was only five. So he was a good father, a loving father."

It was a sweet story, but Lotte Wieland was leaving out so many answers, I had no choice. I would have to press her, ask the questions that she might refuse. I was not here for reminiscence.

"If Oliver Godolphin wanted a son so badly, why didn't he and his wife have another child?" I tried to make the question sound as gentle as possible.

"Because she couldn't, Alexandra. Not after the daughter. Oliver told me there could be no more children." She didn't seem offended.

"Then why, since his daughter was practically grown up, didn't he divorce Alexandra and marry you?"

"There was never any question of that. Oliver did not believe in divorce."

"Was he Catholic?"

"He was loyal." Her eyes flared slightly.

"And you lived in that Left Bank apartment, you and Hans Florian, for ten years?" I eased off.

"Yes. It was a very nice apartment. It was our home."

"Who paid for it?"

"Oliver."

"How?"

"With money," Lotte Wieland was not enjoying my interrogation. "He paid for everything. There was more money than we could use, and though Oliver was quite wealthy, I told him there was no need to spend so much on us, but he just laughed and said that it had all been arranged. Why do you have to know this?"

"Bear with me and I'll explain in a moment," the sun was setting and I could see that she was chilly. "How did he give you the money? Did he write you a check?"

"The money was deposited into my bank."

"Which bank?"

"The Credit Lyonnais."

"Do you know Danny Speers?"

"Who?"

"Danny Speers, an American film producer."

"No," she looked puzzled. "Why?"

"It doesn't matter." I didn't think she would appreciate the joke. "You said that when you met Oliver Godolphin, he didn't speak German. Did he learn the language with you?"

"No. He never tried. He wasn't interested," Lotte Wieland said, then leapt ahead of me. "Now you want to know about the German language in the book. That is very simple. He wrote in English and I would translate those parts into German. We both thought that was very funny. But he knew that we had carried it too far and that most of it would have to be put back into English, particularly that long talk between Lulu and Jordan at Schloss Fuschl, the one before she takes him to bed. Oliver was having a small joke on his publisher."

"And he never was here at the Café Winkler?"

"Never here, never in Salzburg, never in Vienna, never in Austria," she said. "I described it all for him over the years. He would have me close my eyes and in my mind I would go back to Austria. Then he would tell me what he wanted me to do and have me describe what I saw, like when I was a young girl and how I walked to school. It was everything. He started with my first memories here in Salzburg, all the way to when I moved to Vienna when I was seventeen and what my life was like there. It was a game we played."

A mesmerizing game to say the least. Was this something else Godolphin learned from the natives while he was in the Foreign Legion? After all the personal accounts from Sheffy to the unfortunate Danny Speers to the beauteous Alexis to Baby Habibi and now to Lotte Wieland, I still had no real idea who Oliver

Godolphin was. It seemed as if everyone had described a different person. The man had led a double life. Did he have multiple personalities?

"Why did you leave Paris?" I forced myself back to the point.

"It was too painful to remain and as my parents still live here, I thought it was important for Hans Florian to have some family since he no longer had a father."

"It must have been a very difficult time."

"Yes, there were many problems. Hans Florian spoke German, of course. But he was a French school boy, and it is provincial here. And my father still had not forgiven me. For the first year, he refused to acknowledge his grandson. Even after that, they were never close. Hans Florian was not a disciplined Austrian. He was an excitable Parisian, always talking too much, always saying he didn't like it here, always claiming that the French were better. Fortunately, there was enough money to buy our own house, but still I was an unmarried woman with a rebellious child. That did not make life easier."

"But you stayed."

"My parents were getting older and my mother needed me here, so I took over my father's jewelry shop on Getreidegasse. I suppose, it has become a habit." She shivered suddenly. "I'm sorry, but it is cold now."

"Shall we go inside?" I gestured at the Café restaurant.

"No. I think it would be better if we went to my house. I can give you something to eat if you are hungry."

"Whatever is convenient for you."

"Nothing is convenient for me, Mr. Maltese," she said sadly. "It is too late for that. But it is necessary."

"Yes," I said. "If the book is to be published, it is very necessary."

"You don't understand. You see, if it weren't for that book, Oliver would still be alive."

3

We drove down from Mönchberg in Lotte Wieland's Opel, which I guessed was several years old, then over a bridge to the right bank of the city, neither of us having spoken since her last ominous remark. I knew the rest of the story would come out now, but she would tell it on her terms and in her own time. I was convinced that everything she had related this far was true, but I would still need more than just my convictions to arrive at an undeniable provenance. How would Alexis react to all this? Since she had said that there could be no happy ending to this story, she must have been anticipating much worse than I had heard this far, except for Lotte Wieland's final comment at the Café Winkler. If it weren't for the book, Oliver Godolphin would still be alive. Why? I had the feeling that, unfortunately, Alexis was right.

"We are almost there," Lotte Wieland said, as we drove through an elongated square in what seemed to be a newer part of the city. "You have been to Salzburg before?"

"No, this is my first time."

"It is quite pretty, but it is small, not at all cosmopolitan like Vienna."

"Do you go to Vienna often?" I was ready to maintain my end of the small talk.

"No," she said and lapsed back into silence.

A few minutes later, we pulled up in front of a small house on a residential street and I tagged after Lotte Wieland to the front door, waited for her to find her key, then followed her inside. The furnishing appeared out of place, more Swedish modern than Austrian bucolic, framed prints on the wall, a shelf of books and even from a distance I could spot the row of Godolphins, the complete Alexandra dedications in Lotte Wieland's home. It seemed a little strange. Why would Oliver Godolphin continue dedicating his books to his wife after ten years of his mistress's company, particularly since, according to Alexis, Alexandra didn't want them? Another riddle.

"Yes," Lotte Wieland had observed my visual inspection. "I brought the furniture from Paris. I thought it would be good for Hans Florian to have something familiar. Would you like something to drink?"

"Whatever you have will be fine."

"Schnaps?"

"Please."

Lotte Wieland walked out of the room, giving me the opportunity to check the books more closely and one by one I flipped open the collected Godolphins, looking for an inscription. Nothing. Not even a signature. Why wouldn't he sign the books at least? The man had fathered her child and if he wouldn't give his name to his son, he could have given her an autograph. Obviously, I had not grasped the nature of their relationship.

I moved away from the bookshelf and prowled some more. This was the house that Danny Speers had paid for and yet Lotte Wieland had never heard his name. On a corner table there was a small framed photograph of Hans Florian, a few years younger, hair much shorter, glaring with open hostility at the photographer. Definitely an unpleasant boy at the time. I had difficulty relating the person in the picture with the young man I had intimidated earlier that day in Battersea Park. Perhaps his adolescent anger had been spent by the marijuana and painted girls on Charlie Cunliffe's bus? I did not regret my act of violence.

"Here," Lotte Wieland had returned, wearing a cardigan sweater and carrying two small glasses.

"Thank you." I accepted my glass and we both sipped without toasting.

"You were looking at his photograph. Does Hans Florian look different now? Older yes. The picture was taken two years ago. But is he well?"

"His hair is longer." I decided to equivocate. "And he did not look as angry as he is in the photograph."

"Yes." Lotte Wieland took another sip. "Hans Florian was very angry then. It was just before he started running away. The first time he managed to go all the way to Paris. Of course the happy childhood he was searching for was no longer there, which only made him angrier. Please, sit down."

I accepted her invitation to take the couch and she sat in the chair opposite, pulling the sweater around her, still feeling a chill, the deep sadness reflected somehow in her every gesture. If I succeeded in establishing so solid a provenance that Alexis would have no choice other than withdraw her threat to sue Farrow & Farrow and allow the book to be published, what would Lotte Wieland do with all that money? Easily a four million dollar advance, Rupert Farrow had said, and since the instructions were for all monies to be sent to Pierre Rougemont, I thought it was a fair assumption that, for whatever reason, Oliver Godolphin had nominated Lotte Wieland as the recipient. But, I realized, that also presumed that Oliver Godolphin had some premonition of his death. Why? Instead of this intricacy becoming clearer, it had become even more complex.

"Why," I had to pursue the point, "did you say that if it weren't for the book that Oliver Godolphin would still be alive? Because he wrote the book for you?"

"No, not that at all," she said then paused. "It is difficult to explain. There are certain things that I do not know and some things that perhaps would be better if I did not know. I worry about telling you this."

"I will be discreet. I give you my word."

"No, no." Lotte Wieland almost smiled. "I worry about what it will do to you."

"To me?" I took a swallow of schnaps. "Why to me?"

"To give you the burden, the responsibility. You see, Oliver never spoke to me of his other life, his life with Alexandra and Alexis, as I am certain he never spoke to them of us. But you have told me that you know Alexis, and now you know me. And you have met Hans Florian."

"Yes?"

"I have already been hurt by my knowledge, so that is not important. But if I reveal these things to you, then you will have to decide what you must reveal. That will not be easy."

"I will reveal only as much as is required to establish that Oliver Godolphin wrote the book."

"But how much is that, Mr. Maltese?"

"I don't know."

Lotte Wieland removed her glasses and rubbed her eyes. For a flash I had an image of how she must have looked when she was in her twenties and without the pervading sadness. Why would she worry about how her information was going to burden me? I suddenly wished that Pierre Rougemont were here. His ebullient spirits could give us both a lift. Suppose Lotte Wieland received the money, would it help?

"All right," she put her glasses back on. "After the book was finished, Oliver told me that he was going on holiday with his wife and daughter and would be gone for a few weeks. That had happened before and I did not mind. He even suggested that I take Hans Florian away on a pleasure trip during that time, so the boy would not feel abandoned. But we were happy in Paris and had no need to go anywhere. Oliver brought presents and said good-bye and I thought that he had already left when he came to the apartment late the next night. He was wild, crazed, and I did not know what was wrong. Then he finally told me. Alexandra had destroyed the manuscript. She had thrown the pages into the fire."

"Why?" I interrupted without thinking.

"Out of anger."

"About you? Because he wrote the book for you?"

"I don't know. But Oliver was so beside himself because of the destruction of his work that finally I told him, I confessed to him what I had done."

Lotte Wieland finished her schnaps and placed the empty glass carefully on the table, pausing for several moments before she continued.

"Oliver used a typewriter when he wrote and he would make a copy of each chapter for me to do the translation, telling me to just write out the German on the page. Then he would take the chapter back when he brought me the new one. I had never done this kind of translation and I was anxious that my work would not please him, so I made a photocopy in case I was sloppy or made a mistake. I did this without his permission and so I was afraid to admit what I had done. I had promised myself that when the book was finished that I would throw my secret copy away, but I didn't. I loved Oliver and it was part of him that I could keep with me all the time."

"And this secret copy had the German translations as well?"

"Oh, yes. Those were the pages that I worked on. After each chapter, I would make a neater copy. I wanted him to think that I was perfect. This is what I confessed to him that night, a confession that I had betrayed his trust."

"What was his reaction?"

"He just stared at me without saying a word and then he laughed and he said, 'This is your book, Lotte, now it is all yours.' Then he kissed me and he left, taking my copy with him. That was the last time I ever saw him."

There were tears in Lotte Wieland's eyes. She removed her glasses to wipe them away. "The last time."

I sat there as Lotte Wieland wept silently, barely able to hold my own tears back. Why was I so moved? For her to have lived with this wound for seven years, losing her lover and now her son, was more than an unhappy ending, it was heartbreaking. And, worse, there was no cure. But at last Oliver Godolphin's promise would come true. The book, Lotte Wieland's book, would be published. I would see to that. But why did Godolphin wait for seven years to have the manuscript delivered to Farrow & Farrow?

"I am sorry," Lotte Wieland said finally, rising to her feet. "I will make us something to eat."

I just sat there on the couch, trying to elevate my thought process over my emotions. What would I tell Alexis? Her mother had destroyed the manuscript, but her father's mistress had made a copy. Was that so bad? Alexis had been afraid that I would discover something terrible about her father. And did having an illegitimate son fall into that category? That was not so terrible, there were many men with bastard children, but few as loving and caring as Oliver Godolphin, at least loving and caring toward Lotte Wieland and Hans Florian.

No, the most difficult part would be telling Alexis about her mother destroying the manuscript. But Alexis had voiced no anxiety about my discovering something awful about Alexandra Godolphin. Still, since there was a copy, even if unknown at that moment, was Alexandra's action too horrible to reveal? Had other writers' wives destroyed manuscripts in rage. I would have to research that question, but I was reasonably sure I could find a precedent. There were numerous tales of painters' wives who slashed canvases in fury, though I couldn't think of a specific example immediately, but those didn't really apply.

"Mr. Maltese." Lotte Wieland called me.

We ate in the small kitchen at a formica-topped table, large bowls of steaming Gulaschsuppe, chunks of heavy local bread, and a chopped tomato and onion salad. Lotte Wieland had produced a bottle of Blauburgunder, a heavy red table wine which we drank out of water glasses, neither of us talking, unable to pick up the conversation at the point where it had been so emotionally terminated.

"Proof," I said finally. "I shall have to show them some physical proof."

"Yes, I have that as well," Lotte Wieland answered.

"And I will need you to write a statement. Nothing complicated. Just what you told me."

"All right."

I couldn't think of anything else to ask and we finished the simple meal in silence. How many silent meals had Lotte Wieland eaten in this kitchen? How many lonely hours?

"When the book is published," I tried to bring up a happier subject, "there will be a lot of money, quite a lot of money."

"Is that why you think I am doing this, Mr. Maltese?" She looked at me. "For the money."

"No," I said. "But it will provide you with choices. You could move back to Paris or Vienna."

"Why should I do that? My home is here now. I shall remain here."

"Perhaps Oliver Godolphin wanted you to have a better life."

"What Oliver wanted then does not matter now. Does it?"

"What do you want?"

"I want what I once had and can have no longer." Lotte Wieland began clearing the table. "Wait. I shall bring the album."

Would all this have been different if the manuscript had been delivered without the seven year delay? Yes, I decided, much different and with much less pain. Suppose Lotte Wieland had decided to remain in Paris instead of returning to Salzburg to give Hans Florian a sense of family, would the boy still have been so rebellious? Where would he have run away to? She had made an emotional choice at the time and, I thought, a bad one. But few things were easier than finding fault with history. Lotte Wieland was in Salzburg, in this little house, and what, I wondered, could I do to help her? Nothing came to mind.

"Here," Lotte Wieland returned, carrying four thick albums. "You may look at these and I will make coffee."

Family photographs. Lotte Wieland pregnant by the window of the apartment in Paris. Oliver Godolphin sitting on the couch with a newspaper, looking up surprised. The baby Hans Florian in his mother's arms, then in his father's arms. Family groups in the apartment. Godolphin and Hans Florian with a ball in a park. A full frontal nude photograph of Lotte Wieland framed in the bathroom doorway. A series of Christmases, gaily-wrapped packages under the tree, and the recorded opening of the gifts. Birthdays, holidays, winters, springs and summers with the family group.

Oliver Godolphin certainly was not camera shy, and if it hadn't been for the history, it would have appeared to be a very normal family album. I turned the page. Lotte Wieland was at a writing desk, pages of a manuscript in front of her as Oliver Godolphin looked over her shoulder, photos taken from several angles.

"What's this?" I asked.

Lotte Wieland came from the stove to look over my shoulder.

"That's when we were working on the book. Hans Florian took the photos. Go to the next page."

I flipped the album page and there was a clear photograph of Oliver Godolphin and Lotte Wieland, smiling into the lens and holding a single sheet of paper. "SAKURA by Oliver Godolphin," the words could barely be made out. But there it was. Proof. Though I had not doubted a single word Lotte Wieland had said, this was the provenance. What could be more evident? I leaned back in the chair, suddenly exhausted.

"I will have to borrow some of these photographs," I said.

"Yes, you may take what you need. Return them to me. That is all I ask."

"You will be hearing from a banker in Geneva whose name is Pierre Rougemont. In fact you may have to go there with proof of your identity." I yawned uncontrollably. "But he is a very good man and he will make things as easy and as simple as possible.

This will probably take a week or so. Do you understand?"

"Of course."

"If there is any problem, I will hear about it and I will contact you to get it straightened out," I said and yawned again. "Now we have to do the statement, if you don't mind."

"What hotel are you staying at, Mr. Maltese?"

"I'm afraid I don't have one. I came straight to meet you."

"Then you shall stay here. In Hans Florian's room. You are very tired. You go to sleep and I shall write the statement. If it needs to be corrected, we can do that in the morning."

"It's no trouble for me to go to a hotel. Really."

"There is no need. The bed is comfortable and the sheets are clean." Lotte Wieland smiled. "I still change them every week."

The room was small and cluttered with Hans Florian's mementos, a large collection of rock and roll tapes and a poster of Roddy Startle taped to the wall. But even that could not keep me awake and I slept soundly until four in the morning, awakening with the realization that Lotte Wieland had not actually answered my question. Yes, if she hadn't kept her secret copy of the manuscript, the book would be gone, but why did she say that if it weren't for the book Oliver Godolphin would still be alive? We seemed to have glossed over that point. Or had I missed it?

I stretched out in Hans Florian's bed and reviewed the entire dialogue, front to back and then back to front. The only possible connection was the secret copy. If Lotte Wieland hadn't kept it, there would be no book, but since she had, there was a book, so why did Oliver Godolphin have to die because of it?

By dawn I knew the answer and at that same moment understood what Lotte Wieland had meant about my assuming the burden of that knowledge. She had wanted me to figure it out by myself, because she had not been willing to actually say the words. Now I had no choice but to speak them. I dressed and washed and went down to the kitchen. Lotte Wieland's handwritten statement and the selected photographs were on the table and I turned the flame on beneath last night's coffee, then began to read.

Her statement was clear and concise, reflecting everything she had told me in a very comprehensible style. She had signed her name and added the date at the bottom of the last page, leaving out only what she had left to my speculation, which was certainly nothing I would want to see written on paper.

The reheated coffee was bitter, but I drank two cups and finally Lotte Wieland came into the kitchen, a bathrobe over her nightgown. Silently, she poured herself a cup of the bitter brew and sipped at it, sitting across the table from me. Obviously, she was waiting for me to begin.

"The statement is very good," I said. "But I have some difficult questions."

"Yes, I know."

"If you had not kept your secret copy, would Oliver Godolphin still be alive?"

"Yes," Lotte Wieland answered in a whisper.

"Do you consider yourself responsible for his death?" This was not easy to ask.

"Yes." Again a whisper.

"Why?"

"Why do you think?"

"What I think," I began the dreaded speech, "what you have led me to think, is that Oliver Godolphin told his wife, Alexandra, that there was a copy of the manuscript, the original of which she had destroyed, and that he had already sent it somewhere beyond her reach. Does that sound right?"

"Yes. This is what Oliver would have done."

"And then he told her that the book would be published and that the book was not only dedicated to you, but that he intended that you were to receive the monies from that book. Does that also sound right?"

"Yes." It came out as a shuddering sigh.

"But this last part, he told her in complete privacy, in a place where no one else could hear them. In a helicopter."

"Yes."

"And how do you think Alexandra reacted?"

"Like this." Lotte Wieland shot her hand straight out, as if pushing something away.

"She sent the helicopter into a dive."

"That is what I believe."

"First she destroyed the manuscript. And when he revealed your secret copy, she killed him."

"Yes."

"But you believe his death is your fault?"

"What else can I believe?"

"Anything but that," I told her.

Lotte Wieland drove me to the airport and we parted outside. She was still sad, but I thought—at least I wanted to think—that, after tormenting herself with this terrible guilt, she now felt some degree of relief at sharing this secret at last. Now what was I going to do?

As the plane lifted off from Salzburg, I realized that I had not spoken a single word of German.

LONDON

1

It was pouring, the rain coming down in sheets, as if the sky were practicing for Wimbledon. I sloshed my way across the sidewalk toward Farrow & Farrow's Victorian red brick home, intentionally arriving a half hour late for dramatic purposes. After returning from Salzburg, I called Stephen J. Thurston and instructed him to arrange the meeting in three days time and to inform Alexis Godolphin that I requested her presence, saying only that I would then demonstrate the final provenance of the novel *Sakura*, but giving no indication of which way it would go.

Later that day, I went back to Great Russell Street to see what the British Library had to say about the history of matrimonial manuscript destruction. But the only example I came up with was Isabelle Burton's burning of Sir Richard F. Burton's English translation of the Arabian erotic classic, *The Perfumed Garden*, which did nothing to help my case. Besides, I knew that a precedent meant nothing here and I was only trying to delay my own unpleasant task.

I rented a typewriter and secluded myself at the Rembrandt, giving the hall porter the now familiar information that I was not accepting calls. Writing a meticulous provenance report has never been easy for me, as I choose each single word with care in my attempt to avoid even the slightest misinterpretation. The results are dry and often difficult to read, but my goal is accuracy, not entertainment.

But, as difficult as other reports have been, they flowed easily in comparison with this one. My emotions had become involved and I had to excise any personal feelings and simply present the facts and the progression through which I reached my conclusion. Since so many of the steps I had taken to follow this trail were emotionally motivated, the separation was almost impossible.

I struggled and, after reading the first few pages, realized that I had failed. Was it really necessary for me to include the fact that it had been Fiona who arranged my introduction to Sheffy Eccleston, Oliver Godolphin's former secretary? Sheffy certainly played a major role, steering me first to Danny Speers and then to the crucial meeting with Hans Florian. But how could I bring Sheffy in without mentioning Fiona, and just mentioning Fiona meant that I had to explain who she was. Was Roddy Startle going to appear in the Godolphin provenance too?

I ripped the pages in half and started over. By the time that hunger drove me to hike over to Wolfe's on Park Lane for a hamburger and french fries, I still had not succeeded in writing a single page that survived reading. What was the problem? A provenance report was simply a straightforward presentation of the facts, so why did my every attempt turn into some intimate confession? And I had just touched upon the beginning of the statement. What would I do later on when I got to the part about Baby Habibi? Could I leave Maury out? And how could I write about Alexis in a way that would not reveal my feelings? I couldn't even bear to think how I would handle my visit to Salzburg.

With my hunger, though not my turmoil, assuaged, I plodded back to the Rembrandt and, glancing up for some reason, noticed for the first time that the hotel was not on Cromwell Road. It was actually on Thurloe Place, the same street, but a full block before it became Cromwell Road. I didn't even know where I lived. With that unrelated but unsettling thought, I returned to the typewriter for another three frustrating hours, typing and tearing, before I gave up, took a hot bath and went to bed.

Perhaps there didn't have to be a written report. Perhaps I could just do it verbally. Yes, and make an absolute fool of myself by weeping at the sad part. No, I decided, I would write the report the only way I could, leaving nothing out, sparing no one, particularly myself. Perhaps, if I were lucky, someone would throw it into the flames.

"They're all waiting for you," the Farrow & Farrow

receptionist scolded. "You're late."

I hung my sodden Burberry on the coatrack and carried the briefcase I had purchased to protect my precious documents up the stairs. Then I opened the double doors to the conference room without knocking, my sudden appearance making them all turn. My eyes, of course, went immediately to Alexis and she was, impossible to imagine, even more beautiful.

"Oh, Mickey," she said with relief. "You're so late. I was afraid you'd been in an accident."

"Sorry." I smiled at her, then turned to look at Rupert Farrow and Stephen J. Thurston. "If you will excuse us, gentlemen, but I must speak with Miss Godolphin privately before we begin."

"I say," Farrow objected sullenly. "You do, after all, work for us."

I just stared at him, until Thurston got to his feet and took Farrow's arm.

"Come on, Rupert. Let's not make an issue of this."

Reluctantly, Farrow let himself be led to the doors and they went out with no further protest. I made sure the doors were firmly shut and then walked to the table and sat across from Alexis, placing the briefcase in front of me.

"Your father has been trying to get in touch with you," she said.

"I know."

"And so have I. You never returned my calls."

"Forgive me."

"Have I done something to offend you?"

"No," I said. "You are the most wonderful and beautiful person that I have ever met, and I'm afraid that I am going to do something that will not only offend you, but cause you to never see or speak to me again."

"Oh, God." Alexis was shaken. "What is it?"

"I have determined the provenance of *Sakura*. There is no question that your father wrote it. I have all the documentation in this briefcase, and I don't want to show it to you. I don't want to show it to anyone."

"Is it that bad? Is it that terrible?"

"No, it is not." This was not true, but I had to try. "There are some things that will shock you, but I would rather tell them to you personally than have it all come out in a formal session."

"If I didn't know you better, I would think this sounds like blackmail," Alexis said.

"I am only trying to protect you. I hope you believe me."

"I do."

"Then what shall we do?"

"Tell me," she said softly.

"All right, and after I tell you, if you still want to see what is in this briefcase, I will show it to you."

"Tell me, Mickey."

"Eighteen years ago, your father met a young Austrian woman in Paris. Her name is Lotte Wieland. They had an affair and, as a result, Lotte Wieland had a son. His name is Hans Florian Wieland. This relationship continued until your parents' death. Lotte Wieland translated the German parts of your father's last novel, and he dedicated the book to her."

"Was my father in love with her?" Alexis interrupted.

"Yes, he was," I could only make that assumption. "And Lotte Wieland was very much in love with him. Your father supported his mistress and son very generously. But I'm afraid that you owe Danny Speers quite a lot of money, as he was the conduit for these funds."

"Have you met her, this woman?"

"Yes."

"What does she look like?"

Instead of answering, I opened the briefcase and took out the photograph of Lotte Wieland and Oliver Godolphin holding the title page and smiling. I handed the photo across the table to Alexis, hoping that this would be all the proof needed to convince her, but knowing that she would still have questions. So far, it hadn't sounded bad. Anything further would be painful. Alexis studied the photograph for a long time, hurt and anger in her beautiful eyes.

"She was very pretty." Alexis dropped the photo on the table.

"Yes."

"Does this get worse?"

"Your father also assigned all royalties on the book to Lotte Wieland." I had to tell her that.

"Why?"

"Because she was basically his guide to Austria. Your father never went there and he used Lotte Wieland's descriptions of Salzburg and Vienna as his point of view, his research. Also, I believe he wanted to financially look out for her and his son."

"I suppose you've met him, too."

"Yes."

"I think that I had better see what else you have in your bag of horrors," Alexis said with a sharpness I had never heard before.

"That's your choice," I said somehow keeping my voice calm and reasonable. "But, and I know you're angry now, let me ask you a few questions first. Please."

"Go ahead then."

"Do you believe now that your father wrote this book?"

"Yes. That picture doesn't leave much room for question. You've done a very good job, Mickey. Very thorough. You should be proud."

"Do you think," I ignored her insult, "that the publication of this book will in any way harm or damage your father's reputation?"

Alexis took a moment to think it over, then shook her head.

"No."

"Do you object to Lotte Wieland receiving the royalties from this book?"

"In principle."

"But it will not damage you financially."

"No," she admitted.

"Then why do you want to see what's in my briefcase? Your father had an affair. He had an illegitimate son. What's so terrible about that? He didn't hurt or deprive you or your mother, did he?"

"No."

"But you feel betrayed now and I understand that," I said. "Believe me, I know what betrayal feels like."

"You think that Maury betrayed you," she said suddenly.

"We're talking about your father, not mine," I snapped.

"Mickey, your father didn't betray you." She raised her voice.

"You don't know anything about it!" I shouted. "You don't understand a thing! Your father was a decent and honorable man, God damn it! My father is a crook!"

The double doors slammed open and Farrow and Thurston hurried in, both of them wide-eyed with alarm.

"What in heaven's name is going on in here?" Farrow asked.

"Get out," Alexis answered. "Both of you get out."

"Look," I said after Farrow and Thurston had made their hasty retreat, "you have been given a gift, Alexis. Since your parents died, you have been alone in the world. Now you have a brother. He's seventeen, estranged from his mother and he misses his father even more than you do."

"How can you know how much I miss my father?" Alexis asked coldly.

"All right," I backed off instantly. "That was presumptuous and I apologize, but you were twenty-seven years old when your father died. He was ten. I know you went through a lot of pain and grief and I don't mean to diminish that in any way. Believe me. And now you have a very good life. All that Hans Florian has is hurt and anger."

Alexis looked down at the photograph of her father and Lotte Wieland again, then she turned and stared out the window for a long time. How had I become so passionate, so eloquent? This did not involve my life, yet here I was pleading in desperation. Of course, I was trying to protect Alexis, trying to protect everyone involved, but if I failed and the whole provenance was revealed, the only person involved who would remain free from pain was me. So why was I caught up in such a vehement defense? It was, after all, just another provenance.

"Do you have a picture of Hans Florian?" Alexis turned back to me.

"An old one." I reached again into my briefcase.

I handed her the photograph of Oliver Godolphin kicking a ball with the eight- or nine-year-old Hans Florian in the Bois de Boulogne. Alexis studied the photo and I could see the sadness invade her expression. I didn't want this to go any further and I willed Alexis to surrender.

"Oh God, Mickey," she said finally. "This is all true, isn't it?"

"Yes."

"And if I agree to allow the book to be published, to all the terms, what happens to what you have in there?" She pointed at my briefcase.

"I'll burn it all," I promised. "Except for the photographs. I gave my word to Lotte Wieland that I'd return them."

"I know I can trust you not to tell what you know, but what about her?"

I hadn't thought about that, too concerned about my own obligations to Sheffy. What would Lotte Wieland do? She would have the money, so there would be no reason to sell her story to a tabloid. But what about her pain, her sadness? No. Revealing her history would not end that. What did she want, other than the resurrection of Oliver Godolphin and the return of her son? She wanted her book.

"I suppose you can make her guarantee of silence part of the agreement," I said. "But I don't think it's necessary."

"Why did she wait seven years before she sent the manuscript?" Alexis was not going to let go.

"Lotte Wieland never knew what became of the manuscript. She was totally taken by surprise when I told her that it had arrived," I was getting onto dangerous ground here, but there was nothing I could do except tread very lightly. "Apparently, your father sent Pierre Rougemont's bank the manuscript along with the specific instructions."

"Why?"

"I have no idea." I had reached the line that I could not cross.

"What about your provenance? What about all your work?" Alexis asked.

"What about it?" the question threw me.

"If you burn it, then no one will know what you've accomplished," she said. "That's not fair to you, Mickey."

Fair to me? With all this she was thinking it wouldn't be fair to me. Who was this incredible woman? I felt myself starting to choke up and fought it down.

"Alexis," I said quickly. "Nothing in the whole world would give me greater pleasure than to burn my provenance. Believe me. As that last page goes in the flames, I will feel a satisfaction that you can't imagine. I swear to you."

"You are, without doubt, the strangest and sweetest person I have ever met," Alexis smiled. "And I don't understand you at all."

"That's okay. Neither do I."

"Does Fiona?"

"Fiona?" I was aghast. "How does Fiona come into this?"

"After you vanished from Marbella, Maury and I were worried. Baby told us that Fahid had driven you to the airport to catch the London flight, and your father and I talked about you a lot."

"He told you about Fiona?"

"I asked him. You said you still loved her and I was curious."

"Maury doesn't know anything about Fiona." I knew my voice was getting loud.

"He told me they had dinner a few months ago."

"That son of a bitch!" I exploded.

The double doors flew open again, but this time Farrow and Thurston only peered in anxiously.

"The two of you getting on all right?" Thurston asked tentatively.

"Fine," Alexis said. "You might as well come in now. It's all settled."

Farrow and Thurston hurried to their chairs, as Alexis handed me the two photographs, giving each of them a quick, final glance, I slipped the photos into my briefcase and snapped it closed. How could Maury have told Alexis about his dinner with Fiona? What gave him the right? Another betrayal. The final betrayal. I would never speak to him again. Let him die a lonely old man with his forgeries and his deceits. To hell with Maury Maltese.

"I beg your pardon," Farrow was staring at me strangely.

"Mickey," Alexis cautioned at the same time.

"Oh," I forced a smile. "Sorry."

"After reviewing the provenance that Mr. Maltese has prepared, I now agree that my father was indeed the author of the manuscript you have in your possession," Alexis spoke very precisely. "Therefore I withdraw my objection to its publication and consent to the financial arrangements that were requested."

"Oh, that is splendid news," Farrow rejoiced.

"And I want you to know that you owe Mr. Maltese a far greater debt than you realize," Alexis added.

"Jolly well done," Farrow was carried away by the moment.

Alexis got to her feet, prompting the rest of us to stand, said her farewells to Farrow and Thurston, adding if there were any release forms for her to sign they could mail them. Then she walked gracefully to the door before she turned and gestured for me to join her. She took my hand in both of hers and just held it for a moment, looking into my eyes.

"Where is my brother?" she asked softly.

2

I didn't actually burn my confessional provenance and Lotte Wieland's handwritten statement, as my room at the Rembrandt had no fireplace, instead tearing each page into confetti-sized pieces as I sat on the bed with the wastebasket held between my knees. The very last piece, however, I placed in the ashtray and lit with a match, so that, symbolically at least, I kept my promise to Alexis. Still, it was a bit of a letdown.

After Alexis had left the conference room, both Farrow and Thurston pumped my hand in congratulation. Taking advantage of the high spirits, I submitted my expense account. They were a little stunned by the amount, but I explained that good provenance is never cheap and Farrow issued me a check on the spot. With a smile, I thanked them and prepared to leave.

"But where is it?" Farrow asked.

"Where is what?"

"The provenance."

"It's in here." I held up my briefcase.

"Well, aren't you going to give it to us?"

"No," I said.

"But we paid for it," Farrow objected. "It belongs to us."

"As a result of my provenance, Alexis Godolphin has agreed to the publication of the book," I pointed out. "That's what you paid me for."

"Now hold on," Farrow was becoming agitated. "I paid for that document and demand possession of it."

"Demand all you want, Rupert, old chap." I was enjoying this. "I won't give it to you."

"Stephen," Farrow turned to Thurston. "Do something."

"See here, Maltese," Thurston blustered on cue.

"Get stuffed, Thurston," I turned and walked to the door before delivering my final word. "By the way, Rupe, I've never met your wife."

Leaving Farrow to draw his own conclusion, I went down the stairs, pulled on my wet Burberry and plunged out into the rain on Henrietta Street. There were taxis everywhere, but none of them empty, making me think that when it rained in London people just got into cabs and rode around until it stopped. I slogged my way to Leicester Square and caught the tube, which, as I was no longer on expenses, was the thrifty thing to do.

After a quick stop at Barclay's Bank where I deposited my check and instructed them to transfer most of my funds to my New York account, I then purchased an economy ticket for the next morning's flight. I emerged from the South Kensington underground station as drenched as a water rat and just as miserable. I was sick of London rain, fed up with Europe, finished with the Godolphin provenance, furious with my father, hopeless with Alexis and helpless with Fiona. It was, clearly, time for me to go home.

Back at the Rembrandt, after a hot soak and a brisk toweling off, I began to feel better. At least I was out of it, out of the madness and emotional tumult of the past two weeks and I looked forward to immersing myself in some quiet, scholarly pursuit. I would avoid foreign films and exotic restaurants. The Met perhaps by now realized that, while taking an inordinate amount of time with the *faux* Michelangelo sketchbook, I had saved them both money and embarrassment. They might even have a job for me. If not I was confident that I could find something short term. I was, after all, an authority. Someone would always need my expertise.

So, with my confidence bolstered, I set about taking care of the loose ends, first destroying the provenance and Lotte Wieland's statement, then writing to Pierre Rougemont to say that my investigation had been successfully concluded, the authorship of the book no longer in question, Lotte Wieland identified and suggesting that Rougemont contact her in Salzburg as soon as possible, adding that her spirits were low and word from him would be uplifting.

Then I wrote to Lotte, returning the photographs. I told her that they were the final proof and that if she didn't hear from Pierre Rougemont in Geneva very soon that she should call him. I wished her well, then added a postscript informing her that Alexis was going to contact her half-brother, Hans Florian, which I hoped would be helpful. I put no return address on either envelope.

Now came the difficult part. I had to phone Sheffy. Without her help, I might be still stumbling around in my quest for truth, but now I could not reveal the truth to her. It was ironic at best, but at least my motivation, my justification seemed to me more ethical than my lying about the "Donatello" with Baby Habibi. I had no excuse for that.

"Amicus?" My call had been put through instantly.

"It's all over, Sheffy," I said. "Alexis Godolphin realized that the book was written by her father and agreed to let it be published."

"Crikey," she said. "But what about Godolphin's son? What about all the mystery?"

"It was just a misunderstanding. It's all settled now."

"Damn. I thought this was hot." She sounded very disappointed.

"So did I, but it doesn't have the serious potential that we thought."

"No."

"That's show business," I said. "But if I come up with any new stories, you'll be the first person I call. And that's a promise."

"I'll hold you to it."

And that was it. I was off the hook and out of literary provenance forever. The game was far too exciting, and though I had emerged victorious from the arena, I promised myself that I would never enter it again. The art world was where I belonged. From now on I would stay within its boundaries, and with that thought I pulled on my still soggy Burberry and made a dash through the rain to pay my farewell visit to the V & A across Thurloe Place. At last I had it right, not that it really mattered.

Bastianini's Savonarola was waiting for me in Room 46, and again I admired the genius of the work marvelling at the captured expression, the intensity. How could some people say his bust of Lucrezia Donati was a superior work? If anything came close it was Bastianini's terracotta bust of Girolamo Benivieni, the Florentine poet and friend of Savonarola. The Benivieni bust was auctioned in Paris in 1866 and bought by the Louvre for 14,000 Francs, a very large sum considering that they had only paid 6,000 Francs for the Venus di Milo forty-six years earlier. The Benivieni was given a place of honor in the Louvre's collection of Renaissance masterpieces, attributed to everyone from Donatello to Verrocchio, but the fraud was revealed after only one year.

When questioned, Giovanni Bastianini not only admitted that he was the artist, he announced that he had sold it to a dealer for 350 Francs, which he thought was a reasonable amount for the little time it had taken him to make it. The Louvre, of course, then banished the work to a cupboard. Poor Bastianini, a man whose genius, whose gift, cannot be questioned, scrambling for money to survive and seeing only the smallest fraction of what his work was sold for by the dealers.

Art dealers. Who could be more deceitful? And who typified the breed better than my father? How much had Alceo Dossena received for his "Donatello" and how did that amount compare to what Baby Habibi paid Maury? How unfair. How cruel. How dare they?

By 10:00 I had eaten a rubbery room service omelette to avoid the rain and allow my Burberry a chance to dry out. I also repacked my suitcases for the voyage home. I was ready to leave for the airport eleven hours ahead of schedule. It was going to be a long wait. I had discovered Mrs. Bettina Sachs's soporific synopsis and thought that I would use it to put myself to sleep. But I had met the real Lulu von Hofmannsthal and had heard the real story and didn't want the reminder, so I confettied those pages as well, stirring them into the collection already in the wastebasket for additional security. I would remain the only person who knew the truth. Was Lotte Wieland right to worry about giving me this burden? Before I could answer my own question, there was a knock at the door.

Who could it be? Had my father come to London to involve

me in another swindle? Since he had succeeded with his false "Donatello," did he think the time was ripe to strike again? That would fit right in with Maury's style. Well, this time I had a few choice words to say to him and I strode across the room to yank open the door.

Fiona was standing there, raindrops sparkling in her glorious red hair. Fiona. I was speechless. What had happened to "I want you out of my life. Forever!" What had changed? Had Roddy Startle thrown her over? Or had she thrown him over, having suddenly come to her senses and returned to me?

"I tried to ring first, but they said you weren't taking calls," Fiona explained with her wonderful smile, stepping past me and into the room. "So this is where you live. Not very cheerful."

"Fiona," I managed to speak, letting the door close.

"I just ran into Sheffy Eccleston at a party and she told me you were in town," she said, then noticed the suitcases. "Are you leaving?"

"Tomorrow."

"Then thank God I came tonight." Fiona sat on the bed and patted the place beside her. "Come sit down. There's something we have to settle."

Settle? My heart was pounding, my pulse racing. What did this mean? I was afraid to ask. Numbly, I walked across the room and sat next to her. Didn't Fiona know what she was doing to me? Didn't she understand that another rejection would be more than I could bear? I was at the end of my emotional endurance.

"Fiona," I began to warn her, but she silenced me by pressing her fingers to my lips.

"Now you do what I do," Fiona said and then began unbuttoning her blouse. "Come on, Mickey. You're not keeping up."

"What are we doing?" I asked with the last of my breath.

"What do you think we're doing, silly?" Fiona laughed, opening her blouse to reveal that she wasn't wearing a brassiere. "We're going to bed."

The combination of the sight of Fiona's lovely breasts and her words was more than enough to awaken Polyphemus and turn into a lustful, amorous flag pole. Reason fled and there was no time for buttons. An instant later, Fiona and I were on the bed, locked in a naked, passionate embrace, my hands moving over

her body, wanting to feel everything at once, kiss and taste every
part of her flesh, desperate to be inside her, outside her and
envelope her all at the same time.

"Fiona. Fiona. Fiona." I was so ecstatic that I didn't know
whether I was speaking or thinking. "Fiona."

After what seemed to be only an instant, Fiona slipped out of
my embrace, rolled me onto my back, then straddled me, taking
me slowly into her. She placed her palms on my chest and, with
her eyes closed, began to rock slowly back and forth. I reached
up to caress her breasts, but she brushed my hands away, and I
understood that I was simply to lie there. Fiona wanted to make
love to me. This was a precious gift, a bestowal I had never
dreamed of receiving.

"God bless you, Fiona," I whispered.

Maybe she heard me, because the tempo of her rocking
increased and she began to make little cries, which became louder
as she moved faster. There was a line of sweat on her upper lip
and I wanted to lick it away, but Fiona's hands were pressing
down on my chest, her fingernails digging into my skin, as she
drove her body against mine with total concentration, her cries
full voiced and growing louder.

"Two times two is four," I forced myself to think. "Eight
times eight is what?"

It had been a very long time and I couldn't hold back any
longer, my body pumping up at Fiona and at that same moment,
she screamed and we shuddered and collapsed together. I heard
alarmed voices in the corridor, footsteps running up and down
and realized that Fiona's final cry had been misinterpreted by my
neighbors, but I was not about to explain.

"Oh, thank God," Fiona whispered breathlessly.

"Yes." I agreed from my heart.

"You see," Fiona said, "I've been going to Mephistopheles."

"Mephistopheles?" This time I thought Fiona had really gone
too far.

"Mrs. Stopheles," Fiona enunciated. "She's this wonderful
Greek psychic on Black Friars Lane. I've been having this little
sexual problem again, you know, like you and I used to have.
Actually, it only happened in Cap d'Antibes, but I decided to take
care of it at once, so this afternoon I explained the whole

situation to her. And she said that it was all very clear. Let me get up."

Fiona disentangled herself from my arms, rolled across me and got out of bed.

"She could see that I was on the path to happiness." Fiona started getting dressed. "But she could also see that there was this big letter M blocking my way, and so if I wanted to continue on the path to happiness, I had to overcome the M. Well, that was pretty obvious. And we did it, Mickey. I'm so grateful."

"Where are you going?" I asked dully.

"Back to the party." Fiona made it sound so natural.

"Can't you stay a few minutes?"

"I've got a taxi waiting," Fiona said. "Isn't this weather beastly?"

I was the big M, the weather was beastly and she had a taxi waiting. Where was this path to happiness?

"There's something else I have to tell you." Fiona ran a brush through her flame red hair. "Roddy and I are getting married."

NEW YORK CITY

1

I don't know why I had worked so late at the Met that night, but when I left it was well after closing. The night guard had me sign the sheet before, grumbling, he unlocked the door to let me out. It was springtime in New York, the night air soft and balmy, and I descended the steps in a light and carefree fashion, without a worry in the world. At first, the sight of the blue Rolls Royce Silver Cloud parked at the curb signified nothing, then I realized that the man standing alongside was Fahid.

"Good evening, Mr. Maltese," he said, beckoning me and then opening the rear door. "Please get in."

The Rolls' interior lights were off, but I could see that there was someone sitting on the far side. I hadn't heard from my father in eleven months. Was this, at last, going to be his approach? Without hesitating I entered the rear of the Rolls. The man sitting there had a car blanket over his knees. His beard and hair were white, a few old scars visible on his face despite the wide framed dark glasses. Then I noticed his hands, paralyzed permanently closed and heavily scarred. He turned to look at me through the inky lenses and I knew instantly who he was.

"Oliver Godolphin," I said.

"That is no longer my name." His voice was hoarse and raspy, as if there had been some damage to his vocal cords.

"I had a feeling that you weren't dead," I told him.

"Yes, you have been very intuitive," he waited until Fahid got behind the wheel and the Rolls pulled smoothly away. "And I want to thank you, Mr. Maltese, thank you not only for what you

did, but even more for the way you did it. You protected everyone."

"I only did what I thought best," I said.

"I was watching all the time," he said. "And if you had started
to go wrong, I would have pulled you back somehow. That would
have been very dangerous, but fortunately it wasn't necessary.
You were very gentle, very kind with Lotte. That meant a lot to
me. I'm sure you understand."

"Yes."

"And with Alexis, too."

"I tried."

"Oh, you did more than try, Mr. Maltese. I suspect you have a
special feeling, a special attachment for her."

"I do," I said. "I hope you don't mind."

"No," he said. "As long as you never tell her all you know.
That would be too painful, a pain that she does not deserve. Some
things are best left alone."

"Then Lotte Wieland was right about what happened in the
helicopter." I had to know.

"My dear Lotte was right about many things," he smiled. "I
miss her sometimes."

"She misses you constantly," I told him. "Isn't there any way
you can let her know?"

"That I am still alive?" he laughed. "No, that is quite impossible. You are the only one who knows, who will ever know. Is
that too great a burden?"

"I'm used to it."

"Yes. I know you are."

"But let me ask you one thing." I knew I was pushing it.
"After you took the secret copy that Lotte Wieland made and sent
it with your instructions to the Rougemont Bank, why did you
have them wait for seven years before sending the manuscript to
Farrow and Farrow?"

"I'm surprised you ask, as you have already given Alexis the
answer." He looked down at his useless hands, then turned to
look at mine. "I see that you are still wearing your father's
watch."

It was, of course, a dream.

But I had been having these strange dreams since I saw the

photos of Fiona and Roddy's marriage in *People* magazine. Two weeks after I arrived in New York, still trying to water the house plants back to life, I saw a small, boxed story on the front page of *The New York Times* and almost didn't bother to read it because it seemed to be about baseball.

MET'S DIGGER FINDS
LOST NOBEL NOVEL

The last, long lost novel by Nobel Laureate Oliver Godolphin was unearthed recently by Amicus Maltese, the provenance expert for The Metropolitan Museum of Art. Both Farrow & Farrow, Godolphin's longtime British publisher, and Alexis Godolphin, the late author's daughter, have confirmed the discovery, but refused comment, other than to say Amicus Maltese was "instrumental" in bringing the work to light. All attempts to contact the elusive Mr. Maltese have failed, and while the Met acknowledges that he is in New York, they claim to have no way of contacting him. A U.S. publisher will be announced shortly.

I had already changed my phone number, but *The New York Times* story drove me underground. Alexis, I was certain, would think the leak had come from me. At a stationery store, I purchased a rubber stamp and an ink pad, so when the letters came I would simply stamp RETURN TO SENDER on the unopened envelopes and drop them back in the mailbox. I would be unreachable, invisible, until the time that I could face the world again. Once I had wanted fame, but only to impress Fiona and now that, in a minor league way, I had achieved it, not only was it too late, it was humiliating.

The Met on my return, but before *The New York Times* story, was not particularly thrilled to see me, but they assured me that they would let me know if anything came up. I made my rounds of the dealers, but no one was in need of provenance, so I was left with a lot of time on my hands during the long, hot New York summer. I went for walks, sentimental journeys, past the Park Avenue apartment where I grew up, past the jewelry store

on Lexington that once had been Maltese Antiqué Silver, through
Central Park, giving my bruised heart time to heal.

Fiona had treated me very badly, and the memory of our last
love making in my room at the Rembrandt made it even worse. It
was over. Finally finished. We would never be together. I would
probably never see her again. So be it. I had held on to that foolish dream for many years, and, at last, I let it go. The only problem was that I was still in love with her, and whoever said that
love knows no pain doesn't know what he's talking about.

In September, there was a letter from Maury in London and
two from Alexis in Cap d'Antibes. I stamped them both and
dropped them in a mailbox immediately, before my curiosity
could overwhelm my intentions. I tried not to think, but that was
difficult. I had been so involved that it wasn't possible to pretend
that none of it had happened.

Had Alexis found Hans Florian? If the boy could be rescued by
anyone, that person was Alexis with her warm and wonderful
personality, her understanding. Had Pierre Rougemont contacted
Lotte Wieland? Had she received the money? Had her life
improved? Of course I didn't know any of the answers, but the
questions remained. It was either good or bad or both, but no
matter, there was nothing I could do. I had done all I could. I had
finished my part. I had left the stage and the only applause I
received was in my dreams.

In November, I went back to the Met, reasonably certain that
The Times story had been forgotten, only to be told that the
Director was in Europe on a buying trip and that there might be
something for me on his return. I was brought in for an opinion
by a dealer who had a mystery client who was considering selling
his "Viscount Lepic and His Daughters" by Edgar Degas. It was
a beautiful painting of a bearded man in a top hat, smoking a
cigar and carrying what appeared to be a rolled umbrella. His two
identically clad young daughters faced in the opposite direction.
There was a dog behind them and an elegant spectator standing at
the edge of the frame, the use of movement exceptional, captured
on canvas, creating the impression of a frozen instant in time.

Another second and they would all walk away. Degas had
painted it in 1873. But was this the original? It was hard to tell
because when I looked it up, instead of naming the collection or

Museum, it stated "Location unknown." Since the dealer would not reveal the identity of the mystery client, a full provenance would mean going back to France and starting at the beginning and I wasn't up to that. I felt the texture carefully, examined the back of the canvas.

"Have you done the X-rays?" I asked, still scrutinizing.

"Perfect," the dealer said. "Ultra-violet and infra-red."

"Chemical analysis?"

"That's the problem, Mickey." The dealer sighed. "The client won't allow it. Not even an alcohol dab."

"Mmm." I looked carefully at the frame and it passed inspection easily.

"Well, what do you think?"

I stepped back and studied the whole painting again. It was magnificent, truly a work of genius.

"I think it's a beautiful painting," I said.

"Yeah, but is it by Degas?" the dealer asked the basic question.

"I don't know," I told him. "But if it isn't, it's by somebody just as good."

"You want to do the provenance?"

"Save your money."

It wasn't until I had walked for several blocks that I realized what I had said, and at that moment almost turned to run back and agree to dig out the truth. But I had meant it. If the painting had not been done by Degas, it had been done by somebody just as good. My attitude had changed. How? What had happened to me? Had I become a connoisseur overnight? By that one statement, by that one act, I had destroyed my credentials. What had provoked me? Me, the cold master of provenance? I had to have a hot dog.

Emerging from Nathan's with a satisfying burp, I still could not explain to myself what I had done. The "Viscount Lepic and His Daughters" was an exceptional work of art, and if I had been told that it was by Edgar Degas, I wouldn't have questioned it. But now the question had been asked and I had responded that it didn't matter. Then what point was there to provenance? There were many proven famous paintings by many proven famous painters that I didn't care for at all. Yet there were works by

Bastianini and Dossena that I admired enormously knowing that they were false. But they were originals, created in Renaissance style, not copies. That was the difference.

To view Albrecht Dürer's self-portrait alongside Wolfgang Küffner's copy left no room for comparison. The copy was skillful, the original a masterpiece. So, I told myself with some relief, I was not condoning forgery, and since I had not had the opportunity to compare the possibly false "Viscount Lepic and His Daughters" with the theoretical original, I could only judge by what I saw and what I had seen was a beautiful painting. It was the original Degas. It had to be. If it hadn't been, how could the mystery client have refused chemical analysis?

It was certainly not a foolproof system if the forger used the correct materials, which was not difficult for a painting done in 1873. Zinc white was first used in 1780 and ultramarine and cobalt have been basic since 1820, which makes Renaissance fakes generally easy prey for spectroscopy, but not for the Degas.

No, "The Viscount Lepic and His Daughters" was real and knowing it was real, the mystery client hadn't hesitated to refuse chemical analysis, and therefore a provenance would have been a waste of time and money. I had made the right choice. Still, I was bothered by my statement that if the painting had not been done by Degas, it had been done by somebody just as good. Why did I say that?

The telephone was ringing as I entered my small apartment on East 84th Street and, since no one had the number, I knew it couldn't be for me.

"Hello?"

"Good evening. My name is John Wilson and I'm with Intercosmo Polls. We are conducting a survey of television viewing habits, and if you could spare thirty seconds of your time, it would be most useful."

"Could you say that again?"

"Certainly, sir," and he repeated his spiel without changing a word.

I thought I had recognized the voice the first time and now I knew. Billy Lutzenberg, captain of my boarding school football team and ringleader of my tormentors. He had been the one who had organized my humiliation at the hands of Four Finger Sally

Sears. The last I'd heard he was going to Amherst, based on a generous parental donation more than on academic standing. Now he was doing telephone surveys. I couldn't resist.

"Do you know who you've called?" I asked casually.

"No, sir. Our system is totally impartial. We're fully automated and computerized."

"Is there any way you can redial this number?" I wanted to be absolutely certain.

"No, sir, the computer picks the numbers. It's all random choice. Now, if I may proceed with the questionnaire."

"Not yet."

"What?"

"You are in serious trouble, Mr. Lutzenberg."

"What?"

"I can tell from the level of your voice that both your cholesterol and your blood pressure are dangerously high. Have you seen your physician lately?"

"Who is this?"

"The symptoms are at the risk point and I would advise you to abstain from all physical exertion. Sex, of course, is totally out of the question, as there's a good ninety-nine percent chance that the act will cause a massive heart attack. How much do you drink a day?"

"Who the hell is this?" There was panic in the voice.

"If you smoke cigarettes, you must stop immediately," I hung up and waited to see if the phone rang again.

It didn't, but I wouldn't have answered anyway. I knew it was cruel, but a visit to his doctor was a small price to pay for the agony he had caused me. And, coincidentally, it had happened just at this time of year, right before the Thanksgiving Holiday. Thanksgiving. What would I do? Before Mary Frances died, it was always a festive occasion, a big turkey golden brown from the oven, sweet potatoes with marshmallow melted over them, peas and, of course, pumpkin pie.

It was generally a peaceful time, particularly if Maury was away on business and Mighty Mel carved the bird in his place. And there was no anxiety about giving or receiving presents. Elisa and I would argue over the wings and Mary Frances would give us each one, along with a slice of white meat and scold me gently for trying to pick all the giblets out of the stuffing. I don't think we knew what the holiday celebrated or the meal signified. I certainly didn't. With a sigh I put my family memories aside and picked up *The New York Times* to find out what my television viewing habits would be that night. As usual, there weren't any.

My bank statement arrived in the beginning of December and, though I had been spending as little as possible during this period of unemployment, my funds were getting low. I had not earned a penny in six months. What could I do? Other than provenance, I had no skills. Work in a gallery? I didn't think anyone would hire me and, besides, I knew I wouldn't make a very good salesman. I decided to check with the dealers again and, bundling up warmly, went out to walk in the snow. Even if there was no work, it would be good just to talk to people. I had been spending too much time alone. Everyone was very friendly, but no one was in need of provenance and, on impulse, I went back to visit "Viscount Lepic and His Daughters," deciding that if the job were still available, I would take it. Not only was there no job, there was no Degas.

"After all that, the son of a bitch decides he doesn't want to sell it," the dealer complained. "You should've taken the provenance, Mickey. You could have had the advance and not done a lick of work."

"Easy come, easy go." I smiled. "You wouldn't happen to have anything else for me?"

"Sorry, pal. Have you tried the Met? They usually keep you busy."

"The Director's on a buying trip in Europe."

"Oh, yeah," the dealer remembered. "I heard something about that, like he's come up with a big find and now he's in a pissing contest with the Getty and the National."

"A big find?" I had a horrible thought. "Where? I mean, in what country?"

"How the hell would I know? Those guys don't talk to me."

A big find? A "Donatello," perhaps? I would have to warn him. I took a taxi to the Met, rushed up the stairs then hurried to the Director's office.

"Oh, Mickey," the secretary said. "We've been trying to find you for days. There are six Impressionists in the basement on consignment and the Director wanted you there when they uncrate them. He thinks they're good, but he's not buying anything until you check them out. So, you're back on payroll. Merry Christmas."

"Where is he?" I asked. "Can I get him on the phone?"

"Why?"

"I heard a rumor on the street that he was negotiating for a major piece and if it's what I think it is," I had to be circumspect here. "Well, I'd just like to talk to him privately."

"If the Director's negotiating anything, it's the slopes in St. Moritz," she laughed. "He's gone skiing for the holidays. Now will you please get down to the basement so we can get those crates open."

"Right away," I said.

"Nice to have you back."

This was wonderful. The timing couldn't have been better. But if I hadn't gone back to see "Viscount Lepic and His Daughters," I wouldn't have heard about the "big find" and that was what brought me to the Met, a place that I had no previous intention of visiting. Someone was looking out for me, I smiled as I made my way to the basement. Six Impressionists. That could take quite a while.

2

Mirouet, Vautrin & Lambert
Avocats

9, Rue de Balzac
Paris VIIIe, France

Cher Monsieur,
  Suite à la demande de Mlle Alexis Godolphin, nous vous infor-
mons par la présente que tous les efforts de restitution envers Mr.
Danny Speers ont echoué, ce dernier ayant trouvé la mort l'année
dernière, dans un accident de bateau, près de l'île de Malta.
Malheureusement, Mr. Speers était décédé intestat et nous n'avons
réussi à trouver ancun héritier, les régistres indiquant que Mr.
Speers n'était jamais marie et qu'il n'avait aucune progéniture.
  Mlle Godolphin nous pria de vous assurer que tous les efforts
possibles ont été faits.
  Veuillez agréer, cher Monsieur, l'expression de nos sentiments
distingués.

                              (scrawl)

The letter had been addressed to me in care of the Met, post-
marked in December but, due to the usual holiday season postal
pandemonium, it didn't arrive until the first week of January. I
only glanced at the light blue air mail envelope, then shoved it
into my jacket pocket to take home, rubber stamp and return to
sender. But that night curiosity got the best of me and I opened it.
The gist was clear and I was shocked enough to pull out my
French/English dictionary to make a definitive translation.

Dear Sir,
  Following the demand of Miss Alexis Godolphin, we inform you
hereby that all the efforts of restitution toward Mr. Danny Speers
have failed, as he found death last year in a boat accident near the
island of Malta. Unfortunately, Mr. Speers was deceased intestate

and we have not been successful in finding any heir, the records indicating that Mr. Speers was never married and that he had no children.

Miss Godolphin entreats us to assure you that every possible effort was made.

Be pleased to accept, dear sir, the expression of our distinguished sentiments.

I was stunned enough to crack open the bottle of Chivas Regal (my Christmas present from the Met) and pour myself a good three fingers. Danny Speers dead in a boating accident off Malta. My God. Well, I thought after the first finger, if he went down, I was sure he went down swearing. The accident must have happened during my reclusive period or I surely would have read about it in *The New York Times*, as the passing of a man of Danny Speers's eminence, at least in Hollywood, could not have gone unnoted.

"Here's to you, Danny Speers." I raised my glass, then knocked back the last two fingers. "Give them hell, wherever you are."

But what about the children? I suddenly remembered the conversation in the bar at the Grand in Rome. I agreed to leave out the part about Abramowitz to make it easier for the kids. Obviously, there had been a mistake. The lawyers had not done a careful provenance. It was terrible enough that Danny Speers' children should lose their father, but for them to also be deprived of their inheritance was more than I could tolerate even though I was no longer involved in the Godolphin affair.

I rolled a sheet of paper into my typewriter and, giving the Met as my return address, wrote to Mirouet, Vautrin & Lambert to inform them that Danny Speers was actually Danny Abramowitz from the Bronx, New York, and, in fact, that there were children, suggesting politely that they conduct a further investigation in light of this new information, all this, of course, in English. If Maury had insisted that I learn French instead of German, it would have been far more useful. Nevertheless feeling that I had acted responsibly, I allowed myself another finger of Chivas.

Then, a little tipsy, I went out to eat a sausage and onion pizza, which required drinking a couple of Miller Lites. That night I dreamed of Fiona. She was acting in a play and her name was

Strawberry and the rest was very hazy. Walking to the Met the next morning, I tried to find some meaning to the dream, but if there was any significance, it eluded me.

The six Impressionists were a breeze and, since no one pressed me, I milked it, piling up facts, accumulating detail after detail and carefully writing one long and dry provenance report after another. They were all originals, though minor works, and I knew the Met would purchase them. When they finally did, I would be out of my little basement cubicle and back on the street, a prospect that did not appeal to me at all. So I continued to dawdle and no one seemed to mind. All in all, I was at last feeling better in my soul, my wounds healed and my spirits level, never soaring, but never plummeting. My life was a plateau and I desired neither mountains nor valleys. I knew, of course, it wouldn't last.

Once again it was *The New York Times* that made the announcement. *Sakura*, the long lost novel by Oliver Godolphin was about to arrive, the initial printing of five hundred thousand copies already ordered and another two hundred and fifty thousand were being printed. Fortunately, the story of the Godolphin provenance was not mentioned. Even so I held my breath, realizing that I had somehow blocked out the knowledge that there would be an explosion of publicity when the book was published. Would the spotlight swing slightly in my direction? Would there be questions? The week the book came out in the beginning of February, I decided to stay home with the flu.

Sakura, of course, was hailed by the critics and had gone instantly to the top of *The New York Times* best seller list. There appeared to be no further interest in why the novel's publication had been delayed for seven years and I decided it was safe to reappear. I returned to my basement cubicle at the Met, accepted sympathies about my fraudulent illness, and, not able to delay any longer, began writing my provenance report about the last Impressionist. Perhaps the Met would keep me on. If not, I would make my rounds of the dealers, though not as desperately as my finances had recovered somewhat. I could get by until spring and surely something would come up then.

I left the Met just before closing time and was halfway down the stairs, when someone moved suddenly to block my path. A tall, young man, expensively dressed with blow-dried red hair. Red hair?

"Hi, guy," he grinned. "You sure are one tough dude to find."

"Hans Florian?" I gaped at him.

"Here." He handed me one yellow rose wrapped in cellophane with a ribbon around it. "From Alexis. She wants to see you at eight o'clock tonight. We're at the Hotel Pierre, just down Fifth Avenue. You know where it is?"

"Alexis is here?"

"Yo, bro." Hans Florian turned and started down the steps.

"Wait a minute," I called. "How's your mother?"

"Same old bitch," he said over his shoulder and continued away.

For a moment I thought it might have been better if I had left him with Charlie Cunliffe. But why was he in New York, and, more importantly, why was Alexis here and why did she want to see me? It had been five months since I had returned her letters rubber stamped and unopened. Now she had sent me a yellow rose, which did not indicate anger. I wanted to see her, longed to see her, but was I up to it emotionally? My wounds had taken this long to heal and, though Alexis did not inflict them, she certainly could reopen them. I looked down at the single yellow rose. I had no choice.

It was snowing again, so I left my rent controlled home on East 84th Street early and trudged down to Fifth Avenue hoping to flag a cab. Not a chance. So, snow blowing in my face, I trudged the twenty-some blocks to the Pierre and arrived a few minutes late, stamping my feet and shaking the snow from my overcoat before I entered.

"Miss Alexis Godolphin, please." I announced myself at the desk.

"Yes, sir. She's waiting for you in the dining room."

I checked my coat and, wiping the fast melting snow from my hair as best I could, walked down the steps into the Pierre's dining room. There she was. The beautiful Alexis, sitting alone at a corner table, her expression not revealing the slightest hint of anger. Still I approached warily.

"Good evening." I smiled. "You look wonderful."

"Mickey," she leaned forward for a kiss, and I managed to

drip on her in the process. "Sorry, but it's snowing out."

"Sit down and have a drink," she said, then caught me looking at her Evian. "It's all right. You can have a drink."

I ordered a large Chivas with soda, no ice, then looked back at her. She was wearing a dark blue top with a white blouse beneath, the single tear-drop diamond at her throat. I didn't know what to say.

"Hans Florian has certainly grown into a young man." This seemed safe. "He looks very different than the last time I saw him."

"Yes," Alexis said. "It hasn't been easy. I'm afraid that, in order to compensate for the past, I've spoiled him."

"Where is he, by the way?"

"Out at some club. He's very independent."

"I gather he saw his mother."

"Yes. That didn't work out too well. He has so much resentment."

The waiter brought my Chivas and soda. I raised the glass to Alexis.

"Thanks for the yellow rose." I smiled.

"It was the only way I could think of to force you to come," she said. "I don't understand why you ran away, why you refused to see me."

"It's a long story, and now that I'm here it doesn't really matter."

"It matters to me. You come into my life, you make me laugh, you dazzle me, you do something very important and then you disappear before I have a chance to thank you. Why?"

"I had some personal problems, Alexis. It had nothing to do with you."

"I realize," she said gently. "It had to do with Fiona. I know about that."

What did she know? That I was the big M and that Fiona had a taxi waiting while we made love?

"There was a lot of publicity about the wedding," Alexis continued. "I thought about how much that would hurt you."

"I'm totally over that now," I hoped it sounded convincing. "And I've been very busy at the Met. How's Marcel?"

"Marcel and I separated several months ago. I wrote to tell

you. I wrote twice, but my letters were returned."

Fortunately, the waiter arrived to take our orders before I would have to dissemble my way out of that. Alexis ordered a veal paillard with asparagus to start. I followed suit, as usual, accepting the offer of another Chivas.

"Are you seeing anyone?" she asked.

"Not on a regular basis," I said, then felt compelled to tell the truth. "Actually not at all."

"You're so funny, Mickey," she smiled. "I knew that no matter what I ordered, you would have the same thing. Why?"

"I guess I just want what other people have." It was an honest answer.

"And suppose someone wants what you have?" Alexis looked me in the eyes.

What I have? What did I have? A crooked father? A hateful sister? My strange dreams? I didn't know how to respond.

"Who would want that?" I answered lamely.

"Suppose I did?" Alexis asked evenly.

"Wanted what?" I didn't know where she was going with this.

"Never mind," she dismissed my response. "You're making it into a game."

"Alexis," I protested. "You can have anything you want."

Except the truth, I thought. Is that what was holding me back? Lotte Wieland had been right. It was a burden. Why wasn't I telling her amusing stories? What had happened to my eloquence?

"How do you see me?" she asked.

"Extraordinarily beautiful, wonderful to be with and totally unobtainable," I said. "Beyond reach."

"I'm not beyond your reach, Mickey," she said. "Have you tried?"

"No."

"Then try." She held out her hands, palms up.

Slowly, I reached my hands toward hers and nervously took them in mine, our eyes locked, a smile on her lips. My heart began to pound furiously. Hadn't I lived this scene before?

"You see," Alexis said very softly.

The asparagus arrived with my fresh Chivas and soda, forcing our hands to let go, and we ate in silence, Alexis's eyes remaining locked with mine. What was she really saying? Were we talking about love? Did I love her? My emotions were very strong. But this was not the way I felt about Fiona. Another kind of love? I had a flash image of myself living with Alexis in Cap d'Antibes and wearing white linen suits. Could I be charming to her friends? What would I say to them? No, I would make a fool of myself and ruin everything. And what would I do about Maury?

"What about your father?" Alexis asked. "You just said it out loud."

"My thoughts pop out sometimes." I reached for the Chivas.

"I've noticed," she said. "Well, what about him?"

"I really don't want to talk about my father."

"He wants to talk to you. He knows how upset you are."

"You've seen him." I should have guessed.

"Of course," Alexis said easily. "People who care about you worry when you disappear. It's only natural."

"Alexis, don't have anything to do with my father. Please. He does a lot of damage to the people around him."

"Mickey, you are his son and he loves you very much. We've talked about it. He feels terrible that, for some reason, things always end up so badly between you."

The veal paillard was served and, feigning an appetite, I attacked mine voraciously, trying to evade any further discussion, but Alexis was persistent.

"I know you think he betrayed you in Marbella."

"Mmm." I chewed the veal without tasting anything.

"He doesn't know why," she said seriously.

"He's a liar," I said after swallowing, then shoved another piece of veal into my mouth.

"And you always tell the truth?"

"Mmm."

"Did you tell me the truth about my father?" Alexis asked.

I closed my eyes and tried to wish myself back to my apartment on East 84th Street. I had been hiding from *The New York Times,* away from the newspapers in general, out of fear that I would be asked about Oliver Godolphin, about the awful secrets I possessed, but how could I hide now? Was this why Alexis had come to New York? Was our tentative hand clasping only preamble to her question? I opened my eyes and I was still in the Pierre restaurant.

"Did you?" she asked again.

"You know I did," I told her.

"But not everything."

"No."

"Well," Alexis seemed very determined, "the secret about Lotte Wieland is secret no more. The book has been published and that means it's all over. So now you can tell me the rest of it."

"I destroyed the provenance." I tried to slide past it.

"But you know what was in it. And I want you to tell me."

"I can't," I said. "I just can't do that."

"Why?"

"I promised."

"Who?"

This was not going to be easily answered. I ran the options quickly in my head, trying to find a reasonable alternative, but none of them were acceptable.

"Your father," I said and saw Alexis pale. "In a dream."

"My God." Alexis closed her eyes, putting her fork down blindly, then raising her hand to her face.

"I'm sorry," I said quickly. "I shouldn't have told you."

She didn't move and I didn't know if she had heard me, her eyes remaining shut, her breathing fast and shallow. I thought she was going to faint and readied myself to leap forward to catch her. Why did this have to happen in a restaurant? I glanced around quickly, but no one else seemed to have noticed the drama at our table.

"Alexis?" I whispered. "Are you all right?"

"No," she replied, then lowered her hand, her eyes opening. "If that was meant as a joke."

"It wasn't," I said before she could finish.

"You dream about my father?"

"Only once."

"And in your dream you promised him that you would never tell me." Her eyes penetrated mine.

"That's what he wanted." I didn't blink.

"Was my mother in your dream?"

"No. Just your father and Fahid."

"Fahid?" Alexis leaned back. "You dreamt my father was in Marbella?"

"No. It was here in New York. Fahid was driving Baby's Rolls," I said. "I know that doesn't make a lot of sense, but dreams are hard to explain. It was very real, though."

"I can't believe this." Alexis looked away. "You dream about my father, whom you have never met and who has been dead for almost eight years, and you promise him that you won't tell me what you know. Don't you think that's a little strange?"

"Yes," I answered when Alexis looked back at me.

"But you are going to keep the promise, this dream promise."

"I have to."

"Yes, I should have expected that." She picked up her fork, then put it down again. "I'm afraid I have lost my appetite."

"I'm sorry I upset you." That sounded like a feeble apology, but I didn't know what else to say. "I wish I was better at this."

"Better?" Alexis almost laughed. "Mickey, if you were any better, I couldn't stand it. You prove my father wrote the book, you manage to persuade me to allow its publication without showing me one piece of evidence and now you close it all off by making a promise in a dream. *Bon Dieu!!*"

I wasn't sure if that was a compliment or a criticism, but in either case it didn't seem to require a response, so I just sat there silently while Alexis called for the check and signed it. At her gesture, we got up from the table and walked out of the restaurant without exchanging another word. Somehow the moment of our holding hands tenderly seemed like it had happened a long time ago, a moment that would never be recaptured. I felt my wounds begin to throb.

"Where are you going?" Alexis asked when I went to retrieve my coat. "I want you to come up to the suite. I have something to show you."

She turned and walked toward the elevators and, obediently, I followed. We ascended in silence, standing several feet apart, both of us watching the floor numbers change, strangers in an elevator. I had the uncomfortable feeling that I had bungled everything and was now about to pay the price and the even worse feeling that whatever fate awaited me I probably deserved. Did other people lead such emotionally tangled lives, or was I the only one? How had the dinner conversation gone so wrong? I had tried so hard to protect Alexis and now I was the one who had hurt her. It was like a curse. The Maltese curse. Maybe the horrible Sally Morgan was right after all.

The elevator door opened and I stayed a half step behind Alexis as we walked down the corridor, then waited as she unlocked her door. The suite was enormous, the reflection in the mirror over the fireplace making it seem even larger. I closed the door, made a small advance forward, then just stood there, waiting for the worst. Alexis walked across the room and took a sheet of paper from the pile on the desk before she turned to look at me.

"Sit down, Mickey," she said.

I sat on the edge of the couch, my leg muscles tensed to leap when the ground fell away. Alexis approached and sat next to me, so close that I could smell her perfume, making me instantly remember her handkerchief when I disgraced myself on the Highway of Death. My emotional balance was vibrating and I knew that I had come out of seclusion prematurely. One nudge from Alexis now and I would go to pieces.

"Here." She handed me the sheet of paper. "I thought you should see this."

Zelberg, Bamberg & O'Casey
Attorneys at Law
1 Avenue of the Stars
Century City, California 90067

Louis Lambert, Esq.
Mirouet, Vautrin & Lambert
9, Rue de Balzac
Paris VIIIe, France

Dear Lou,

I've finally run the Speers/Abramowitz allegation to the ground and it's a pretty strange story. The late Danny Speers was born in New York City at St. Vincent's Hospital and his full name at birth was Daniel Quentin Speers, Jr., as you can see from the enclosed photocopy of his birth certificate. The Abramowitz fabrication, however, appears to have some basis in fact, as when Speers came to Hollywood, he began telling people that he was Jewish and had changed his name, in the hope that a different ethnic background would help him get ahead in the business. I have heard of many, and personally know quite a few Jews who have "Americanized" their names for a variety of reasons, but this is the first time I've ever heard the flip side. In any event, our conclusion remains unchanged. The late Danny Speers was never married, had no heirs and died intestate.

I hope this settles the question once and for all, but if there is anything else you require, please do not hesitate to contact me.

                    Best regards,
                    (signed) Zippy
                    Alan D. Zelberg

P.S. Pretending to be Jewish? The guys in the office can't believe it.

I was totally confused. Whatever Danny Speers may have pretended in Hollywood was one thing, but why did he lie to me? Didn't anyone tell the truth? Was the whole world based on falsehood? Was life itself a forgery? A lawyer named Zippy Zelberg on Avenue of the Stars? None of this could be real. But this was the first signature I had been able to decipher in ages.

"Satisfied?" Alexis asked.

I nodded numbly.

"When you wrote to my lawyers, you thought you were doing the right thing."

I nodded again.

"You always try to do the right thing, don't you, Mickey?"

Another nod.

"It's not easy, is it?" Alexis said gently.

"I believed Danny Speers and now I feel like a fool."

"Why?"

"Provenance means discovering the truth, the origin, where something came from, and Danny Speers didn't come from the Bronx. I failed."

"Is that so important? That one small mistake? Does it change anything?" Alexis moved even closer.

"No," I admitted.

"Then just kiss me, Mickey," she said.

I did and then a few minutes later, the kiss somehow unbroken, we were in bed. Everything was in slow motion, everything was tender and gentle, everything perfect and unhurried. There was no taxi waiting and the big M was not only on the path to happiness, he was inside it as well.

"You'll stay the night?" Alexis murmured as, still embracing, we finally drifted into sleep.

The next morning was cold and crisp and clear, the snow still white, as I floated up Fifth Avenue, suffering from an excess of happiness. Alexis had still been asleep after I had quietly showered and dressed, but I couldn't leave without kissing her. She smiled without opening her eyes and only responded with a soft, sweet sound when I whispered that I would call her later.

"You'll stay the night?" I remembered her somnolent words. A thousand nights. A lifetime of nights. Why had Alexis taken me to bed? What did she see in me? She had everything and I had nothing. Why would she choose me? Was last night, perhaps, just an act of gratitude?

I slipped on the icy pavement and, both feet flying out, landed on my back, my head thumping the sidewalk painfully. The other pedestrians kindly walked around me instead of stepping on me and I finally managed to pull myself back to my feet to continue uptown. Actually I felt better, the fall knocking away my negative thoughts and punishing me with a swelling bump on the back of my head for even having them.

I scrounged up some aspirin, cadged a cup of coffee and went to my basement cubicle to work on my last Impressionist. By 11:30, I had accomplished nothing and could wait no longer. I picked up the phone and dialed the Pierre.

"Miss Alexis Godolphin, please," I requested.

"I'm sorry, sir, but Miss Godolphin has just checked out."

"What? Where did she go?" I demanded.

"Let me connect you to the front desk."

This had to be a mistake. After last night she wouldn't have just left without saying anything. But I had disappeared from both Marbella and London in similar fashion. Could this be retribution? No, Alexis was not a vengeful person.

"Front desk."

"Yes, I'm calling Miss Alexis Godolphin, and the operator said she checked out." I sounded a little panicky.

"That's right, sir."

"Where did she go?" I forced myself to be rational. "Listen, my name is Mickey Maltese. Did Miss Godolphin leave a message for me?"

"Hold on, sir. I'll check."

If she was really gone, then there had to be a message. Where would she go? Why would she go?

"Mr. Maltese?"

"Yes?"

"Would you please telephone Miss Godolphin at Kennedy Airport in the British Airways Concorde Lounge between one and one fifteen."

The Concorde? Alexis was on her way to London. What about Hans Florian? I knew that something terrible had happened. There was an hour and a half before I could call and sitting in my cubicle would not make the time pass faster. I rubbed my face and felt the stubble. I would go home and shave.

By 1:00, I had shaved, changed my shirt and tie, washed and dried the few cups and dishes in the sink, watered the plants and generally tidied up my East 84th Street nest. I composed myself, picked up the telephone and dialed having also gotten the number from Information in the interim.

"Good afternoon, Concorde Lounge," a cheerful British voice answered.

"I'd like to speak with one of your passengers, please. Miss Alexis Godolphin."

"Just a moment."

Suppose she wasn't there? I would call back. The traffic to Kennedy was probably jammed by last night's snow and the icy roads. Suppose she wasn't on the passenger list?

"Mickey?" I wilted with relief at the sound of Alexis's voice.

"Hi. I got your message at the hotel. What's up?" Talk about casual.

"I was so worried that you'd be worried, but there was nothing I could do," Alexis said. "There was a problem with Hans Florian. He got himself into serious trouble last night, so I have to get him out of the country."

"What did he do?"

"I can't talk about it now, but call me at home tomorrow."

"All right."

"I'll think of you. And, Mickey," she lowered her voice, "thank you for last night."

It sounded as if she blew a kiss into the telephone before she hung up, but I wasn't sure. Thank me for last night? No, Alexis, thank you for everything and forgive me for bringing Hans Florian into your life. She had to get him out of the country, and herself away from me at the same time. What had he done? Forgive me, Charlie Cunliffe.

I was back at the Met before 2:00 and headed down to the basement in much better shape then when I left. Alexis and I were all right, despite whatever problem Hans Florian had created, and that meant I was all right. I would finish the last Impressionist, splurge on a plane ticket to Nice and take a week or so to work out some definition of the relationship. What, I wondered, did Alexis have in mind?

"Ah, Mickey." The Director was at the bottom of the stairs. "I've been meaning to tell you how much I've enjoyed your work on the five Impressionists. Can't wait for the last one."

"I hope to finish it today." I knew I would.

"Good, good," the Director walked with me. "There's something else I've been meaning to say to you. I reacted badly on that Michelangelo business. You were absolutely right, of course, and you saved us a lot of money and enormous embarrassment. So I want you to know that from now on you have a home here at the Met."

"Thank you, sir." I was amazed.

"Here," the Director took my arm and steered me through a doorway. "Let me show you our latest acquisition. Quite a coup."

It was, of course, the "Donatello." I fainted.

LONDON

1

The Concorde nosed down through the dark gray clouds on its descent into Heathrow. It was May and, naturally, it was raining. The trip had taken just over three and a half hours, which was not only amazingly fast, but also very fortunate, as when I took my aisle seat I discovered that my traveling companion was John Lipscomb, Fiona's third husband.

"Mickey Maltese?" It had taken him a few seconds to place me.

"Hello, John," I smiled politely. "How's the oil business?"

"Not like it used to be in the old days," he said. "Still, I can't complain. How's Fiona?"

"I haven't seen her in ages," I said. It was, after all, almost a year ago. "She's married again, you know."

"Yes, to that singer fellow. I'm surprised that stopped you. It certainly didn't when she was married to me."

"I'm sorry if I caused you any problems," I was contrite.

"All for the best." He waved my apology away. "Still in the art field? Weren't you working for some museum in New York?"

"Until recently," I answered, recently being about two weeks ago.

When I had come to on the basement floor of the Met, someone had elevated my feet and placed a cold cloth on my forehead. The Director was gone, but the "Donatello" Madonna was still there. What was I going to do? I didn't have time to consider because the paramedics arrived to check my vital signs and when I was approved, two Met assistants, at the Director's personal request, drove me home with the instructions that I was not to return until I was totally recovered. The last Impressionist could wait and, clearly, I had been working too hard. I thanked them weakly and crawled up into the security of my apartment after assuring them of my speedy recovery.

What recovery? The Director had just given me a home at the Met and I could not go home again. Was the "Donatello" there on consignment or had it been paid for? The Director wouldn't buy the six Impressionists until I had done my provenance, how could he have bought the "Donatello" without one? And for how much? He had used the word acquisition and that implied the worst.

Now, if I exposed the piece as a Dossena, what would happen? And if the Director asked me for an after-the-fact review of whatever provenance Maury had concocted, what would I say? Could I admit that I had already seen the statue at Baby Habibi's ranch? No, because I had, with all my disclaimers, attributed the work to Donatello at the time. Besides, I would have to explain what I was doing in Marbella and that would open up the whole Godolphin story again. I was trapped.

Despite the early hour, I opened the bottle of Chivas and didn't bother with a glass. My father had done this to me. Any meticulous research would trace the work back to him. He was the one who had arranged for the Madonna to be shipped out of Italy in a coffin supposedly carrying a deceased Savelli. There would be records, the story not that difficult to discover and the fraud destined to be revealed. If I, independent of my involvement, had been given the provenance assignment, I would have been able to expose the swindle in a few weeks.

Had Baby Habibi been the open seller or had he remained anonymous? And why would he have gotten involved? Not for the money, the man had millions. And why sell it to the Met? My father knew of my connection. He had even arranged it. Was this a plot? I took another swig of the Chivas.

What were my options? I could resign because of ill health and go to the South of France. The Director would hire someone else, and if that person started examining the "Donatello's" history, where would that lead? To Baby, to Maury and to me. If put on the witness stand and asked if I had identified the Madonna as being by Donatello, I would have to answer, "Yes." My career would be ruined, my reputation dishonored. Then someone would dig up the story in *The New York Times* and the whole Godolphin provenance would be questioned, Lotte Wieland tracked down and ruthlessly interrogated until the unspeakable truth was revealed. What would that do to Alexis? More Chivas.

No. I would have to stay. I would have to keep anyone from prying into the "Donatello's" provenance and then just hope that, after it was put on display, no one would bother to check. That would entail a lot of research and I doubted that anyone would want to take the time. The Met would have its moment of glory, the other museums would seethe with jealousy, and it would all blow over, become forgotten just like the Godolphin provenance. Besides, it was truly a beautiful work of art and, in the end, that's what counted. Another sip.

My plan to fly to Nice for a week or so would have to wait. The definition of Alexis and my relationship would have to be postponed. That was painful, but it was a sacrifice that had to be made for the sake of the future. I would explain that I was involved in some very important work, without going into detail, and Alexis would understand. Perhaps we could do some definition on the telephone? All was not lost. I raised the bottle to toast the happy thought and guzzled.

I woke up on the floor at 9:00 that night, my head splitting and the Chivas bottle empty. But I was still at the Met on time the next morning, even more determined to watchdog the "Donatello" and prevent disaster. I finished the last Impressionist without much difficulty, sent it up to the Director and waited. Nothing happened.

It wasn't until I left the Met at closing that I remembered that I had forgotten to call Alexis, but when I phoned her the next morning, she didn't seem at all irritated. Hans Florian, she told me, had bought some cocaine at a disco and had become involved with some unwholesome people, whom he had invited over to the Pierre. There had been some unpleasantness with the management, who had called the police. Fortunately no drugs were found, but Hans Florian had acted rudely and announced that he was intending to disco again, so Alexis decided it was time to go.

She was very understanding about how the importance of my

immediate work prevented me from coming to France. I had no choice but to be equally understanding about her inability to come to New York and leave Hans Florian on his own. There was no definition and no talk of the future. The conversation ended on a friendly note, but nothing more than that, leaving me both relieved and disappointed.

Weeks went by and I sat in my cubicle every day with nothing to do except guard the "Donatello" with my presence while the preparation for its unveiling was underway. Nobody came to pry and no one asked any questions. I called Alexis regularly and her friendly tone continued, at least in terms of our relationship. She was quite concerned about Hans Florian, who had now wrecked her car and whose behavior was becoming more and more hostile. When I suggested that she relieve herself of the responsibility, as Hans Florian had already celebrated his eighteenth birthday, Alexis simply said that she couldn't. There was no further mention of my visiting her or her visiting me. The love affair was on hold, which clearly made it easier for both of us under the circumstances.

April 10th was the date announced for the "Donatello" to make its first public appearance and the news stories had not provoked any suspicious inquiries, so when April arrived, I began breathing easier. A few days later, the Director's secretary came down to my cubicle with a thick folder and said that the Director had asked me to look over the contents for form's sake, adding that she was supposed to have done this last week and requesting me not to mention the delay. It was a photocopy of the "Donatello" provenance and it was just as Maury had described it, substituting some Italian name for his own as the crafty dealer, filled with specific details of the Savelli family history and their financial reasons for disposing of this ancient possession in such an unusual fashion.

There were the usual documents and notarized statements, all in all, at least to an eye less jaundiced than my own, pretty convincing. Besides who would be looking at this? The Met didn't exactly hand out provenance reports at the door. No one would examine it unless there was a problem, and if there was a problem, it would be too late. I waited until April 9th, then sent the folder back to the Director with the comment that it looked good to me.

The "Donatello" was hailed by the critics and the Met praised for its achievement, crowds of culturally appreciative New Yorkers came to comment knowingly, and in less than three weeks, the fraud was exposed. Alceo Dossena, feeling an understandable pride about his work, had the habit of photographing some of them in his studio at Via Margutta 54 before selling them, and unfortunately, the "Donatello" was no exception. Some clever curator in Cleveland had managed to acquire a copy and had been waiting as patiently as a cobra for the work to emerge. The rivalry between museums being as vicious as it is, there would have been less satisfaction in denouncing the false Donatello immediately, so the Cleveland curator waited for the enthusiasm to peak before striking.

The results were, of course, disastrous, the Met the laughing stock of the art world, the board livid, the newspapers refusing to let the story die, and I knew that heads would roll. Dossena's Madonna in the style of Donatello was returned to the obscurity of the basement, the Director resigned, and I was fired, an event made public in a small and inaccurate story in *The New York Times* headlined "Met's Digger Strikes Out," and which attributed the faulty provenance to my hand. It was an awful week, made even worse by Alexis's news that Hans Florian had run away, and that she was going off in search of him.

I holed up on East 84th Street and waited anxiously for the Godolphin connection to be made. But the story faded overnight and no one noticed, my relief far greater than the hurt of my disgrace. My career was over, even though I had nothing to do with the "Donatello" provenance, other than maintain my silence. Still, I had been unprofessional and I could justify no resentment. But what would I do for the rest of my life?

A week later Alexis phoned. She had traced Hans Florian to Aubagne, just outside Marseilles, where he had enlisted in the Foreign Legion and which meant that he would be gone for five years. Alexis seemed upset, feeling that she had failed to salvage him, but I was enormously relieved and explained to her that, in effect, it was destined. Hans Florian was simply following in his father's footsteps and what path could be more natural?

And now, since my obligations to the Met had been terminated,

I was free to visit her. Alexis agreed and said she would meet me in London the following Thursday, adding that I should take the early Concorde that morning which would get me into London in time to meet her in the Ritz bar at 8:30.

The Concorde was very convenient, but it was still a little out of my price range. Alexis said no, I was her guest and she was sending me the ticket. There would be no argument. What was my address? Without thinking, I gave her East 84th Street, the same address from which her letters had been returned. If Alexis made the connection, she made no comment, saying only that there was something very important that she could only tell me in person. Another friendly conversation.

Alexis, with her perfect timing, was rescuing me from my ignominy in New York. Perhaps I could find work in London, though I was sure that news of the "Donatello" scandal had already traveled across the Atlantic, but the British were more forgiving about such peccadillos as they had experienced so many of them.

"You're a pleasure to travel with, Maltese," John Lipscomb said as the Concorde rolled smoothly to a stop. "Can't stand people who chatter all the time."

"Yes, I know what you mean." He should have heard what had been going on in my head.

"Car picking you up?"

"No. I'll just take a taxi."

"Nonsense. I'll give you a lift. Where are you staying?"

"At the Athenaeum on Piccadilly." I couldn't face going back to the Rembrandt.

"I'm at the Savoy," he said. "It's right on the way. The Athenaeum, eh? I always thought that was more for people in the film business. Thinking of changing your line of work?"

"The thought has crossed my mind," I admitted.

"Well, best to be careful then. I hear they're a tricky bunch."

I was in my room at the Athenaeum at ten past seven, exactly one hour since the Concorde had arrived, which was amazingly fast considering that I had left New York just under five hours earlier. This was the only way to fly, as long as someone else was paying for it, but next time, providing there was a next time, I hoped it wouldn't be Alexis.

Could I look her in the eye and say, "I love you"? I didn't know. Certainly my feelings for her were very strong, but was it love? The friendly tone of our phone conversations had me confused. What was she going to tell me? I took a hot bath. By the time I pulled myself out of the tub and wrapped myself in one of the Athenaeum's huge towels it was already 8:00. I would have to hurry. I put on my best Brooks Brothers shirt, my Yale tie and my Paul Stuart blazer and was on my way to the door when the phone rang. It had to be Alexis. No one else knew I was in town. Perhaps she was running a little late.

"Hello?"

"Mickey, this is simply incredible. Mrs. Stopheles told me that I would see you very soon and then I ran into John at the Savoy and he told me you were at the Athenaeum." Fiona made it all sound like one sentence. "Listen, darling, we have to talk. I mean this is terribly important. You know I left Roddy."

"No," I said.

"Oh God, yes. It turned out that he was basically a homosexual. There were always these boys around and I can't believe it took me so long to find out."

"Fiona, I'm sorry, but I have to go now."

"Where?"

"I'm meeting Alexis Godolphin at the Ritz bar and I'm already late."

"Get rid of it."

"What?"

"I said get rid of it and I'll meet you there. I have to see you."

"Fiona, I can't. I'll see you tomorrow."

"It can't wait till tomorrow. Oh God, Mickey, I've been such an awful bitch and you've always been so patient, waiting and waiting for me to come to my senses. When I think how dreadfully I've behaved it makes me cry. I'm crying right now. Can you hear it?"

"No," I croaked.

"Well, I am. Really."

"Don't cry, Fiona."

"But I have to. I've hurt you so much, Mickey. Can you ever forgive me?"

Fiona asking forgiveness? And why this sudden confession? I

felt my wounds tearing open, this time never to heal again. Tread lightly, my dear, you're standing on my heart.

"Fiona, please be careful," I began.

"Ever so careful," she interrupted. "Always, darling. Always and forever. You're not the big M, Mickey. The big M is Sally Morgan. You are the path to happiness. Don't you understand? That's the way it was always meant to be. I love you, Mickey. I've always loved you. It was just a silly misunderstanding. Do you love me? Do you?"

"Yes, Fiona." There was no way to deny the fact. "I love you."

"Then it's settled. Get rid of Alexis whoever she is and I'll meet you at the Ritz."

Click.

I was shaking, my heart beating like a snare drum. Sally Morgan was the big M and I was the path to happiness. And Fiona said she loved me. But she also said she was coming to the Ritz. What would I do with Alexis? I ran out of the room, waited frantically for the elevator, then rushed through the lobby onto the street. It was still raining and I had no time to search for a taxi, so I raced down Piccadilly at full speed toward the Ritz. Panting and drenched I rushed into the bar. Alexis was sitting there. With Maury.

"Alexis, we have to go." I was breathless.

"Sit down, Mickey and be calm. Your father is here at my request. What I have to say concerns him as well."

"You don't understand. We have to go. Now." I made it sound as urgent as I could.

"Relax, Amigo," my father said. "This is something we both have to hear. If you want me to leave afterwards, I'll go. So just sit down."

"It's not that. It's worse than that," I tried to explain.

"Mickey, please sit down," Alexis said firmly.

I sat down. The whole world was about to come to an end.

"I'm pregnant," Alexis said. "And I am going to have this child. Your child, Mickey, and your grandchild, Maury."

"Congratulations," my father said.

"Can we go now?" I asked Alexis

"I'm not finished." Alexis gave me a forgiving smile. "I know this comes as a shock to you, but I want you to understand that this does not put you under any obligation. I choose to be a single parent and the amount of involvement that you have with our child is totally up to you. I want to make that very clear."

"You're going to have a baby?" I suddenly realized what she was talking about. "Oh, my God. That's wonderful."

I got up to walk around the table to kiss Alexis and Fiona chose that moment to arrive and I kissed her instead.

"Darling," she said to me, then turned to kiss my father on the cheek. "Maury, it's so good to see you. And you must be Alexis. I'm Fiona. Has Mickey told you the good news?"

"He hasn't had the chance yet," Alexis told her pleasantly.

"Good, because I wanted to be here," Fiona smiled at everyone. "Mickey and I are getting married."

2

"For the last time, will you stop laughing," I shouted angrily.

"I'm trying, Amigo. I swear I'm trying," Maury let loose another gale.

The rain had diminished to a light drizzle and we were walking back down Piccadilly. Alexis had suggested that the two of us leave for a while so that she and Fiona could talk, a suggestion I welcomed instantly. My father had made it out of the Ritz before he surrendered to his laughter.

I didn't think there was anything to laugh about and his amusement only aggravated me. Alexis had announced that she was going to have my child and Fiona had announced that she was going to marry me, and I was given both these pieces of information as a total surprise. What was I, just a shuttlecock to be banged back and forth across the net? Didn't I have some say in these matters? And here I was walking with my father who was laughing away as if this were some joke.

"You set me up, you son of a bitch," I said.

"Amigo, I had no idea that was going to happen tonight. How could I?"

"At the Met, you bastard. You set me up with your fake Donatello at the Met."

"Yes," Maury said. "As a matter of fact, I did. I had to do something to blow you out of that rut. What were you going to do, spend the rest of your life working for those fools, taking their little handouts, being grateful for their crumbs? No, Amigo, it's time that you and I talked about real business."

"Monkey business."

"I need you. I've been training you all your life for this, and together we will be the best."

"You have another Dossena you want me to sell?"

"That Madonna is a beautiful work of art, isn't it?" My father turned to look at me.

"Yes, it is," I had to agree. "Why didn't Baby keep it?"

"I guess he just wanted to double his money," Maury shrugged. "That pompous idiot from the Met couldn't write the check fast enough."

"Don't tell me you weren't in on the sale."

"No. I only made sure that someone whispered to the Director where the Donatello was, using a dealer in Madrid, of course. Baby's name never came into it. What did you think of the provenance?"

"Only fair," I said.

"I know you could have done a better job," Maury said amicably. "God knows you've had the practice."

How had my father managed to ruin my career? What had he done? The answer was obvious.

"You sent the photograph to Cleveland."

"I arranged it," Maury smiled. "Look, Amigo, when Baby showed you the Madonna at the ranch, you knew it was a Dossena, didn't you?"

"Yes."

"But you said it was a Donatello. Why?"

"I don't know. For you, I guess."

"That's when I knew you were ready. I've been waiting a long time. Then you had another chance to expose it at the Met, and you didn't."

"No."

"There you have it, Amigo." My father held out his hand and, without thinking, I took it. "Welcome to the family business."

"Wait a minute," I yanked my hand away. "I haven't agreed."

"What else are you going to do? After all, you've got a family to support. Two, in fact." My father started laughing again.

Art dealers were the people I despised most. Could I become one? I certainly knew enough, but did I have the raw courage to do what Maury did? No, at the crucial moment I would fluster and radiate guilt. What did my father actually want me to do? Write false provenances for his forgeries? I certainly could do that, though not with a clear conscience, and I had to earn a living. I could be the sorcerer's apprentice. Suddenly, that didn't seem like a bad idea.

"Come on," my father took my arm when we reached the front of the Athenaeum. "I'll buy you a drink."

We went into the bar and the friendly barman took our orders with enthusiasm. Maury nibbled on the nuts until the arrival of the drinks, mine a large vodka and his a Knockando malt whiskey. We touched glasses and sipped.

"Well, Amigo, what are you going to do with these two women?"

"What can I do?"

"How do you feel about them?"

"Alexis is the most spectacular person I've ever met in my life," I said, then sighed. "She's beautiful, warm, intelligent, funny and tender. And Fiona is Fiona."

"And you're still in love with her?" my father was serious.

"I can't help it," I admitted. "I never could. Not from the first moment I saw her. It just happened."

"Then marry her, son. If that's what's meant to be."

"But Alexis's going to have my child."

"Amicus, I didn't know you were in town." Sheffy strode toward our table. I was pleased to see that her face had fully recovered from the mugging.

"Sheffy." I kissed her cheek. "I'd like you to meet my father. Amour Maltese. Sheffy Eccleston."

"Amour and Amicus? Crikey, that's wonderful," she laughed.

"Please join us," my father said and we all sat down.

"I'm his agent," Sheffy told my father. "We were onto something that had very serious potential last year, but it didn't pan out."

"An agent." Maury leaned toward her. "That must be very interesting work."

A half an hour later, Maury and Sheffy were still talking and I knew it was time to return to face the music at the Ritz. But when I interrupted Maury to tell him, he replied that this was one meeting I would have to handle on my own. He was staying at the St. James Club and I could reach him there tomorrow. Walking back to the Ritz, I realized that my father was right. This was my problem, not his, and the only thing he could do was be a witness, which would only add pressure to the situation. I would deal with it alone. Deal with what? Alexis's reaction to my marrying Fiona? Alexis didn't want to marry me or she wouldn't have said that she chose to be a single parent. Fiona's reaction to Alexis having my child? That might be a problem, but the conception had occurred while she was still married to Roddy. Roddy a homosexual? That was startling news. When I entered the Ritz bar, Fiona and Alexis were gone.

"The ladies have gone into the restaurant, sir," the waiter said. "They've asked that you join them there."

Things must be going well. I walked down the wide corridor and looked cautiously into the restaurant, and there were Fiona and Alexis in animated conversation, punctuated with bits of laughter. What was so funny? Maury and Sheffy were engrossed at the Anthenaeum, and here were Fiona and Alexis having a grand time at the Ritz. What about me? I walked over to the table.

"Maury sends his regrets." I smiled.

"Sit here, darling," Fiona indicated the chair alongside hers. "Alexis was just telling me about the wonderful work you did in connection with her father's last book. I read it as soon as it came out. I couldn't put it down. It was simply breathtaking. And so romantic."

I nodded. What about the baby?

"We're having the grilled sole," Alexis said. "If you want to eat, you'd better order soon."

"Yes," I signaled for a waiter and ordered a medium rare steak and a large vodka, knowing I would need the strength.

"And," Fiona went sailing on, "Alexis told me that you took her out to dinner at the Eden Roc. Roddy and I were there probably just a few days later. Isn't that a coincidence?"

"Mmm," I agreed.

I had anticipated an emotional scene, but here was Fiona chattering away as if nothing unusual had happened. My entire life had just been changed and everyone was taking it a little too casually. My father admitting that he had manipulated my disgrace at the Met, Alexis announcing her pregnancy and Fiona announcing that I was getting married, and none of them realizing what I had been going through. There was something wrong. But what? I was basically getting it all, everything I wanted, so what was the problem? The waiter brought my large vodka and as I raised the glass, I caught Alexis's eye and she winked. Winked? What did that mean? I took a hearty belt of vodka.

"And so we thought that since you were going to be Daddy," Fiona was talking to me, "I would have to be something and Alexis suggested Auntie. Auntie Fiona. I like that. What do you think, darling?"

That was it? Alexis had told her about the baby and all Fiona was concerned about was her title? How could it be this easy? Daddy and Auntie Fiona?

"Mickey, are you in there?" Fiona nudged me.

"I think it's perfect," I said and started to laugh.

After dinner there were hugs and kisses. Alexis was flying to Nice in the morning, but she promised she would call regularly. Fiona and I took a taxi to the Athenaeum and she waited while I collected my suitcase and checked out, assuring them that there had been no problem, and then the taxi took us home to Chester Square. Fiona kept chattering as she unpacked my suitcase, not approving of my New York wardrobe, and then we went to bed and made love slowly and familiarly, as if we had been doing this for years. Tomorrow, I thought sleepily, we would have to go to the local for a drink.

3

"Did you ever see him do it?" The rain had finally stopped and Maury and I were walking along the Victoria Embankment, idly watching the traffic on the river.

"Did I ever see who do what?" my father glanced at me.

"Mighty Mel. Did you ever see your father bend a silver coin with his fingers?"

"Christ, you still remember that story?" Maury laughed. "No, Amigo, I saw my father do many amazing things with silver, but bending a coin wasn't one of them."

"You mean it's not true?" I was disappointed.

"I don't know if it's true. I heard the story when I was a child. I think I even asked my father, but I don't know. Mel was over forty when I was born."

"Why were you and he always fighting?"

"We didn't see eye to eye." Maury shrugged the question off.

"About what?" I persisted.

"About a lot of things."

"Come on, Maury, will you tell me?"

My father looked off at the river thoughtfully. I had carried so many questions in my head for so many years, and now I was determined to get the answers. The time had come. Maury continued to look at the Thames and I continued to wait.

"What did you think of your grandfather?" he asked finally.

"I loved him. I thought he was wonderful."

"He was a wonderful silversmith," Maury said, "and he was probably the best silver forger in the world."

"Forger?" I blinked. "How could he have been a forger?"

"Where do you think all that beautiful antique silver came from? Mel was an expert at lifting hallmarks. He'd take one from a small piece and put it on a larger one, turn an urn into a cup, a paten into a tray, then take all the leftover pieces and make something else from them. He had a huge collection of hallmark stamps and that way he could attribute the work to anyone he chose."

"Mighty Mel?" I was stunned.

"My father," Maury confirmed. "He tried to teach me smithing when I was young, but I just didn't have the gift. I was clumsy and Mel would be furious with me, saying I wasn't trying hard enough. The more he shouted, the more I refused and our relationship never recovered. He stayed angry at me for the rest of his life. He felt that I had betrayed him."

Maury clumsy? I couldn't put the thought together. My father did things seemingly without effort. My father knew everything. I was the one who was clumsy. Was this some story he'd invented to enlist my sympathy?

"Why were you and Mighty Mel still fighting when I was a kid?" I wanted the question to throw him.

"Over you, Amigo." My father looked at me sadly. "Since I had failed him, Mel wanted someone to whom he could pass on his skill. He wanted me to apprentice you to him, and I refused. Oh, I let Mel have his time with you to see if you had any interest, but you were even less curious about the silver trade than I was, so I refused."

"All those Saturday lunches," I said softly.

"Yes, all those Saturday lunches," my father nodded. "Besides, I knew you had the eye for painting. You were quite precocious, Amigo, the way you saw details, were able to identify technique."

"You forced me."

"I encouraged you to learn."

"You've manipulated me all my life." I was starting to get angry.

"I prepared you," my father said.

"To be a crook." My voice was louder. "We're a family of crooks."

"We're survivors," Maury said calmly.

"Where did we come from? When Mighty Mel came to New York, where did he come from?"

"What does it matter, Amigo? We're here now, and that's what counts."

"What counts," I jabbed my finger at him, "is that I am not going to be a crook."

In a rage, I turned and stormed away. It was bad enough that my father sold fraudulent works of art, but my grandfather was an actual forger. I had dishonest blood in my veins, deceit in my genes, deception in my soul. I would defy my heritage. The family history was finished, over, ended. I was my own man and I would not fall into this trap. As Maury had refused to join his father, I would refuse to join mine. My own guilt about my behavior regarding the Dossena Donatello would remain locked in my heart along with the Godolphin secrets. At least I had Fiona as my companion in life. Though I could never reveal these ugly details to her, she would give me strength and courage.

Of course I would have to find a job. Even with all my funds transferred back to Barclay's Bank from New York, life with Fiona was expensive. We had been dining and dancing at the Elephant on the River, the Dorchester Grill and a variety of other costly places and my account was running low.

"Don't be silly, darling. I've got scads of money," Fiona had said when I mentioned my dwindling finances.

"I can't live off your money, Fiona," I had replied honorably.

"Well, then I'll put it in your bank and then it will be your money. What difference does it make?" Fiona had dismissed the subject and I hadn't brought it up again.

Perhaps I could find a place at the V & A, something quiet where I wouldn't have to travel, a normal nine-to-five job that would pay for the basics. There would be questions about the scandal at the Met, but I would be forthright and admit that I had been fooled—not altogether an honest answer, but a reasonable one. What did they say about the British sense of fair play? And if not the V & A, there had to be a place for me.

I decided to prepare a resume and I knew it would read impressively. When I reached the house on Chester Square, I stopped and took a few deep breaths for control. The news about Mighty Mel had hurt me and I couldn't let that show.

"Hello, darling," Fiona said then kissed me. "That's from Alexis. She rang about an hour ago and we had a marvelous talk. She's feeling absolutely fine and says her tummy's starting to grow. Isn't that exciting? How was your talk with Maury?"

"Interesting," I said.

"He's such an interesting man, your father. I absolutely adore him. Everybody does. And it's so exciting that the two of you are going to be working together. I think that's an absolutely fabulous idea," Fiona began to chatter and I tuned out.

I hadn't spoken to Alexis in weeks, since that night at the Ritz, but she and Fiona spoke almost every day. How had they become such close friends? I couldn't think of two more different people, yet here they were engaged in a relationship beyond my understanding. What could they possibly have to talk about? And why wasn't Alexis speaking to me? Had I done something to offend her, other than planning to marry Fiona? I was, after all, the father of her child. Had Fiona usurped our relationship?

"I'm going to take a bath," I interrupted Fiona's chattering.

"I've made reservations at Scott's," she said as I headed out of the room. "Eight o'clock. I'm simply dying for some caviar."

Caviar? At Scott's on Mount Street? This was going to cost a fortune.

Fiona's divorce from Roddy became absolute in the beginning of June and we posted the banns immediately, agreeing on a simple, private ceremony out of town. At first Fiona had suggested that Maury attend since he had missed our original wedding, but I persuaded her that if we invited him then we would have to invite other people as well. There were no plans for a honeymoon as what, other than the London weather, could be better than Chester Square? There was also no way that I could afford it, my funds now almost totally depleted.

I rented a typewriter and went to work on my resume, the first draft running eleven pages, which I thought was excessive and with some careful pruning got it down to seven. Reading it over, I decided that I would hire me. I had copies made and, without mentioning it to Fiona, sent one to the V & A. They replied quickly and courteously, stating that my credentials were most impressive, but, alas, they had no opening at this time. When my American Express bill arrived, I didn't have the money to pay it and Fiona wrote me a check for a thousand pounds which was all I would accept. Still, I felt like a worm.

"Where's Maury?" Fiona asked out of the blue as we were having dinner at L'Écu de France on Jermyn Street. "Have you seen him lately?"

"He's been busy," I said. "I don't think he's in town."

"Oh." Fiona let it go at that.

Did my mother know what Maury did for a living? She must have realized something after the indictment, but did Maury ever discuss his business with her? And what about Mighty Mel? Was she aware that her father-in-law was a forger? Was this ever discussed openly or was it as hidden as it had been from me?

Both Fiona and Alexis liked Maury and I wasn't speaking to him, just as he and his father had not spoken. Was this the Maltese curse? The next day when Fiona went out to have her hair done, I phoned Cap d'Antibes.

"Allo?"

"Alexis, it's Mickey. How are you? Both of you?"

"Mickey." She sounded happy to hear from me. "We're both fine. Are you all right?"

"Well, I've had this falling out with Maury," I had to tell somebody.

"I know," Alexis said.

"You know?"

"We've spoken. He told me."

Maury talking to Alexis? Fiona talking to Alexis?

"Your father is very upset," Alexis continued. "He doesn't know why you are so angry at him. If the two of you could just sit down and talk without one of you losing your temper, maybe you could come to an understanding."

"Understanding about what? The man is a fraud, Alexis."

"Mickey, I love you and I like Maury enormously. I don't want to see you in such conflict."

"You love me?" I couldn't believe my ears.

"Of course I love you," Alexis said. "But I'm not in love with you. Fiona is madly in love with you, and you are with her."

"Yes, but I love you, too."

"I know you do and that's why it hurts so much that you and Maury continue this endless fight when I know that you love each other. It just doesn't make sense."

"No," I admitted.

"Then will you call your father and try to work this out? I really want you to do this, Mickey. It's very important to me."

"All right." I caved in and a moment later we said good-bye.

Why did Alexis have such a calming effect on me? The sound of her voice was like a warm current of soothing air. How had she so effortlessly persuaded me to call my father? I dialed the St. James Club. Maury had checked out the day before.

Fiona and I were married on June 30th in the Registry Office in Exeter, Devon, the simple ceremony performed by a Justice of the Peace, with no guests invited. It was very emotional.

"Do you, Amicus Maltese, take this woman for your lawful wedded wife?"

I looked at Fiona and she was glowing, her glorious red hair in perfect contrast to her tailored cream suit. I was marrying Fiona. Again.

"Answer the man, darling," Fiona cued me, then when I still hesitated she continued. "Alexis may choose to be a single parent, but I don't."

"What?"

"I'm pregnant."

"I do."

GSTAAD

1

My father is dead. The immortal Maury Maltese is dead, and I am rich. So rich that we are now living in a large rented chalet in this high valley in the Bernese Oberland while we wait for our lakefront house in Vevey to be remodeled. Our residence permits, Pierre Rougemont assures me, are only a formality, having paid US$3.7 million for the house in Vevey and with a letter from Rougemont & Cie stating that we shall not become a financial burden to the Swiss Government.

The air is very pure here at 1000 meters up, but it is September and there is the slightest hint of fall approaching. Alexis is seven months pregnant and, Fiona four, both of them quite chubby now. Fiona has, of course, kept the house in Chester Square and I shall use it on my trips to London, despite the bad memories.

The tragedy had happened in July, just two weeks after the wedding. I had been out, secretly talking to the dealers and leaving my resume behind in the event that some employment opportunity should arise. When I returned to Chester Square, Fiona gave me the good news. Maury had called and we were all going to Le Gavroche for dinner the next night, as he had just flown in from Malaga with Baby Habibi and would not be available until then. He was at the St. James Club again, in case I wanted to phone.

I thought about it, thought about my promise to Alexis, and did not make the call, even though Fiona had told him of her pregnancy. Tomorrow night would be soon enough, I thought. But tomorrow night never came. Instead there was a banging on the door at 2:00 in the morning. Fiona and I pulled on our robes and hurried down the stairs to investigate the cause of this alarm. I opened the door and a grief stricken Baby was facing me.

"Ton pere est mort, mon cher Mickey. Je suis désolé." He spoke in French for some reason, perhaps thinking it was the language of diplomacy.

Stunned and shocked we sat on the floral couches in the drawing room, while Baby explained the details. They had eaten at Crockford's, a private club on Curzon Street, a late meal, and then had gone to the Salle Privé to gamble. Maury was on a hot streak, winning one hand of blackjack after another and finally betting the whole fifty thousand pounds on what was agreed to be the last play. The dealer dealt him the Ace and then the Jack of spades. Maury laughed and then collapsed with a massive coronary, dead before his head hit the table.

"Maury went out with a winning hand," Baby said. "He was a happy man."

Yes, but I had not seen or spoken to him since losing my temper on the Victoria Embankment. My eyes filled with tears. My breath came out in jarring gasps. I nodded because I could not speak. Dead? How could my father be dead? It was impossible. Maury would live for a hundred years and when the Angel of Death at last arrived, Maury would sell him a fake Rembrandt. Why had I been so stubborn? My tears began to fall and, though Fiona held me tightly, I found myself wishing that Alexis were here.

"I loved your father," Baby wept, too.

So, for a while, all we did was cry, then Fiona made us some tea. Baby announced that he would notify Maury's lawyer and have his people take care of all the unpleasant details and that I should not worry about anything, a generous though meaningless statement. When he finally left, he left behind a briefcase containing 125,000 pounds, Maury's last winning hand.

"Come back to bed, darling," Fiona said gently. "There isn't anything you can do now."

She was right and so we went to bed, but not to sleep. The sudden thought that Baby Habibi had been present not only at my father's death but Oliver Godolphin's as well started the wheels of coincidence turning in my head. How had all of this become so intertwined? At dawn, when I drifted off into an uneasy sleep, I still had no answer. Why hadn't I phoned my father? Why hadn't I called? Why? Now it would never be settled.

All men, to one degree or another, carry their fathers with them all their lives, but not to the extent that Maury carried Mighty Mel. In the closet at the St. James Club, clearing out my father's possessions, I found a new unopened box of business cards from Smythson's on Bond Street, the sample card on top elegantly printed and on the finest linen stock, and next to that another, larger box. I opened it and inside there was a sealed metal container labeled, "Cremated Remains of Mellos Maltese." Now, I understood why I had not attended my grandfather's funeral. Maury had been carrying Mighty Mel's ashes with him all these years. Was my father trying to somehow achieve a peace with his father? I knew exactly how he felt.

I buried them both in Highgate Cemetery, as far as possible from Karl Marx, as there seemed no point in creating a reunion in New Jersey. There were seven women in black at the funeral, Fiona, Alexis, Sheffy and four distraught women I had never seen before. Baby was there and so was, to my astonishment, Pierre Rougemont. I wept and wept and finally had to be helped back to the limousine by two pregnant women.

Except for the four strangers, everyone came back to Chester Square for drinks, the moment where we began putting our grief behind us and looking once more to the future. Alexis and Baby were deep in conversation, Fiona making certain that everyone's needs were being looked after and chattering to Sheffy at the same time. Pierre Rougemont sat next to me and smiled. I was delighted to see him.

"Thank you for coming, Pierre." I was in reasonable control by now. "But how did you know?"

"I think this will explain," he said pleasantly. "But I would suggest you read it in private."

He took a thick envelope from his jacket pocket and handed it to me. This would explain what? I had so many questions, were all the answers here? I slipped the envelope into my jacket pocket.

"I am very sorry about your father," Rougemont continued.

"You have my deepest and sincerest sympathies."

"Thank you," I had to go see what this envelope contained. "How's Lotte Wieland?"

"I do not know. We maintain the account for her, but she does not call upon our services very often."

"Have you seen her?"

"No. I offered to go to Salzburg to discuss how she would prefer for us to handle her financial situation, but she said it wasn't necessary. She sounded very sad."

"Yes."

So I had been right. The money hadn't helped. Poor Lotte, holding on to the past, to the secret that we shared, never letting go. I could almost see her eating lonely dinners in the kitchen, sitting on the furniture from the apartment in Paris and telling herself the same tragic story over and over again.

"If you are feeling well enough, I would enjoy taking you to lunch at the Connaught tomorrow," Rougemont said. "There are several matters we need to discuss. Would one o'clock be convenient?"

"Fine."

"Again, you have my sympathies," Rougemont got to his feet and made his farewells, Sheffy leaving with him.

A few minutes later Baby announced that he would be godfather to Alexis's child, with our approval, of course. Daddy and Auntie Fiona agreed that it would be a fitting and wonderful idea, and soon Baby, too, was gone. Alexis was staying with us in Chester Square and she and Fiona made sure that I was not left alone for an instant. I kept fingering the envelope inside my jacket pocket.

That night Fiona cooked, roasting a chicken, *mange-tout* ready for a quick steaming and, while the three of us sat in the kitchen, Fiona produced another shower cap from the George V and fried her fabulous potatoes. It wasn't until everyone was asleep that I managed to retrieve the envelope and tiptoe to the drawing room to finally rip it open.

June 20th

My sweet Amigo, my dear son,

Don't be upset. I have known this was going to happen for over a year now, the first two heart attacks indicating that a massive one was inevitable. I hope I went out with a bang. I'm sorry about our unpleasant scene on the Embankment, but I hope we have made peace before you read this. I love you, Amigo, but everything I told you that day was true, a truth I have held back from you for years, knowing how badly you would take it. You were always a sweet child and I could never understand that and now you have become a sweet man and I love you for that as well. I wish we had been closer, but looking back at my relationship with my father, I think that I understand the reasons. Maybe we will have a chance to bridge this gap together. If not, know that I have bridged it for myself and now you must, too.

I know that you are surprised by the identity of the bearer of these pages, but Pierre's father, Phillipe, was my dear friend for many years. Also, my banker, as now Pierre shall be yours. The Corot, by the way, is real, and I will leave you to wonder about the ones in the Louvre and the National. Perhaps old Camille painted three versions, who knows? But back to the point. There is between sixteen and eighteen million dollars in the Rougemont bank, which you may share as you see fit with your sister. I don't think she will accept the money, so I suggest you have Pierre send her fifty thousand and see what she does with it. My guess is that she will give it away to some odd organization, but if she doesn't, then I will leave the division up to you.

Attached you will find a list of your personal inheritance. There are thirty-two paintings and four pieces of sculpture, all of them beautiful, all of them (from your point of view) questionable. The time has come, Amigo, to put your questions to rest. Forget about New York. Its time has passed. Concentrate on London and Munich, for those are the real marketplaces. I took a gamble when I forced the German language on you, but you will find that gamble will pay off.

Start with the Renoir, as it is perfect and will pass any test. I have been saving this for you. This will make you known and, believe me, people will seek you out. As you sell, replenish and be patient. The Renoir has been waiting for thirty years, so never hurry, there is no need.

Leave something for your children. We have not had good luck with our women, but luck enough to carry us into the next

generation. Barely. I am confident that you will change that, as
none of us have had two before, as I am confident that someday
you shall have a son. Teach him well, but be more gentle than I
was with you, then perhaps you will not have to wait this long to
tell him what I am telling you.

Base your family in Switzerland, spend time in Munich and in
London, but spend most of your time with your family. And above
all, enjoy your life. It's time for you to start that, too. Enjoy each
day, each passing moment. I have.

> Your loving father,
> A. Maltese

When Fiona and Alexis found me on the couch later, I was still
sobbing. By the time I met Pierre Rougemont at the Connaught,
this long, long crisis had finally passed. Over a delicious salmon
trout and a bottle of Cuvée de la Chevalerie Saumur '68, we went
through the details and I explained what I had in mind.
Rougemont listened and though he took no notes, I knew he
would not miss a point. There should be no difficulty was his
only comment before he mentioned the chalet in Gstaad. It was
owned by a client and it was for rent. We could move in at any
time.

On my way back to Chester Square, I prepared my answers for
whatever questions Fiona or Alexis might have, but they simply
accepted my announcement without challenge. There was no
mention of Alexis returning to Cap d'Antibes. The next few days
were spent putting the Chester Square house in order, clothes
shopping and packing. I took the last afternoon for myself,
retrieving my resumes, then, with two dozen yellow roses, I went
to Highgate Cemetery for a final farewell. This time there were
no tears.

That night, at Fiona's suggestion, we had dinner at Le Gavroche and the next morning left on the early flight to Geneva.
Pierre Rougemont was at Cointrin to meet us and insisted on personally driving us up to Gstaad, the luggage following in the new,
large BMW I had ordered. By the time we reached Lausanne,
Rougemont's infectious good spirits had us all feeling quite
merry.

When he mentioned the lakefront house that was for sale in
Vevey, we agreed that, since it was on the way, we should stop

to see it. The house had six bedrooms, a large living room with a beautiful view of Lake Léman, and a comfortable study for me. Fiona and Alexis agreed that the kitchen and the bathrooms had to be redone and the entire interior repainted in brighter colors. We then had lunch at the Hotel Trois Couronnes dining room before leisurely continuing to Aigle and then up to Gstaad.

The chalet, of course, was everything and more than Rougemont had said it would be. Madame Auger, the house-keeper, waited to welcome us. She had spent the morning at market and had filled the kitchen with delicacies. Fiona and Alexis were enchanted with the place and the spectacular sight of the surrounding green mountains. I knew that I had made the right decision. Rougemont said that he would let us know when he had concluded negotiations for the house in Vevey.

"How is your wife?" I asked as I walked him to his car.

"No better, no worse," he smiled and shrugged. "There is no change."

"I'd like it if you'd visit us," I said. "As often as possible."

"Then I shall," he opened his car door.

"The Corot is real," I told him.

"I know. Otherwise your father would not have given it to mine." Rougemont got into his car and drove away.

Why had he allowed me to see the "Page Missing"? While I might have resolved the Godolphin provenance without seeing the L.W. dedication, it had certainly spurred me on. Should I thank my father for that, as well? There were many things that I would never know, many questions never to be answered. Who was Oliver Godolphin and who was Mighty Mel Maltese? Had Fiona been one of Jimmy Fitzhugh's party girls and what about the red Aston Martin? But I did know that I had no need to know, that it no longer mattered.

Life settled quickly into an easy pattern. After Pierre Rougemont called to say the Vevey house was ours, Fiona and Alexis would travel down the mountain frequently to supervise the painting and remodeling and ordering the furniture in Lausanne. In the evenings, Alexis gives French lessons to Fiona, and she has picked up the language with surprising speed, her accent far better than mine.

There is a constant discussion about the children's names,

Alexis favoring Alexander for a boy and Jerusha for a girl, while Fiona seems to have settled on Maurice Anthony or Catherine Anne. I smile and express no preference, but when the moment arrives I will then announce my decision.

True to his word, Pierre Rougemont visits us often and never fails to add to our pleasure. He and I go for long scenic walks and, though it is unspoken, we both know that we shall repeat our fathers' friendship. Fiona and Alexis enjoy his company so much that they are always a little disappointed at his departure, so I always make an extra effort to maintain the atmosphere of happiness and contentment at those times. It isn't difficult. What man could have a better life? But these were all small steps. The first big one was yet to come.

In the end of August, I told Fiona and Alexis that I would be in Geneva for a few days on business and that they could reach me at the Richemond if necessary. I would take the train, leave them the car and drive back with Pierre on the weekend. Fiona and Alexis thought it was an excellent plan and drove me to the small Gstaad station in the morning. The train ride was pleasant, the Richemond welcoming. I retrieved the Renoir that afternoon.

After bolting my door, I unwrapped the painting cautiously, positioning it on a chair by the window so that I could view the work in natural light. "Woman on the Bank of the Seine." It was signed and dated 1878, making it a relatively early work, done well before Renoir's violent break with the Impressionists. The woman was standing, one hand on her hip, with her back to the river, her expression typically blank, dark eyes staring straight out of the canvas. In the background, men in striped shirts were paddling sculls nonchalantly, the painting giving the impression that the woman had just turned away, bored by this lazy race.

If I had been shown this work as an innocent viewer and asked to identify the artist, there was no question that I would have instantly replied, "Auguste Renoir." The painting, like Renoir himself, was sensitive but reserved, the woman portrayed caught unaware, the background paddlers indifferent to the moment, as if the artist had somehow managed to be a hidden observer.

I got down on my hands and knees to study the signature. I could not fault it. Though I knew Renoir had not painted this canvas, I wondered what his reaction would have been on viewing it.

Distressing, probably, as when dissatisfied with his own work, Renoir would not only refuse to sign it but would even deny that he had painted it. Would he have signed this?

By the time Pierre Rougemont picked me up to return to Gstaad, I had made all the necessary arrangements. He had heard, indirectly, from my sister. Maury had been right, as Elisa simply endorsed the check and donated it to the Lesbian Defense Fund in Boston, which I found an interesting choice. Pierre and I chatted amicably and laughed often during the drive, stopping in Vevey to see how the work was progressing. The walls were bright and cheerful, the bathrooms in the process of being tiled, the kitchen totally different and only waiting for the appliances to be installed. There was no doubt that we would be able to move in by the beginning of October at the latest, which was a great relief. Though the chalet was a delightful place, I was concerned about Alexis since the baby was due at the end of November.

Fiona and Alexis greeted us enthusiastically, inquiring if my business had gone well and saying how delighted they were to see Pierre again. The chalet brimmed with good cheer and we all sat down to another of Madame Auger's excellent meals, during which Fiona suggested that Pierre be godfather to our child. The suggestion must have taken him by surprise as there were happy tears in his eyes when he kissed her hand and said that it would be an honor. That night, very quietly and very gently, Fiona and I made love for a long time.

Three weeks later, before I went to Munich to witness the auction at Sotheby's and then accept congratulations after the Renoir sold for $7.6 million dollars, I had thrown away my old business cards and refilled my case from the box from Smythson's on Bond Street, which I had realized for some time that my father had ordered for me.

A. MALTESE
Art Dealer

Somewhere, I knew, in Highgate or in Heaven there were peals of laughter.